MURDER ON THE HIGH SEAS
AND
THE DIAMOND BULLET:
THE COMPLETE CASES OF GILLIAN HAZELTINE

George F. Worts

Eric of the Strong Heart

BY VICTOR ROUSSEAU

The Woman of the Pyramid and Other Tales:
The Perley Poore Sheehan Omnibus, Volume 1

BY PERLEY POORE SHEEHAN

A Columbus of Space and The Moon Metal:
The Garrett P. Serviss Omnibus, Volume 1

BY GARRETT P. SERVISS

The Black Tide: The Complete Adventures
of Bellow Bill Williams, Volume 1

BY RALPH R. PERRY

The Nine Red Gods Decide: The Complete
Adventures of Cordie, Soldier of Fortune, Volume 2

BY W. WIRT

A Grave Must Be Deep!

BY THEODORE ROSCOE

The American

BY MAX BRAND

The Complete Adventures of Koyala, Volume 1

BY JOHN CHARLES BEECHAM

The Cult Murders

BY ALAN FORSYTH

MURDER ON THE HIGH SEAS
AND
THE DIAMOND BULLET

THE COMPLETE CASES OF GILLIAN HAZELTINE

GEORGE F. WORTS

ILLUSTRATED BY

JOHN R. NEILL

COVER BY

PAUL STAHR

STEEGER BOOKS • 2019

PUBLISHING HISTORY

"Murder on the High Seas" originally appeared in the November 29, December 6, 13, and 20, 1930 issues of *Argosy* magazine (Vol. 217, Nos. 1–4). Copyright © 1930 by The Frank A. Munsey Company. Copyright renewed © 1958 and assigned to Steeger Properties, LLC. All rights reserved.

"The Diamond Bullet" originally appeared in the January 10, 17, and 24, 1931 issues of *Argosy* magazine (Vol. 218, Nos. 1–3). Copyright © 1931 by The Frank A. Munsey Company. Copyright renewed © 1958 and assigned to Steeger Properties, LLC. All rights reserved.

"About the Author" originally appeared in the January 25, 1930 issue of *Argosy* magazine (Vol. 209, No. 5). Copyright © 1930 by The Frank A. Munsey Company. Copyright renewed © 1957 and assigned to Steeger Properties, LLC. All rights reserved.

Visit steegerbooks.com for more books like this.

TABLE OF CONTENTS

MURDER ON THE HIGH SEAS

Not even in pirate days did a schooner see a more grisly scene of carnage then the affair which brought the survivors of the Jula Jungle to Gillian Hazeltine, the brilliant criminal lawyer

CHAPTER I

A LITTLE SPITFIRE

GILLIAN HAZELTINE WAS standing in the window of his private office, looking down over rooftops at the Sangamo River, when the Jula Jungle hove into view.

It was a lazy sunny morning in spring—the kind of morning that makes a man think of packing a suitcase and starting forth for some distant and adventurous land. And the Jula Jungle came sailing into his vision as if in answer to the vagabond thoughts in his mind.

She was a big black schooner. Her sails were dirty and patched. There were patches upon patches. Her rigging looked slack. Her air was frowzy and disreputable and not a little sinister. There was something of an old weatherworn vulture about her. She might well have been the last of the privateers.

There was a fresh breeze from off the sea, or the black schooner could never have negotiated the harbor.

The famous criminal lawyer knew nothing of the sea but any landman's eye could tell that this schooner was a cargo boat, not a yacht, and that she was making port after a long voyage. If he could have known then that she had beat her way in with a cargo of mystery and terror and amazing surprises and a blood-chilling tale of horrible murders, he would have looked at the schooner with keener interest.

Gillian watched her dreamily until she passed from sight behind a wall of office buildings. Then his brisk, pretty secretary came in with a sheaf of correspondence and an open notebook.

1

For the next hour he was busy dictating, and the slatternly old schooner passed from his mind.

Some minutes after his secretary had finished taking dictation and gone out, Gillian heard a commotion in the outer offices. He heard a shrill voice raised in anger, and lower voices which protested and argued. The voices rose and fell. Then the shrill voice rose to a fine shriek; the lawyer's door burst open and a thin figure in a torn and shabby sailor's suit came flying in.

THE INTRUDER stood panting in the middle of Gillian's luxurious Bokhara rug, reminding him absurdly of a doe at bay. Large brown eyes stared at him, half in fear, half in defiance. Tangled brown hair full of red glints came down to the girl's shoulders. Her color was mahogany. She might have been a South Sea Islander.

Gillian sank back in his desk chair and looked her over with the greatest interest and an almost uncontrollable impulse to burst into laughter. Portions of his startling visitor's bare skin were visible through rents and worn spots in the once white sailor's suit. These portions were white. Remnants of white tennis shoes were tied with pieces of string to her feet. One toe of each foot was visible.

Before Gillian could complete his inspection, the door, which his amazing visitor had slammed on the way in, burst open again and Donald Carter, one of his clerks, came shouldering in, red of face and stammering with angry confusion. A scratch on Mr. Carter's nose was bleeding.

With twinkling eyes Gillian looked from the girl to his big, broad-shouldered clerk.

"This—this creature," panted young Mr. Carter, "forced her way in here, Mr. Hazeltine, before we could s-stop her. I tried to detain her, and—"

"If you lay those paws on me again," the girl announced in a low, husky, venomous voice, "I'll scratch your damned eyes out! Pipe down! I've come to see Gillian Hazeltine, and no white-collared office rat is going to stop me." She whirled like a cat.

*"I'd rather do my talking standing
up," cried the little sea Arab*

"Are you Gillian Hazeltine?"

"Yes."

"The one they call the Silver Fox?"

"My enemies sometimes call me that."

"You're the great criminal lawyer who buys judges and bribes
juries and—"

"Mr. Hazeltine," interrupted his angry clerk, "shall I call a
policeman?"

The telephone bell on Gillian's desk now added its silvery
voice to the uproar. The girl in the tattered sailor's suit edged
over and made a short dash which brought her behind Gillian's
chair. From this refuge she glared at Mr. Carter. The young man
later swore that she then stuck out her tongue at him, but it is
possible that he was exaggerating.

Gillian picked up the receiver and said hello.

An excited voice crackled in his ear: "Gill? This is Josh
Hammersley. Who's the wild woman who just hotfooted it up
to your office?"

Josh Hammersley was a reporter on the Greenboro *Times* and one of Gillian's closest friends.

"We've only just begun to introduce ourselves," Gillian replied. "You'll have to give me time to catch my breath."

"I'll call you in a few minutes," said Josh. "Unless I'm crazy, this is the hottest story that has broken in these parts in years. That girl just came off a schooner that has put into port with a wild yarn of murder on the high seas. The entire crew is under arrest. Will you hold that girl until I get up there?"

"I can't promise anything," said the Silver Fox.

"Don't let any other reporters get at her, will you," Josh pleaded.

"I'll do my best," Gillian agreed, "but unless I'm mistaken, this situation is going to be difficult to control."

HE HUNG up the receiver and gravely said, "Don, I think you can safely leave me with—where in the devil did she go?"

"She's behind your chair, making faces at me!"

"I am not!" the girl cried. She stepped out from behind his chair.

"You can go, Don."

"Yes, sir."

"Stand outside the door and keep everybody out. Tell the switchboard girl I'm not to be disturbed."

"Yes, sir."

When his clerk had gone, Gillian opened a golden humidor and extracted therefrom a plump blond cigar. He carefully bit off one end of this and lighted the other. Through rising clouds of fragrant blue smoke he gazed at the girl. She had walked over to the middle of the Bokhara rug again, and now stood facing him with small brown fists planted on hips, small feet planted wide apart. She reminded him of a musical comedy version of a pirate.

In the low, throaty voice which would soon be thrilling hundreds of spellbound people, the beautiful sea Arab was saying:

"My name is Carolina Dawn. You knew my dad."

Gillian was wondering how old she was. His first guess had been twelve his next, sixteen. He revised his guess upward to twenty.

"Caleb Dawn," she said, "once saved your life off Martha's Vineyard when you were out sailing in a dory and got caught in a storm. He ran up beside you and threw you a rope. He towed you into port and saved your life. You told him when you stepped ashore that you would be indebted to him as long as you lived— that any time he needed your help, he should call on you."

"I remember," Gillian nodded. "And later I did my best to pay the debt. Caleb Dawn was one of my first clients. He killed an Italian fisherman and I defended him. I got him off."

Carolina Dawn stood on his Bokhara rug with feet planted apart as if she were on a deck, bracing herself against the rolling and pitching.

He asked her to sit down.

"I'd rather do my talking standing up," she said. "Let's settle this old murder case. My dad killed that knife slinger in self-defense. It was proved at the trial. You got paid for defending him, didn't you?"

Gillian nodded.

"Then aren't you," she said triumphantly, "still under obligations to him for saving your life that time off Martha's Vineyard?"

The lawyer chuckled. This girl was a fighter.

"Very well, Miss Dawn. We'll grant that I am still under obligations to Caleb Dawn. What can I do for him?"

"Nobody can do anything for him. He's at the bottom of the Atlantic Ocean. He was murdered Sunday night. Someone with an ax sneaked down into the after cabin while we were all asleep and chopped off his head. Then the murderer sneaked into the first mate's cabin and chopped off *his* head."

Gillian, in his astonishment, almost swallowed his cigar.

"Who," he managed to ask, "is the murderer?"

"I don't know."

Gillian looked incredulous. "You don't mean to say that on a boat as small as that, a man could kill two of his shipmates and not be discovered?"

"I mean just that. I do not know who committed the murders."

"How many are there now in the crew?"

"Five."

Gillian shook his head. "It simply isn't credible, Miss Dawn. Was there any one else aboard?"

"A passenger."

"Man or woman?"

The girl drew a deep breath and said, "A man."

"That makes six and yourself from whom the murderer is to be selected?"

"Yes, sir."

"It's the most amazing story I ever heard. Weren't any of the crew on watch when it happened?"

"Yes, sir; a man was at the wheel—the second mate, Hans Larssen."

"What did Larssen see?"

"He says—"The girl stopped. Her fists were clenched at her sides. Her eyes had suddenly become narrow. "Larssen is a liar!"

"What does Larssen say?"

"That Roger Pawling did the killings! But he's a liar! Roger didn't!"

"Who is Roger Pawling?"

"The passenger. He is interested in oceanography. He wanted to make the trip on the Jula Jungle to experiment with deep-sea nets and grapples, to find out if a boat her size would be suitable for that kind of work. His father is Chester Pawling, the Boston millionaire."

"Chester Pawling," Gillian informed her, "died three or four days ago. The papers were full of it. I remember distinctly the mention of a son who had run away to sea. The son was the black sheep of the family. In his will, his father cut off Roger Pawling with exactly one dollar."

CHAPTER II

WHITEWASHED SUSPECTS

CAROLINA DAWN'S FINE dark eyes were blazing. "I don't care a damn what the papers said. Roger is not a black sheep. His father didn't understand him. He wanted Roger to be a bond salesman. I know all about it. Roger is the finest man I ever knew. We're engaged to be married!"

"Where was Roger when these murders were committed?"

"Asleep in his cabin."

"Where was it located?"

"Across the dining saloon from mine, which is at the forward end of the cabin. Roger's was between my dad's and First Mate Dirk Morton's, in a row along the aft end of the cabin."

"When did the murders take place—what time of day?"

"A little after two o'clock in the morning."

"That was Sunday night, you say."

"Monday morning, to be exact—two o'clock Monday morning."

"Four days ago," Gillian said, "Where was the schooner bound?"

"For Halifax. We were light—in ballast. We were eight days out from New York when it happened. We ran into head winds and calms."

"Let me see," Gillian suggested, "if I have this straight: At about two o'clock on Monday morning, Larssen was at the wheel. You, your father, the first mate, and Roger Pawling were asleep in your respective cabins. Presumably, the rest of the crew was in the fo'c's'le. Some one with an ax crept into the after house and chopped off the heads of your father and the first mate. Is that right?"

Miss Dawn looked down at her ragged shoes, then tossed her head.

"The crew say they weren't "in the fo'c's'le. They say they saw Roger commit the murders.

Gillian spread open his hands with a gesture of hopelessness and finality.

"My dear girl, if these men saw Roger Pawling commit the murders, how can there be any doubt about it? What can I possibly do? What do you want me to do?"

"Prove that they are liars and that Roger is innocent! It's a deliberate frame-up."

"It's always," Gillian said impatiently, "a frame-up. I've met few murderers in my career who didn't swear they'd been framed."

"I haven't finished," Miss Dawn said grimly. When those murders were committed, Roger was in his room. After the killer was through with my dad and Dirk Morton, he tried to batter in my door, then he tried to smash down Roger's door. He smeared blood all over both doors. That's enough proof, Isn't it, that Roger is innocent?"

"Was your door locked?"

"And bolted. You'll realize why when you've seen those jail-birds."

"How about Roger's door?"

"It was locked so that it wouldn't rattle."

The lawyer's cigar had gone out. He lighted it. His hand holding the match was shaking. The more he heard of this case, the more astounding it became.

"Who do you think committed the murders?"

"I don't know. Any man in the crew."

"Do all five claim that Roger committed the murder?"

She nodded. "Whoever is guilty—one man or more—is being

shielded by the rest. They simply banded together against Roger to save the guilty one's neck—or necks. They've had time to work up a convincing, airtight story, and they will convict Roger with their testimony if something drastic isn't done.

"That's why Roger and I brought the Jula Jungle in here. I knew that if anyone could sift the truth out of all this, you could."

"IT'S BEGINNING to look to me as if no man alive could sift the truth out of it," Gillian replied. "Were you awake when the murders were committed? Did you hear voices?"

"No, I didn't wake up until that ax came smashing against my door. I thought that someone in the crew was trying to break into my room. That's the kind they all are. I was scared stiff. I heard the ax smash against Roger's door, and I think I began to scream."

"Then you opened your door?"

"No, not then. I was still scared and bewildered. I didn't open my door until everything was quiet. Then I peeked out. The dining saloon—it's a huge room—was completely dark. Just as I struck a match, some one else did. It was Roger."

"Wait a minute. Was there any blood on him?"

"No, sir. He had a blue flannel bathrobe over his pajamas. I saw his hands. There was no blood on him anywhere. I held up a match and saw a stream of blood flowing out from Dirk Morton's room. That was my first intimation that there had been any killing. I suppose I screamed again. Then I saw a big splash of blood on the wall in my father's room."

"His door and the mate's were open?"

"Yes, both of them."

"What happened then?"

"I fainted. When I came to, all the crew were in the dining saloon."

"Blood on any of them?"

"No. Roger and I are sure of that. And I'm sure that not more than three minutes elapsed from the time the ax smashed on my door until all of us were in that room. The murderer would not have had time to clean up. He might have worn gloves and a slicker. Oh, we've thought of just about everything—and got nowhere."

"Did the crew immediately accuse Roger of the murders?"

"Yes. They put him in irons and took him to the chain locker. They had it all arranged beforehand—I'm sure of that. But their only reason for doing it was that Roger had been having some trouble with my father and with Dirk Morton."

"What kind of trouble?"

"Quarrels. Dad didn't like Roger at first because he was a landlubber, and he was always picking on Roger. Roger took it as a joke at first until, one night when he was asleep, dad threw some of his deep sea nets overboard."

"What did Roger do about that?"

"He was awfully mad."

"Did he accuse your father?"

"No, but he suspected dad did it. And father—well, when dad found out that Roger and I were in love, he just hit the ceiling."

"What about Dirk?"

"Dirk Morton was nothing but a big bully. I was afraid of him and I hated him. He was always pawing me and trying to kiss me. Ever since I was a kid, he talked about marrying me. And dad was all for it. He thought Dirk was grand. He thought I was joking when I said I loathed Dirk. He didn't see how anybody could loathe a man as wonderful as Dirk. Ugh! He didn't know some of the things I knew about Dirk.

"Last winter, while the Jula Jungle was in dry dock in Brooklyn, Dirk met an old friend named Jake Harper, who used to sail with him. Jake Harper had recently married—a big-eyed baby blonde. Dirk and she flirted. She must have fallen terribly hard for Dirk. Anyway, she and Dirk ran off to Atlantic City for a weekend. Jake Harper said he'd get Dirk some day; but Jake Harper was only one of a small army that had threatened to get Dirk 'some day,' and for good reason.

"I was beginning to think that all men were like Dirk when Roger came on board. I hadn't had any experience with men who weren't sailors. I was born at sea and I'd been at sea all my life. Men were all right until I was about fifteen, then they began making love to me. But Dirk was the worst. It gave me the creeps to hear him tell me how much he loved me. He wanted to marry me, quit sailing, go to Shanghai and start a saloon.

"Things were pretty awful when Roger came. And the minute I laid eyes on him I knew that all men weren't the same. You may not believe in love at first sight, but I do. I fell in love with Roger the minute I saw him!"

GILLIAN SMILED. What did Dirk Morton do about it?"

"The minute he found out that Roger and I loved each other, he began to insult Roger. It got worse and worse, and they finally had a fistfight. Dirk knocked Roger unconscious with a belaying pin. When Roger came to, Dirk told him that he would beat him up worse if he hung around me."

"How did Roger take that?"

"He tried to beat Dirk up, but Dirk knocked him down again with the belaying pin. Then Roger said he was going to kill him. That's what the crew pounced on, after the murders, when they put Roger in irons and took him to the chain locker."

"A few minutes ago you said that you and Roger brought the Jula Jungle in here. Now you've just said that Roger was in irons in the chain locker."

"Yes, Mr. Hazeltine. When they took Roger away, I locked myself in my room and sat up the rest of the night with a loaded automatic pistol that dad had given me. I didn't come out until next noon. They had buried my father and Morton—I mean in the ocean. It was a very calm day, so calm that no one had to be at the wheel during lunch hour. They were all in the dining saloon, discussing their plans. As soon as a wind came, they were going to change the course. They were going to Mexico and turn Roger over to the authorities there. Heaven knows what was to become of me.

"When I went out, with the pistol in my hand, Wallaby, the steward—he's a nasty little cockney—was saying that they would get busy down in Mexico."

"What did he mean?"

"I don't know, Mr. Hazeltine. My dad did not own the Jula Jungle; he only owned a three-eighths interest. You see, a sailing ship hardly pays her way any more. Dad owned a comfortable fortune in stocks and bonds, which are in a Brooklyn bank, but he didn't want to touch any of this, because it was for me. So when ready cash was scarce, he often persuaded some of the crew to take their pay in small interests in the boat—a sixty-fourth at a time.

In this way, in time, Wallaby came to own a fourth and Larssen another fourth. Dirk Morton owned the remaining eighth. Together, Wallaby and Larssen owned a half interest. With dad and Dirk both dead, Wallaby and Larssen really had a right to say what should be done with the boat. And Larssen, as acting captain, had a right to order her anywhere he pleased.... That was how things stood when I went into the dining saloon with the pistol and told them all to throw up their hands."

Gillian grinned, but Carolina went grimly on: "They were five terribly surprised men. I told them I would shoot any man who moved—and I would have, and they knew it. It was my only chance to save Roger and myself and bring those jailbirds to justice.

"I made Larssen give me the keys to Roger's handcuffs. Then I ran up the after stairs, locked the door, crawled over the cabin roof to the forward door, and locked that. Before they could break out, I ran forward to the chain locker, and freed Roger. We nailed heavy planks over the portholes and door of the cabin. And from that time until we got into port this morning, one of us has slept outside the forward door with a gun ready while the other took the wheel.

"As soon as we made port, Roger gave himself up to the harbor police, and they broke in and arrested the crew. And the crew is prepared to swear on a stack of Bibles a mile high that Roger is the murderer."

THE LAWYER sat back and gazed at the ragged, beautiful little sea Arab with frank admiration. He was sure she was telling the truth as far as she knew it.

He asked: "Whom does Roger suspect?"

To his surprise, Carolina suddenly dropped into a chair, buried her brown little face in her hands, and began to cry. She looked up presently with blurred eyes and said in a fierce small voice:

"Don't you suppose I realize that everything points to Roger? That's why I came to you, isn't it? Roger had plenty of provocation for killing my dad and Dirk. That's what the crew says. But they're wrong. You've got to find who committed those murders!"

Gillian stood up. He said gently: "My dear, do you realize that any crime committed at sea comes under the jurisdiction of an admiralty court?"

"I do!"

"And that I am not an admiralty lawyer?"

"I don't care!" she cried I'd rather have you to defend Roger than the best admiralty lawyer on earth. Roger is innocent. You are the cleverest criminal lawyer in America. I have plenty of money. I'll spend every penny of it, if necessary, to prove that Roger is innocent and to find the one who is guilty!"

The lawyer sighed. "But you haven't the remotest idea who the guilty man is."

"You will find him," Carolina said confidently.

Gillian smiled. "How? What clues have you given me?"

"There were no clues."

"You must have overlooked them."

"Roger and I went over that boat from stem to stern."

Gillian frowned. "The point that perplexes me most is that every man on board was accounted for within, say, five minutes of the time the murders were committed—and not a drop of blood on any of them. Somehow, I can't take stock in your argument that the murderer may have worn gloves and a slicker. The man who committed those murders was in too violent a mood to think of such details. Let's suppose, for sake of argument, that no one in that room did commit those murders. How about a stowaway?"

"We thought of that. That's why we searched the ship. There was not a sign of a stowaway."

The criminal lawyer groaned. "My dear girl," he said, "do you realize just what you are asking me to undertake?"

He tapped on his desk with a forefinger.

"Three nights ago an unknown man with an ax slipped into your father's stateroom and chopped his head off, then into the mate's room and chopped his head off. He left no clues. He was not spotted or splashed with blood. Was he a ghost? Did he come out of the night and vanish again into the night?"

"One of the crew did it," the girl said firmly.

"You say yourself that Roger was the only man aboard with motives for those killings. That's what the crew says. That's what the Federal attorney will say. He will certainly indict Roger. I am not a miracle worker. I am not even a detective. How can you, as a reasonable girl, expect me to solve such a tangled mystery?"

Carolina sprang up. Under the mahogany tan, she was pale. Her smallness, her raggedness, made her pathetic. Gillian was sorry for her. He was always sorry for the sweethearts, the wives, the mothers, the sisters of murderers who came to him, begging him for help.

She took one of his hands and squeezed it, and Gillian was astonished at the strength of her small hands. Her eyes looking up at him were as trustful as a child's.

"If I hadn't known that you could save Roger and find the guilty man, do you suppose I would have held up those men and brought that schooner up this river? You're my only chance! You've got to take this case!"

The telephone began to ring.

CHAPTER III

CHALLENGE

GILLIAN PICKED UP the receiver. The switchboard operator in the outer office began talking rapidly.

"Mrs. Hazeltine is here and says she has a luncheon appointment with you and wants to know if she shall come in or wait. There have been a dozen calls in the past few minutes from newspaper offices; wanting to know about some murders on a schooner, and there are reporters and photographers sitting around like a flock of hawks in the waiting room. Mr. Carter told me you weren't to be disturbed. The district attorney's office is on the wire now; it's Mr. Yistle himself. I told him you had left orders not to be disturbed, but he insists on talking to you."

Gillian struck a match and relighted his cigar. The day was threatening to be a busy one. He said:

"Have Mrs. Hazeltine come right in. Tell the reporters that I can't see them this morning, but will give out an interview as soon as I have talked to Mr. Pawling. I'll take Mr. Yistle's call. Put him on."

The line clicked and a harsh bass voice came on the wire. Little love had ever been lost between Gillian Hazeltine and Adelbert Yistle. Many lawyers who fight one another in the courtroom are the best of friends outside of it, but this rule did not apply to Gillian and Mr. Yistle. For years they had been the best of enemies.

"Gillian," Mr. Yistle began, "I understand you've been retained to defend the man who murdered the captain and the first mate of this black schooner that just came up the river. What's in this rumor?"

"I'd like to know, myself," Gillian answered. "Who started it?"

"The murderer himself!"

"Does he say I'm defending him?"

"He does!"

Gillian sent a thoughtful glance in the direction of the girl in the tattered sailor suit. Her brown eyes were brightly upon him.

"As a matter of fact," Gillian said pleasantly into the transmitter, "I can't see, Bert, how this affects you. The case won't go through the State courts. It's a Federal issue."

"I am aware of that," said the district attorney. "And it happens that Sherman Fowler, the United States district attorney, has had a nervous breakdown and has requested me to represent him. I have just finished interviewing the five surviving members of the Jula Jungle's crew, and I am firmly convinced that Roger Pawling is guilty of these murders. I would not have touched the case if I hadn't learned that you are to defend him. I consider it my duty to see that that blackguard does not escape justice through any foxiness of yours."

Mr. Yistle loved the word "blackguard." He had often called Gillian a blackguard. Indeed, almost any one who did not agree with Mr. Yistle's views was apt to be added to his list of blackguards.

"I," said Gillian, "am so convinced that Roger Pawling is innocent of these crimes that I consider it my duty to apprehend the real murderer!"

Mr. Yistle's answer to that came sizzling:

"I knew it! You're up to your old tricks! You won't let a chance pass by for personal publicity! That girl is in your office now. You're not thinking of justice! You're thinking of the fun you'll have in spreading her face over the tabloids! You can't resist an opportunity to be a Barnum. I'm telling you, Gillian, that your showmanship won't get you far in a Federal court!"

Gillian chuckled. "Why not? Won't the case go before a jury? When didn't good showmanship impress a jury, State or Federal?"

The ill-tempered man at the other end uttered a snort of anger.

"It's a rotten shame that a man with your instincts is permitted to practice before the bar!" he declared. "It isn't a case with you of justice. It's how much notoriety you can grab! That's all you are—a headline grabber—a publicity hog! All right! I've warned you. Go on and put your head into the noose! Put Roger Pawling's head into the noose! He's going to swing—and I'm going to attend the hanging!"

THE LINE clicked upon emptiness. Gillian was not smiling when he replaced the receiver. Perhaps Mr. Yistle was right. Perhaps Roger Pawling was guilty. Perhaps he would hang. Gillian didn't know. He believed that the younger man was innocent only because he believed that Carolina Dawn had told him the truth. He was acting, as usual, upon emotion. He was so sorry for this pair of unlucky lovers that he wanted to do what little he could for them.

The door opened quickly and Gillian's lovely redheaded wife came in. After five years of marriage, Gillian was still sure that he had married the world's finest, most beautiful woman.

Vee Hazetine's eyes were almost as green as a Ceylon emerald, and they always seemed to shimmer with an inner, secret amusement.

She came around the desk, pecked her famous husband on the mouth, gave his shoulder a little hug and said:

"Darling, am I intruding?"

And Gillian fondly answered, "My dear, your entrance was timed to a split second. We need your expert help. This young lady is Carolina Dawn."

Briefly, Gillian told Vee about the mystery of the Jula Jungle. Concluding, he said: "This romantic tragedy of the high seas has provided me with a tough job. I've taken the job because I am convinced that Carolina is a straight shooter. It goes without saying that in the next few days she will be as popular with newspapermen as catnip is with cats. Obviously, she cannot wander about the streets of this city in that costume. Where is she to stay? How is she to secure clothing without being subjected to embarrassment?"

Vee had been watching him. Now she glanced quickly at the subject of their discussion. Carolina Dawn, for the first time since she had entered the office, smiled. It was an illuminating smile. Her perfect white teeth against the mahogany tan were startling. She was no longer a little sea Arab; she was a hopeful and trusting girl.

"My suggestion," Vee said promptly, "is that Carolina be our guest. I have a bridge tea on for this afternoon. I'll cancel it. My roadster is downstairs. Why can't we slip out of this office the back way, go downstairs in the freight elevator, and escape the reporters? We'll go home. I will telephone various shops for dresses, shoes, hats—everything she needs. When you're ready for her to meet the cameramen, she'll be prepared. Is that what you had in mind?"

"Exactly," Gillian said.

"Of course," Vee went on, "Miss Dawn will wear mourning. And you'll want her to wear mourning throughout the trial."

Gillian nodded. "I'll leave all details to you."

He pressed one of a row of ivory buttons at the back of his desk. The door opened and Donald Carter came in. The young law clerk glared at Carolina Dawn, and she smiled scornfully at him.

Gillian said: "Don, I want you to escort Mrs. Hazeltine and Miss Dawn out the back way to the service elevator and down to Mrs. Hazeltine's roadster. Miss Dawn is anxious to avoid newspaper photographers. If any photographer tries to force his attentions on her, you have my authorization to wallop him in the jaw!"

AS THE law clerk and the two girls were leaving, Gillian's telephone began to ring. Gillian picked up the receiver and the switchboard girl said:

"Mr. Hazeltine, Sergeant Dan Murphy of the homicide squad

is on the wire. I told him you had left orders not to be disturbed, but he says the matter is urgent."

"I'll talk to Dan," the lawyer said. And when the familiar wheezy voice of the old detective came on the wire: "Good morning, Dan; how's your arthritis?"

"Mr. Hazeltine," the detective wheezed, "I've been so busy that I've clear forgot I ever had a symptom. I'm phonin' from the Fourth Precinct station house. Is it true you are after defendin' this bhoy who was a passenger on board that ould hulk that came sailin' up the river a bit ago?"

"Yes, Dan. Have you got him there?"

"I've got every ill-begotten rascal on board the ould hulk here, Mr. Hazeltine. Never in my long life have I clapped eyes on such a pack of cutthroats. When the call came in, I went right down with the wagon. They swear by all that's holy that the bhoy is the murderer, so I let them lodge their charge ag'inst him, then I clapped them in cells on a suspicion charge. And such yellin' and hollerin' as has been goin' on since would make a mule stone deef, Mr. Hazeltine.

"Now Mr. Yistle is here, raisin' the roof because I locked 'em up. He says it is a conspiracy on your part to blacken their lily-white characters as witnesses. I says, 'Well, are they material witnesses, or ain't they?' And he said it made entirely no difference what they were. They are his witnesses, he says, and he is gettin' bail bonds for all of them. He'll have them out of here in two hours, unless you act quick. You tell me what to do and I will do it."

"Change the charge against them," Gillian answered, "and hold them as material witnesses. Have you put a guard aboard the schooner?"

"Yes, sir. The minute we got the call from the waterfront I sent down a detail. They went right aboard, and they're there now."

"I'd appreciate it, Dan, if that boat was kept closely guarded. I don't want what clues there may be spoiled by a mob of curiosity-seekers and souvenir collectors. I'll see you as soon as I've taken a look at the Jula Jungle. How does it all size up from your point of view, Dan?"

"It looks like that bhoy did it, all right, Mr. Hazeltine. All but one of these five pirates claim they were eyewitnesses to both murders."

CHAPTER IV

STUBBORN WITNESSES

THE DINGY BLACK schooner, soon to be made notorious by the press of a nation, was anchored in midstream when Gillian reached the waterfront. Small boats of all descriptions dotted the water about her, and the docks adjacent were crowded with people.

Gillian secured the services of a boy with a punt, who sculled him out to the anchorage. A half dozen uniformed policemen strolled about the Jula Jungle's deck, keeping sightseers at a distance. The officers, recognizing Gillian, permitted him to board. And for the next hour Gillian prowled about the old schooner; inspected it from stem to stern. He expected to find no clues; he wanted merely to familiarize himself with the scene of those two gruesome murders.

He examined each of the rooms in the after house; found black stains which might or might not have been bloodstains.

There were two stairways into the after house, one from the large after deck where the wheel was, and one from the starboard side, forward.

In his quick but careful search of the Jula Jungle, Gillian found but two items of interest, although by no stretch of the imagination could they be called clues. The door of Roger Pawling's stateroom was missing, and the rowboat which had hung between the davits on the after deck was missing. The ropes had recently been slashed.

Satisfied that he was sufficiently familiar with the murder settings to discuss them, Gillian returned to shore and took a taxicab to the Fourth Precinct station house. A mob of reporters met him.

They came plunging down the steps at him, surrounded him. Gillian was popular with newspapermen. He not only knew news values, but he was an artist at creating news. Of a dull trial he had often made a national sensation. As Mr. Yistle said so bitterly, Gillian was a great showman.

This morning the newspapermen threatened to tear the clothes off his back. The story of the Jula Jungle was "hot." It would strike front pages all over the country like an exploding bomb. It was fantastic. It was full of human interest and love interest and it fairly scintillated with dramatic highlights.

They began shooting questions at him:

"Is it true you are taking Roger Pawling's case?"

"Is it true Pawling and the Dawn girl are engaged to be married?"

"Where is she?"

"What's the reason for the hold-out?"

"Who killed them if Pawling didn't?"

Gillian shot answers as fast as the questions came. He was noncommittal; it was still too early in the game to talk. But he managed to stress the love affair. He wanted the public to be sympathetic rather than antipathetic toward the two lovers.

"Can you imagine how the poor child feels—her father brutally murdered, and the man she loves, viciously accused of the deed?"

"Do you know who the murderer is?"

Gillian looked mysterious. He wouldn't answer that one.

WHEN THE reporters would let him go, he went on into the jail. Dan Murphy was waiting for him in his office, a silvery-haired Irishman with keen blue eyes and a fighter's jaw. He looked glum.

"I changed the charge," he told Gillian. "And when Yistle learned about it, he hit the roof. Hear them lousy pirates?"

Gillian heard them. Back in the jail, shouts, yells and roars were making a lively tumult.

"Pirates," Dan growled. "They're yellin' blue murder because I clapped the boilin' of them into cells. 'Ye can't clap innocent men behind bars,' says they. 'Oh, I can't, can't I?' says I. I took enough dirks off of them to start a hardware store. But I can't stop their yellin'. I've threatened to put them on bread and water, and I've threatened them with the steam hose. Yistle will have 'em out of here in another hour, Mr. Hazeltine. If you want them on the carpet, you had better work fast."

"Have you a list of their names?"

"Yes, sir. Right here."

Dan had the names of the Julia Jungle's crew on a sheet of paper, which he gave to Gillian. Gillian scanned the list with interest:

>Hans Larssen, mate.
>Pete Wallaby, steward.
>Ben Carney (black), cook.
>Lester Slick, deck hand.
>Pierre Lohac, deck hand.

"I'll use this office," said Gillian. "Send them in to me one at a time."

"You want the bhoy first?"

"No, Dan; last."

"Yes, sir."

Gillian seated himself at Dan's scarred old oak desk, jammed a cigar into his teeth, lighted it, drew a pad of paper before him, picked up a pencil.

The door opened and Dan's wheezy voice roared: "One more crack out of ye, and you git busted in the jaw."

A man lurched in who could only be described as a human gorilla. Below the medium stature, with massive shoulders and long arms, the resemblance he bore that savage beast was startling. His forehead was low. His eyes were small, beady and close-set. His thick lips were cracked and drawn back from tobacco-stained fangs. His clothes were in tatters.

With his hairy paws carried in half-fists, he came rolling toward the desk. He hitched up his ragged pants, rolled his quid to the other check, and snarled:

"Well, who the devil are you?"

Gillian's steel-blue eyes narrowed and his teeth clicked. Then he smiled.

"Supposing," he said crisply, "we put it the other way around. Who the devil are you?"

"Lester Slick—and what's it to you?"

"The pleasure is mutual," said Gillian. "What's your nationality?"

"United States citizen."

Gillian, glancing at the list of names, saw that Mr. Slick was down as a deck hand.

"Were you ever arrested on a criminal charge?"

Lester Slick hesitated, then snarled, Not me, mister!"

"Let's see your papers."

The gorilla reluctantly obliged. Gillian examined the papers and jotted down notes on the pad. Handing Mr. Slick's papers back, Gillian shot out:

"Who killed the skipper and the mate?"

The beady eyes shifted a little from Gillian's, then returned. Hoarsely: "Roger Pawling."

"Did you see the murders?"

The gorilla spat into the cuspidor by the desk, hitched up his tattered pants and said: "What I know, I know. What I saw, I saw. When the trial starts, I talk—and not five minutes sooner."

Slick placed one hairy paw on the desk and looked down at Gillian with a leer.

"I know who you are. You're Gillian Hazeltine. You're the guy they call the Silver Fox. Go ahead and fox me! Pawling has hired you to get him off. Try and do it! That guy is sewed up in a sack."

"Supposing," Gillian said, "that we found out that Roger Pawling is innocent. How would you like to have those murders pinned on you?"

The gorilla stared at him a moment, and his leathery skin turned yellowish. Then he recovered his composure.

"Blah!" was his comment, "Try and do it. Try and pin it on me!"

"You may have heard," Gillian said, "that I am rough on liars."

"Oh, yeah?" jeered Mr. Slick.

"Yeah," said Gillian. "I'm just warning you. Don't lie on that witness stand."

"Listen," said the gorilla. "I'm so scared I'm shakin' all over like a plate o' jelly!"

Gillian called Dan Murphy and said, "Dan, put this rat back in his cell and bring me another one."

THE NEXT member of the crew to appear was a tall, blond, blue-eyed Swede. He was Hans Larssen, the second mate. He spoke willingly but cautiously, and he did not once remove his mild blue eyes from Gillian's face. Gillian paid particular attention to his hands. They were powerful hands.

Hans Larssen said that he had taken command, as senior officer, immediately after the murders.

"Let me see your papers."

Larssen surrendered them. He proved to be a naturalized United States citizen. Gillian jotted down notes and asked carelessly, "Where were you, Larssen, when the murders took place?"

"At the wheel."

"From where you were standing, then, you could have looked down through the portholes in the after house into the captain's room and the mate's room."

"Yes, sir."

"If there had been a light burning in either of those cabins, you could have been an eyewitness to one or both murders."

"Yes, sir."

"Well—were you?"

"I'd rather not talk, sir, until it's time for the trial."

Gillian puffed thoughtfully at his cigar, and even more thoughtfully gazed at Larssen's large, powerful hands.

"Have all you men," he asked, "decided to say nothing about these murders until the trial?"

"Yes, sir."

"Don't you realize that that attitude is likely to arouse suspicion? It looks to me like conspiracy."

"A seaman doesn't like to say much, in a case like this," was the answer, "to a landsman."

"Has Mr. Yistle talked to you?"

"Yes, sir."

"Don't you realize that all of the information he has secured from you must be thrown open to me?"

"In that case," Larssen quickly answered, "why do you have to ask all these questions?"

Gillian smiled coldly. A glance had told him that Larssen was smart—smart enough to be the gang leader. The lawyer said sharply:

"Larssen, do you want to see an innocent man hang?"

"No, sir: but Roger Pawling is guilty."

Gillian took another tack. "What was the weather the night of the murders?"

"A flat calm."

"Dry?"

"Yes, sir."

"Then you could have left the wheel?"

Larssen's eyes narrowed. "I was at the wheel."

Gillian glanced at Larssen's brawny arms. They were bare to the tattered sleeves of his shirt, above the elbows. Gillian bent forward and looked closer. He saw tattooing and a legion of dark spots.

"What are those dark spots all over your arms?"

"Freckles!"

"Cocaine freckles?"

Larssen growled: "What have they got to do with it?"

"Who knows? How long have you been using cocaine?"

"I can't see that that has anything to do with who killed Captain Dawn and Dirk Morton!"

"We'll let that pass. What kind of man was Dirk Morton?"

"He was as hard as nails."

"An old-fashioned blood-ship mate?" Gillian prompted.

"Yes."

"Did he ever beat men up?"

"Yes."

"Was he a big man?"

"About my size."

"Did you ever fight with him?"

Larssen grinned. "We were like brothers."

"That must," Gillian said ironically, "have been beautiful. You never were tempted to lop off his head with an ax?"

"Never!"

"Were you in love with Miss Dawn?"

"Not me!"

"How did you get along with the skipper?"

"He was like a father to me."

"When he was murdered, did he make an outcry?"

"A gurgling sound."

"How about Dirk Morton?"

"He began to yell. All of a sudden he just stopped."

"Were there lights in the cabins?"

Hans Larssen opened his mouth, then shut it like a trap. "I'll tell it on the witness stand."

"LARSSEN, WHY was the door removed from Mr. Pawling's room and thrown overboard?" Gillian demanded.

"I don't know anything about it."

"Why was the after lifeboat removed from its davits?"

"Was it?"

Gillian had reached the conclusion that Larssen would make a very dangerous witness.

"Larssen," he said, "you and I know that Roger Pawling did not commit those murders. Why weren't you at the wheel when they took place?"

Larssen's jaw was thrust out. His blue eyes were menacing.

"Are you sayin' I had a hand in those murders?"

"I am saying," Gillian barked, "that you are lying. You know that Pawling did not murder those men. I'm warning you, I have no patience with liars. If you go on that stand and lie—you'll suffer."

The Swede folded his brawny arms on his powerful chest.

"If I'm lying, it's up to you to prove it. It's five to one."

"Five liars," Gillian said, "against one."

"What the heck?" the big man jeered. "Try and prove we're lyin'."

Gillian was looking at the tattooed mark on the Swede's forearm. It consisted of a red circle in the center of which was a smaller blue circle. Within the inner circle was a square black dot.

"What does that represent?"

Larssen glanced down at his arm. His air was one of child-like surprise.

"Why, that? What does any tattoo mark stand for? An old man in Tahiti tattooed that on my arm when I was a kid."

"You don't know what it means?"

"I do not."

Larssen folded his arms the other way, so that the tattoo

mark was hidden. He said: "Ask me some more questions. Go on. I'm waitin'."

Gillian called Dan Murphy, told him to put Larssen back in his cell and bring another man.

CHAPTER V

CONSPIRACY?

THE NEXT VISITOR was a whining, sniffling, fish-eyed cockney. He said his name was Pete Wallaby. He had a habit of ducking his head when he answered a question, and of scraping his feet.

"You're the steward of the Jula Jungle?"

"Yes, sir; I ham, sir.' I've been the steward aboard of 'er fer goin' on fifteen years, sir."

"How long did you sail under Captain Dawn?"

"Fer five years, sir—ever since he bought the Jula Jungle."

"How long did you know Dirk Morton?"

"Fer goin' on fifteen years, sir."

Gillian looked at the sniffling cockney with keener interest. "Were you friends?"

"Oh, yes, sir; we was just like brothers."

"H'm. Tell me something about Morton. Was he a cruel man?"

"Well, sir; he was and he wasn't."

Gillian leaned forward. "Don't side-step, Wallaby. I want to know all about Dirk Morton. The truth was, he was a hard case. If a man crossed him, Dirk beat him up, didn't he? Did he ever beat you up?"

"Yes, sir—but I never 'eld it against 'im, sir."

"You mean, you didn't murder him."

"Swelp me, sir, I didn't!"

"Who did?"

"Roger Pawling, sir!"

"Did you see the murder?"

"I—I can't talk about it, sir, until the trial."

"Who told you not to? Larssen?"

Wallaby hesitated. He was clasping a weather-beaten blue serge cap in his hands. Now he was wringing it. Wallaby reminded Gillian very much of a rat.

"Never mind," said Gillian. "I want to know about Dirk Morton. How old a man was he?"

"About thirty-six or seven, I should say, sir."

"Was he a powerful man?"

"Yes, sir. He stood six foot two in his stocking feet, he did. I've seen him pick up a deck of playing cards and tear them in half. And I've seen him take a heavy iron spike and twist it in 'is 'ands sir. And I've seen 'im in fights ashore. I've seen 'im take two big men and bash their 'eads together until they were unconscious. Indeed, he was a powerful man, sir."

"The crew hated him?"

"Yes, sir."

"You own a quarter interest in the Jula Jungle, don't you, Wallaby?"

"I do, sir."

"Did you ever have any disagreements with Captain Dawn as to the kind of trading she was to do?"

"Yes, sir; 'e was a stubborn old man, sir; but they was all friendly arguments, sir."

"You wanted to go into the copra trade, didn't you?"

"Yes, sir; there's good money in copra."

"So, if Captain Dawn was out of your way, you and Larssen could have gone trading in the West Indies? That will come out at the trial."

"Yes, sir; but Mr. Pawling killed the captain and mate, sir."

GILLIAN DISGUSTEDLY sent him back to his cell. With

or without instructions from Mr. Yistle, the, crew of the Jula Jungle had forged a conspiracy against the life of Roger Pawling. Those murders Gillian would not put above any of the men he had so far interviewed. Of the three of them, Wallaby was closest to the murderer type, if there is such a type. He was the sniveling, cowardly kind who would strike in the dark, would stab a man in the back.

The next man to come in was the biggest and blackest Negro Gillian had ever seen. Ben Carney, the Jula Jungle's cook, had large white teeth and very red gums. His attitude was that the whole affair was a huge joke. He was grinning broadly when he came in. He broke into guffaws as he approached the desk. He rolled his eyes until the whites showed. Most Negroes have a natural gift for clowning. Ben Carney was evidently determined to uphold the tradition.

Gillian looked at him steadily. "What's the joke, Carney?"

The Negro stopped laughing. He looked surprised. He stared at Gillian with mock seriousness.

"Whuzzat, white man? Whut joke? Hain't no joke. No, suh. Dis is serious, dis is. Yassuh."

"What do you know about the murder of your captain and Mr. Morton?"

"Whut Ah knows? White man, Ah knows. But don't ask me no questions. Ah ain't in no gabbin' mood dis mawnin'."

"Who killed those men?"

"Da's easy. Roger Pawlin' did."

"Carney," Gillian said harshly, "you're lying. You know you're lying. Do you know what's going to happen to you if you go into court and tell lies?"

"White man," the Negro chuckled, "dey jes' ain't nuffin' gwine happen to dis black boy nohow noway. Ah know who you is. Yo's Gillyum Hazeltine. Folks calls you de Silver Fox. Ah reckon you sho' is foxy, but Ah'm foxy, too."

Gillian looked at Ben Carney's hands. They were big and powerful.

"Where," the lawyer asked, "was the ax kept that was used to kill the captain and the mate?"

"Right outside de galley, by de woodbox."

"You used that ax every day?"

"Yassuh, but not at night! Nebber used dat ax at night. Bad luck to use an ax at night." He chuckled. "Sho' was bad luck fo' de skipper and Misto' Morton."

"How did you get along with Dirk Morton?"

"Jes' fine."

"You were just like brothers, I suppose."

"Yassuh, jes' lak brothers."

"Ever fought with him?"

"Sho', I fit with him. He beat me up good and plenty, first day we sailed. But Ah didn' mind."

Gillian called Dan Murphy and told him to put Ben Carney back in his cell.

THE FIFTH man was Pierre Lohac; a nervous, excitable, anxious Frenchman. A naturalized citizen, Pierre Lohac had sailed in American bottoms for the past twenty years. He had fanatical eyes, lean, strong hands, powerful shoulders. He spoke with hardly the trace of an accent.

As he had done with the others, Gillian asked him for his papers, and jotted down notes on the pad. Then:

"What do you know about the death of Captain Dawn and Dirk Morton?"

"I am not talking," the Frenchman answered.

"How did you get along with the first mate?"

"Nobody got along with the mate. He was too free with the rope's end and the belaying pin."

"Did he ever beat you up?"

"Yes, sir."

"Of course," Gillian said ironically, "you didn't hold a grudge against him."

The Frenchman shrugged. "What good would a grudge do?"

"Perhaps you can tell me what your grudge is against Roger Pawling."

"I have no grudge against Mr. Pawling."

"Then you disagree with the rest of the crew about the killings. Mr. Pawling did not commit those murders—is that what you're saying?"

The Frenchman vigorously shook his head. "He did the killings, but I have no grudge against him."

"Did you see the killings?"

"I will not talk about them."

"Who ordered you not to talk?"

The Frenchman shrugged.

"Mr. Larssen?"

No answer.

"Mr. Yistle, the prosecuting attorney?"

No answer.

"Do you realize that if you go into court and lie, you will be sent to jail for perjury?"

A glimmer of amusement appeared in Lohac's eyes.

"First it must be proved that I am lying."

"You're lying now!" Gillian barked.

"Is it proved?" the Frenchman drawled.

"All five of you are lying. You are going into court, you five men, with a manufactured story. You are attempting to send an innocent man to the gallows. Why?"

"Perhaps because the 'innocent' man is guilty."

"Did you see the murders with your own eyes?"

Pierre Lohac shrugged. "Who else but Roger Pawling had anything to gain by the murders? The captain stood in his way. Mr. Morton stood in his way. What did we, the crew, have to gain by those murders? Perhaps you can answer that."

Gillian felt disgusted and defeated. "Who was being shielded? Larssen? Ben Carney? Lester Slick? Pete Wallaby? This Frenchman? Had the five of them conspired to murder the captain and the mate—and shifted the blame to the passenger? If they had, why had they done it? Why should the crew of a respectable cargo schooner kill off their skipper and mate? What had they to gain?

Certainly, the answers to these perplexing questions were not to be had from the five men. Gillian sent for Dan, and requested him to return Lohac to his cell and fetch Pawling.

CHAPTER VI

A GRUESOME DISCOVERY

THE DOOR OPENED and a tall slender young man came into the room in the station house where Gillian was waiting. Except for bright spots of scarlet on his cheekbones, Roger Pawling's face was pale. But there was fire and fight in his blue eyes. He had a fighter's mouth and a fighter's chin.

He came in long, swift strides to the desk. There was a dauntless something in the way he carried his head that made Gillian take an instant liking to him.

He held out his hand to Gillian and said, "I know you're Mr. Hazeltine. It's a big relief to meet you at last. Is Carolina safe?"

"She'll be here shortly. Sit down."

Roger Pawling sat down and said: "Do you think I committed those murders?"

"I do not."

"Thank God for that," the young man breathed. "I'm not going to let those cutthroats get away with it."

"It's going to be a fight," Gillian warned him.

"Yes, sir! Count me in. This isn't just a case of saving my neck. There's my family to consider, and there's Carolina. She's never doubted me. I've got to come clear for her sake. Now, what's the first thing to do?"

"Whom do you suspect?"

"Every man in the crew!"

"No one man?"

"Larssen or Wallaby or both, because they were part owners of the schooner. They definitely had something to gain with the old man out of the way. But that doesn't explain Morton's death."

"Did Morton want the Jula Jungle to go into the copra trade, too?"

"I don't think he much cared what she traded in."

"Tell me something about Captain Dawn."

"He was the typical old-school sailing captain—a czar of the decks. He was a great disciplinarian, very firm, but absolutely fair and square with the men. He didn't want to trade in copra because he thought there was more money in the lumber and chalk trade, and he hated the tropics. Larssen and Wallaby quarreled with him a great deal about trading."

"How about Dirk Morton?"

"Old-fashioned blood-ship mate. A born bully. He looked it, too. Bright red hair and a pair of the meanest eyes I've ever seen in a human being. Some sailors have girls in every port. He had enemies instead. He was a big brute and as strong as an ox. Every man aboard hated the sight of him. He'd knock a man down on the slightest provocation. We hated each other like a pair of strange pit dogs."

"HOW ABOUT Morton's attitude toward Carolina?" Gillian queried.

"He was mad about her. It was an obsession. It had been going on for years—since she was a kid. He wanted to marry her. I don't think she ever would have weakened. She hated him. But when I came on the scene and we fell for each other, Dirk made out that she had been on the verge of marrying him—and I spoiled his plans. That made the situation pretty uncomfortable, because the Jula Jungle is a small boat—the Leviathan wouldn't have been big enough for Dirk and me.

"Dirk picked on me from the day we left New York. Carolina

*Gillian was met by
Corporal Flaherty*

and I tried to ignore him, but he was the kind you can't ignore. He insulted me every chance he got, and one night we had it out hot and heavy. It was right after supper. Dirk was spelling Larssen at the wheel. I came up on the after deck and filled my pipe and lit it. Carolina took my arm, and we started walking back and forth across the deck.

"All of a sudden, Dirk left the wheel, jumped at me, snatched the pipe out of my mouth and chucked it overboard. Then he hit me in the face. I've done quite a little boxing. I lit right into him. I hit him with everything I had. I had known that a fight would come sooner or later, and I'd made up my mind that when it happened, I would give him the works. I used Dempsey's well-known punch—a straight punch to the stomach and an uppercut to the jaw.

"It seemed to work. He went back about five steps, stumbled and sat down hard. There was a rack of belaying pins handy to where he sat down, and when he came up he had one of them in his hand. I tried to dodge it and get up under it for another punch at his stomach. No use. He outreached me by inches. I caught that pin on the back of the head—went out like a light.

"When I snapped out of it, he was dousing me with buckets of sea water. That was all right. He called me a lot of rotten names, said I was a slick city guy trying to seduce an innocent girl. I got up and socked him again and got the belaying pin again. Did you ever see Babe Ruth swing a baseball bat? Well, that was how that pin looked when it clipped me the second time. I went out, and stayed out for two hours. I thought my head was cracked.

"I stayed in bed most of the next day. It was that night that the skipper and Dirk were murdered."

"Did you ever make any threats against Dirk's life?" Gillian asked.

"You bet I did!"

"Before the crew?"

"Sure! I said I'd kill him the first chance I got."

"Did you ever threaten the captain's life?"

"No, sir! Certainly not. He was a fine old scout. He rode the life out of me, but I think the old boy was honestly beginning to like me. He didn't think much of Dirk, after that fight."

Gillian's cigar had gone out. He relighted it and said:

"You were in your room, weren't you, when the murders took place?"

"Yes, sir. I had a rotten headache from those two wallops with the belaying pin. Carolina had given me some sleeping powders and I was sound asleep."

"What did you hear?"

"Someone trying to smash in my door. I was pretty scared. I waited and when nothing happened, I went out. I met Carolina coming out of her room. We discovered the murders, and a minute later, the crew came piling in. Carolina had fainted and I was holding her when the crew rushed in."

"How long after the murders was this?" Gillian demanded anxiously.

"It couldn't have been more than two minutes."

"Did you see any blood on any one?"

"No, sir. And I looked carefully. I'm certain there wasn't a spot of blood on any of them. And the more I thought about that, the more it puzzled me. How can a man kill two men with an ax without getting a spot of blood on him? It stumped me.

"There were no blood stains on their hands or clothes. When I'd made sure of that, I began looking for clues. Both men's heads had been cut off with an ax. The stumps of their necks looked as if the cutting had been done with one blow. I mean, their heads were cut off clean. The captain's head was lying on the floor near the head of his bed. Dirk's head was missing."

Roger Pawling paused. Gillian was looking at him incredulously.

"Where was it?"

"Overboard. We searched the ship for it. Dirk's head and the ax were never found."

CHAPTER VII

THE MYSTERIOUS TATTOO-MARK

GILLIAN SAID SHARPLY: "Was there a trail of blood from the dining saloon to the deck?"

"Yes, sir. Have you been aboard the Jula Jungle?"

"I looked her over before I came here," Gillian replied.

"You noticed, then, that there are two stairways leading from the after house; one out onto the after deck, the other onto the starboard side of the deck forward of the house. The trail of blood led up this forward stairway—and vanished. Whoever cut off Dirk's head had carried it up—no knowing why—and heaved it overboard along with the ax. There were absolutely no clues. If there were finger-prints, it's too late now to bother with them—everybody in the crew has pawed things over so."

"Who accused you of the murder?"

"The gorilla—Lester Slick."

"What did he say?"

"He said to Larssen: 'There's the guy who did it, Hans.' Larssen, as acting captain, put me in irons and they put me in the chain locker."

"Did you put up a fight?"

"You bet I did! I knocked out Wallaby and the Frenchman. I kicked Larssen so hard in the shins he's still limping. Somehow, my suspicions always come back to Larssen. But I can't prove it. I've worn my brain ragged trying to find motives to pin it on any of them. Mr. Hazeltine, what are the usual motives for murder?"

"There are three," Gillian told him: "hatred or revenge; the hope of gain, and the crimes of passion—the love murder. *Cherchez la femme*—Carolina. Give me what facts you can for each of those motives."

"The men certainly hated Dirk enough to have killed him," Roger answered thoughtfully. "And some of them hated the captain. Lohac, for example, is a Communist. He hated the old man's czarish methods.

"Take the gain theory. By killing off the captain and Dirk, Wallaby and Larssen, each of whom owns a quarter interest in the schooner, would have their way with her. The skipper was a stubborn old boy. He wanted to go into the lumber and chalk trade—taking lumber to Labrador and Nova Scotia and bringin' back chalk or gypsum. Wallaby and Larssen wanted to go into the copra trade. After the murders, these two decided to start without delay for Mexico.

"But there was something mysterious behind that, Mr. Hazeltine. I overheard them—Wallaby and Larssen whispering together several times. They were talking about the Gulf of Mexico, but they weren't talking copra. It might have been rum-running or dope-smuggling or Chink-running. It was something off-color and mysterious, because they were pretty secretive about it. They talked openly enough about the copra trade to the skipper. They quarreled about it a lot.

"Now take the third theory. I've been certain that one or more of those cutthroats wanted the skipper and Dirk out of the way, to be free to go after Carolina. If that was the motive, it was backed up by the fact that, whoever did the killing, next tried to batter down Carolina's door, gave that up, and tackled mine. They didn't get around to Carolina—she beat them to it."

Gillian nodded. "Where does all this bring us? There are no clues—and there are so many motives that the issue is completely confused. Whoever did the killings certainly intended to kill you."

"And decided not to," the young man agreed, "because I was going to be chained up down in that hole and taken to Mexico. But they changed their minds. They decided to kill me, anyway. Wallaby tried to—that same night. Shortly before dawn, Wallaby came down into the chain locker and tried to cut my throat. I had fallen asleep from sheer nervous exhaustion. I woke up with a scared feeling. I could hear the water gurgling under the bows, and—I heard a man breathing hard. I could smell his breath. It was sour with booze.

"A hand came out of the darkness and covered my face. Then I felt a knife at my throat. There I was, Mr. Hazeltine, hand-cuffed to that wood post. Believe me, I acted fast! I drew up my knees and kicked up. My knees caught him in the stomach or the groin. He flew up and came down with a crash near the door.

"I must have knocked the wind out of him. I was scared as the devil; he'd get me—then they'd get Carolina! But he didn't come back. Pretty soon he began to groan. Then he began to puff, the way a man does when his breath has been knocked out of him. Then I heard him crawl away. He didn't come back."

ROGER STOPPED, throwing out his hands in helpless puzzlement.

Gillian got out of his chair. Followed by a trailing plume of cigar smoke, he walked to the window and looked down into the jail yard. He said, in a muffled voice:

"No clues—too many motives." He turned about with a queer smile at his lips and said: "Roger, do you believe in ghosts?"

Roger looked at him solemnly and answered: "Why bother with ghosts when we have five cutthroats to select from?"

"But who else but a ghost could have sneaked into that cabin, killed two men and made his get-away on a ship as small as the Jula Jungle?"

"Don't you mean," the young man guessed, "that you're stumped for some logical explanation of those men appearing in the cabin so soon after the murders without blood stains on their clothes or even a drop of blood on their hands?"

"Also," Gillian went on, "I'm interested in knowing when the lifeboat was cut away from the after davits. The only interesting things I found on that boat were the freshly cut rope ends dangling from those after davits—and the door missing from your room."

The young man smiled. "That last is easy. They took the pins out of the hinges and tossed the door overboard, because it bore evidence in my favor. As for the boat, some of the crew—the murderer or murderers—had cut it from the davits and tied it to the stern by a painter. The murderer was going to make his get-away in the boat, but changed his mind when the crew sided with him in the conspiracy against me. That rope was so short it kept sawing on the rail. The rope snapped while I was at the wheel after Carolina freed me and locked up the crew. There was nothing in the boat but a pair of oars. I had my hands too full to put about and pick it up. I'm afraid that isn't a clue, Mr. Hazeltine."

The door opened and Dan came in, red-faced and almost speechless with excitement.

"Mr. Hazeltine," he wheezed, "I've found the murderer! Bill, fetch him in!"

Roger had sprung up; was staring at the doorway.

Lester Slick, the gorilla-like deck hand, was shoved into the room by a guard. His face was yellow. His small, close-set eyes were glinting like a cornered rat's.

Dan explained: "I caught him in the act of tossin' a note across the corridor to Wallaby. Here's the note!"

Gillian looked eagerly at the scrap of paper Dan gave him. It read:

> If you squeal, you get your throat cut.

Under this dire warning was, in pencil, the symbol that Gillian had seen tattooed on Hans Larssen's forearm—a square dot within a circle within a circle.

He looked from the hasty scrawl to Slick and asked him what the mark stood for.

The deck hand growled: "How do I know? I didn't write it."

"You're a liar!" shouted Dan Murphy. "I saw you write it."

"You saw me throw it. You didn't see me write it. I only passed the note along."

"Who wrote it?" Dan demanded, and Slick snarled the answer.

"Find out!"

"Bring Larssen in here," Gillian said. "Bring them all in here."

Dan departed. He returned immediately with the four other members of the Jula Jungle's crew.

Gillian had been watching Lester Slick. Now he stepped up to him, tore his shirt and exposed, on his hairy chest, the same tattooed symbol he had seen on Larssen's forearm.

"STRIP ALL these men to the waist!" Gillian ordered Dan.

When Dan had complied, Gillian examined the other three. Wallaby had the symbol tattooed on his left biceps. The Frenchman Lohac bore the mysterious insignia on the right shoulder blade. Almost invisible, the mark was found on black Ben Carney's left wrist.

"You men," Dan Murphy said, "might just as well come clean. We know you killed those two men."

"Yeah?" said the gorilla. "Go on and prove it, flatfoot."

Dan turned in despair to Gillian.

"Mr. Hazeltine, I saw this guy throw this note across the corridor to that rat's cell. It fell short and I grabbed it. It proves to me that Slick committed them murders. I'll give 'em all the third-degree. I'll sweat the truth out of 'em.' I'll torture 'em until they howl to confess."

"Wait a minute," Gillian said. "Larssen, what does this mark stand for? It's some secret order, isn't it?"

Larssen glanced quickly at Wallaby and answered smoothly:

"It's nothing but an ornament, sir. As I told you, I had it tattooed on my arm by an old man in Tahiti years ago. These men liked it, and Ben Carney tattooed it on them, and they put it on him to hear him squeal."

Any further questions Gillian might have asked were blocked by the precipitate entrance into the room of Mr. Yistle, the district attorney. He was red with rage. His angry eyes swept down the line-up of prisoners, clashed with the steady blue eyes of Roger Pawling, dealt an optical blow to old Dan Murphy, and came to rest, fairly sizzling upon the bronzed, half-smiling countenance of Gillian.

"What," he hotly demanded, "is the meaning of this?"

When Mr. Yistle was angry, he sputtered. He sputtered now.

A square-built man, with a strong, judicial forehead surmounted by a mop of iron-gray hair, and a massive pair of jaws surmounted by an irongray mustache, Mr. Yistle was a commanding figure. Through sheer force of personality he now endeavored to dominate the present situation.

"Who," he harshly demanded, "is responsible for this? What is the meaning of it?"

"Believe it or not," Dan Murphy grunted, "it's the Wednesday afternoon sewin' circle."

Mr. Yistle ignored this as comedy too low to merit his notice. The full force of his dynamic personality was being projected at Gillian.

"We have been trying," Gillian answered, "to get at the bottom of the riddle: Who killed Captain Dawn and his chief mate?"

"There is no riddle," Mr. Yistle declared angrily. "This fellow Pawling did the killing. I am certain of it."

"You are the only man in this room who is," Gillian said.

Mr. Yistle set his iron jaw. "He will be indicted for those murders. And he will be hanged for those murders. You have no right to bulldoze these men. They are free men. I have bail bonds for the five of them."

"You have no right to turn these cutthroats loose," Dan Murphy broke in. "One of them is the man you ought to indict. Instead of wastin' your time accusin' this bhoy, you ought to be gettin' out indictments for these five pirates. Besides, ain't they material witnesses? Don't the five of them claim they piece together a story—and a tall one it must be!—that will send this bhoy to the gallows?"

"There is no argument," Mr. Yistle snapped. "You men are free."

"**MR. HAZELTINE,**" Dan said quickly, "you swear out five warrants on any charge you want, and I'll book them and clap them back into their cells, bail bonds or no bail bonds."

"Why waste our valuable time?" Mr. Yistle asked cuttingly. "I'll have them out again in an hour on writs of *habeas corpus*."

"But," said Gillian, "any or all of them may clear out. Then where is your case?"

"I'll worry about that," Mr. Yistle said.

"The defense would prefer to have them locked up," said Gillian.

Mr. Yistle snorted. "Defense! You have no defense. You're up to your old tricks. You haven't a case. You're going to go into court without a case—and trust to luck."

Dan had sidled over to Gillian.

Shall I get those warrants?"

"No," said Gillian. "Let them go."

"But the killer is standin' right there, Mr. Hazeltine!"

"Let them go."

"Who cares?" Roger Pawling asked. "Swear out a warrant, Dan, for John Doe; address, Atlantic Ocean occupation, ghost!"

Larssen looked sharply at him, then at Gillian. The Swede's face suddenly lost its color; went yellowish-gray under the coat of sun- and sea-burn. Then he seemed to recover his composure. His color returned in a red flood, stained his heck and even his ears.

Gillian looked at him thoughtfully, very thoughtfully, with narrowing eyes. Then he shot a glance at Wallaby. The cockney was staring at him glassily with his lips parted on discolored teeth. They were finely pointed little teeth, the kind of teeth which have been ascribed to human vampires. In the cockney's face, for a fugitive moment, was a haunting fear.

Roger Pawling seized Gillian's elbow; whispered in his ear:

"Larssen is our man!"

But Gillian shook his hand away. He said:

"Wallaby, I want you to come with me."

Fear returned to the cockney's face. "What for?" he whined.

"Wait a minute," Mr. Yistle cried. "What do you want this man for?"

"I want a newspaper artist to sketch a picture," Gillian said.

"You're up to some of your tricks!"

"Come with me," Gillian invited him.

The cockney went reluctantly, with Gillian on one side, his champion on the other. In the lower hall, among the newspaper men, he found an artist.

"I want you," Gillian said, "to make me a drawing of the tattoo mark on this man's arm."

"What for?" Wallaby whined. "It don't mean nothin'. Swelp me, it don't mean nothin'!"

The newspaper artist produced crayons and a sketchbook. He quickly duplicated in crayon on paper the outer red circle, the inner blue circle, the black square dot.

Mr. Yistle looked on with a contemptuous smile.

"A secret society," he jeered. "Captain Dawn and Dirk Morton failed to pay their dues and were murdered. I won't charge you anything for that idea, Gillian."

"The price is too high," Gillian returned.

A reporter asked: "What's it all about, Mr. Hazeltine?"

Gillian addressed him with gravity: "Here's a mystery for you. Every man in the crew of the Jula Jungle has that symbol tattooed on him somewhere. What's it mean? What's it stand for? I'm anxious to find out. Print it and tell your readers I'd like to have an expert's opinion."

Mr. Yistle was shaking his head dolefully.

"You don't miss a chance, do you, Gillian? This ought to get your name into a lot of papers. Are you through with this man?"

"All through," Gillian said.

GILLIAN AND Mr. Yistle returned to Dan Murphy's office with Pete Wallaby. There, Mr. Yistle calmly announced that the five men were free to leave the jail. "You must not, however, leave the city."

"Where," Wallaby whined, "are we goin' to put up?"

"You'll live in some boarding house until the trial," said Mr. Yistle.

"This boardin' house right here is good enough for the lot of 'em," Dan put in.

"Who," Wallaby wanted to know, "is goin' to look after the schooner?"

"What's it to you?" Dan snorted.

"I own a fourth of 'er, don't I?" the cockney whined. "And Mr. Larssen owns a fourth of 'er, don't 'e? She's in dreadful shape. Captain Dawn let 'er go to the devil, he did. Wot did he care wot happened to 'er? 'E wasn't interested in 'er any more. But I am. And so is Mr. Larssen. She needs paintin' and overhaulin' from cutwater to counter."

"That's your tough luck," Dan snorted, "I've got a guard, day and night, on board that boat, and no one's goin' snoopin' around."

Mr. Yistle said firmly: "I see no reason why these men should not live aboard their schooner. After all, it's the only home they have. And I further see no reason why they should not put in the time until the trial on repairing and painting her. I should say that she is sadly in need of attention. I will also say that the Federal attorney will welcome this chance to save these men's lodging money."

Gillian did not relish the idea.

"Look here," sneered Mr. Yistle. "I'll have these men put up at a hotel for a couple of days. Hire all the detectives you wish to go over the boat for clues. At the end of that time, let these men go aboard and live."

Pete Wallaby was anxiously watching Gillian.

"Very well," Gillian agreed. "But give me two days before you let them go aboard. And I want that guard kept aboard, day and night, until after the trial."

With this understanding, Mr. Yistle and the five sailors departed. When they were gone, Dan said to Gillian:

"There's a couple of things I don't understand, Mr. Hazeltine. What was all this talk about a ghost?"

Gillian smiled. "Who do you think the guilty man is?"

Dan snorted. "Either that gorilla or the nigger."

"Or Larssen or the Frenchman or a pair of them," said Roger firmly. "Why not two of them, Mr. Hazeltine, with Larssen as the leader? Those men are taking orders from Larssen. You know it. He's got them buffaloed. He's smooth and deliberate and colder than a shark's heart. And he takes dope. Why not Larssen?"

"Why not John Doe, the Atlantic Ocean ghost?"

Dan snorted again. Another thing I don't understand is, why did you let those pirates get away? You could have protested bailing. You could have had them held, anyhow, as material witnesses."

"They won't get away," Gillian answered. "They're too confident that they have an airtight case against Roger. All they own in the world is their interest in that schooner."

"But only two of them own interests in her."

"They'll see that the other three don't run out on them. And they're going to be watched, anyway."

"That's another thing, I don't understand, Mr. Hazeltine," Dan said. "Why, if you're turnin' the ould hulk over to them, do you want a guard on board day and night?"

"So that they will be thoroughly watched. When they go ashore, I want them tailed."

"I will attend to that," Dan said. "But I still claim it ain't right for this bhoy to rot away in a cell while those five thugs wander free."

Roger had seated himself. He looked disconsolately at Gillian.

"How much progress have we made?" he asked in a tired voice.

"I don't know," Gillian admitted frankly. He walked over and placed his hand on the boy's shoulder. "Cheer up. We aren't licked."

THE DOOR flew open. Vee Hazeltine came in, followed by a young woman Gillian did not at first recognize. Then he sighed with wonder at the miracles which modistes, manicurists, hairdressers and millinery shops can achieve.

Carolina Dawn, gracious and lovely in a close-fitting black hat, a smart black frock, gunmetal stockings and patent leather slippers, was in mourning, but not too deeply in mourning.

For a moment she stood poised on the threshold. Then she

flew into the room as Roger came out of the chair. They went into each other's arms. They clung together as if they had been parted for years; might never meet again. Carolina stroked Roger's face and his hair and kissed him while tears ran down her brown cheeks.

Vee came over to Gillian and her bright green eyes were shimmering.

She said: "Darling, I think it's dreadful. Love like that ought to be protected and sheltered—it's altogether too rare. She hasn't talked of a single thing but Roger. He's so brave and so fine and so clever! What chance has the poor fellow?"

"It depends on what I can uncover in the next few days."

"Which of those five brutes is the murderer?"

Dan Murphy, overhearing, said promptly: "That gorilla of a Slick!"

And Roger over Carolina's shoulder said: "Larssen! And he's buffaloed the rest of them to stand by him and send me to the gallows!"

Gillian said nothing.

CHAPTER VIII

ABOARD THE MYSTERY SHIP

IN THE LOWER hall, Gillian was again surrounded by a pack of lustily inquiring reporters.

Josh Hammersley literally buttonholed him.

"Gill, what's this ghost rumor?"

Another reporter chimed in: "Yeah! Where do you get this ghost stuff, Mr. Hazeltine?"

Gillian looked from one to another with bright blue eyes.

"What's the rumor?"

"Bert Yistle says you're claiming a ghost came aboard and did those killings. What do you mean?"

"What's the matter with the ghost?" Gillian retorted. "Isn't it a good story? Where's your news sense? Look at the headlines I'm handing you on a silver platter! 'Ghost Murders Captain and Mate of Mystery Schooner, Says Hazeltine. Amazing Disclosures Promised by Police at Any Hour!' What's wrong with that picture?"

"Since when," yelled a tabloid man, "did you believe in ghosts? People will say you're nuts."

"People have already said that," Gillian pointed out.

"Are you trying to tell us," broke in another reporter, "that neither Roger Pawling nor one of those five sailors murdered those two men?"

"I'm saying flatly that Pawling did not."

"Which of the crew do you really suspect?"

"Your guess is as good as mine."

"How far can we go on this ghost story?"

"I can't prevent you from going the limit."

"Oh, yeah?" said a scornful young man. "It's a hot story. 'Ghost With Water Wings Solves Mystery Schooner Riddle. Famous Criminal Lawyer Goes Supernatural! Hazeltine's Happy Haunts Hoax Hoary Herd of Horrid Hop-heads—the hop-heads being us."

Gillian grinned. "Not bad! And you can add: 'While Yistle Yells For Yardarm.'"

He made his way through the reporters and entered a telephone booth. They might kid him to their hearts' content about the ghost—but they would print the story. They would enlarge upon it. Their collaborators with brush, pen and pencil would portray for the sensation-loving public a ghoulish specter, ax in hand, draped with seaweed, slipping aboard the "mystery schooner" in the dead of night to behead the captain and chief mate.

But the results of Gillian's ghost story were destined to be far different from his expectations.

Closing the door of the booth, he called his office and asked for Carter.

To the young clerk he said: "Don, I want you to take down these five names and the information I have on each. I want exhaustive investigations begun at once. Expense is not an object, but time is. Put in a call for the chief of the identification bureau of each of these cities, and get in touch with the Pinkerton agency in each city. I want every scrap of information available."

Gillian read off to him the names of the Jula Jungle's crew and gave to him such information as he had obtained from the five men's papers. Then:

"I'll be sending up a messenger boy right away with the copy of a tattoo mark—a black dot about a quarter inch square inside a blue circle about an inch in diameter, and a red circle about two inches in diameter around that. Have a telephoto of this design, with the colors indicated, transmitted at once to Arnold Blackwood, Crestwood Arms, New York, and tell him to wire me what it stands for. He is the coat of arms expert. Check that and get busy."

EMERGING FROM the booth Gillian secured a messenger boy and sent the artist's sketch to Carter, then betook himself to the waterfront in a taxicab.

It was almost impossible for his cab to move through the thick crowds which were coming and going. Docks lining the north shore of the Sangamo, were solid with people, all staring over the sluggish yellow water at the shabby black hull, the skinny masts which spelled romance and mystery and tragedy on the high seas.

Truly the Jula Jungle was, to the best of her ability, playing her part. The black hull, empty of cargo, perched high upon the yellow water. Her portholes were like furtively-watching eyes. A sinister, forbidding air brooded about her.

It took Gillian a full hour to find a man with a boat to row him out, and the man at first refused to take him; said that hundreds of people had attempted to go aboard and been forbidden admittance by the police.

Gillian was met at the top of the companion ladder by Corporal Flaherty. The lawyer's first question was:

"Has anyone been aboard?"

"No, sir," said the corporal. "Sergeant Murphy gave me orders to let nobody aboard but you and Mr. Yistle and anybody you might give a card to. Hundreds of sightseers have tried, though. How is the case coming, Mr. Hazeltine?"

Gillian shrugged.

"Did that boy do it?" Flaherty asked.

"No."

"Have you got any suspicions?"

"Yes. That's why I'm here."

"If I can be of any help, just let me know."

"Thank you, Mike."

But Gillian did not want any help. The thread of suspicion which he had picked up was exceedingly fine and delicate. It might lead nowhere, or it might lead to a patchwork maze of insoluble "ifs," or it might lead to an amazing revelation.

He went down into the after cabin and opened the doors of all the rooms which gave off the dining saloon. Then he sat down at the head of the table, took out a cigar, lighted it, puffed, and thought. At last, with the cigar almost consumed, he got up.

He went into the captain's cabin and searched it carefully; then, into the cabin where Dirk Morton had met his death. From there he went into and inspected the cabin occupied by Carolina, and the cabin occupied by Roger Pawling.

He climbed the after stairway to the poop deck; took his stand behind the wheel, and looked into the cabins. Leaving the wheel, he went to each porthole in the after wall of the house and looked down inside the cabins from there.

Gillian returned to the cabin, smoked another cigar, then left it by the forward stairway—the stairway up which the trail of blood had led to the starboard side of the deck. He paused at the rail, and his eyes grew dreamy as though he were visualizing the grisly scene of that crime-haunted night two months ago.

BRISKLY, THEN, he walked forward. He went into the forecastle, looked at the bunks; came out and went down into the chain locker where Roger had been held a prisoner. It was a black hole, practically without ventilation or light. Standing in it, he struck a match and looked at the stanchion to which the young man had been ironed by the crew before Carolina had held them up and freed him.

Gillian continued his inspection of the Jula Jungle. It was a much more searching inspection than his first one. He looked into the paint locker. He poked into closets. He descended into each of the cargo holds with a lantern. Gillian wanted to acquaint himself with every detail of the Jula Jungle, below and above water. He poked into every accessible part of the ship, from cutwater to counter, from keelson to pantry shelves.

When he finished, it was dark, and Gillian was covered from head to foot with dirt and cobwebs. His face was streaked with grime. His hands were black. His clothing was torn. He had had no lunch, and he would not eat for hours.

He was weary and he was somewhat disappointed. He had hoped to discover amazing clues, and he had found nothing of great consequence; nothing, it was sure, that would vitally affect the case against Roger.

Yet he was not finished. When darkness fell, the police force lighted lanterns and strung them along the deck. Gillian borrowed two of these lanterns, took them into the after house, placed one on the floor of the captain's room, the other on the floor of Dirk Morton's room. Then he returned to the poop deck, took his stand behind the wheel, and noted what he could see through the cabin portholes in each of the lighted cabins.

In each case, he could see each room almost in its entirety. Behind the wheel, without moving his head an inch, he could see the doorway of each cabin.

A voice in the darkness behind Gillian startled him. It was Mr. Yistle. He was chuckling with amusement. He said:

"Where you're standing, Gill, Larssen was standing that night when the ghost came aboard and chopped off the heads of those two men with his spectral ax! It must have given Larssen an awful start—that green-faced ghost, with the yellow seaweed in his hair dripping brine!"

Gillian eyed him amiably and said: "Where do you suppose Larssen really was when he saw that ghost that terrified him so?"

"At the wheel!"

"But the men all agree that there was no wind. It was a flat calm. The chances were a hundred to one against Larssen's being at the wheel. Where was Larssen?"

"Looking in those portholes, watching the murders!"

"Rot! Another point: Why is a boat missing from these davits?"

Adelbert Yistle snorted with contempt. "Look," Gillian said, going to the davits; "these falls have been slashed. Whoever wanted that boat wanted it in a hurry. Who? Why? When?"

"Easy! Pawling intended to make a get-away in it, but later changed his mind!"

"Wrong! Here are more clues: Why was the first mate's head thrown overboard? Why wasn't the captain's head thrown into the sea, too?"

"Pawling hated the sight of Dirk Morton's face. Murderers do queer things in their maniacal fury."

"WHY," GILLIAN pursued, "was blood smeared all over the girl's and Pawling's doors, but no blood was visible on any man aboard two minutes later? Do you subscribe to the rubber gloves and slicker theory?"

"Not at all. Five eyewitnesses saw blood on Pawling's hands, face and pajamas."

"Why," Gillian asked, "was the door of Pawling's room thrown overboard?"

"He did it himself, to back up his silly argument that it was battered in and smeared with blood! Trot out another clue!"

"Why do Larssen and Wallaby turn green when you mention ghosts in their presence?"

"I suppose," Mr. Yistle answered sarcastically, "it's because they're seeing the ghosts of the two men they murdered! Why not ask a spiritualistic medium?"

One of the policemen on guard approached the two lawyers. Apologetically he said to Gillian:

"I've been rummaging around in the fo'c's'le, Mr. Hazeltine, and I found these under Ben Carney's bunk. Would they interest you?"

He held out to Gillian a yellow slicker and a pair of rubber gloves. Mr. Yistle snatched them. He quickly examined them. Gillian watched him with twinkling eyes.

"There's not a spot of blood on gloves or slicker!" Mr. Yistle triumphantly announced.

"But there is dried salt on both—a crust of it."

"What does that prove?"

"They could have been towed behind a boat. Blood wouldn't cling long to rubber or a boiled linseed oil surface."

"You're miles off the track," Mr. Yistle declared. "You're barking up the wrong tree, Or else you're indulging in your favorite indoor sport—trying to make a sucker out of me! But I've got you licked before you start; and you know it!"

But Gillian was far from licked. He knew that these strange and curiously assorted clues that he had unearthed were leading to an amazing solution of this mystery. His only fear was that they would not lead him to the murderer soon enough to save Roger Pawling from the gallows.

CHAPTER IX

A BACK BAY SNOB

WHEN GILLIAN REACHED home that evening, his first act was to telephone Dan Murphy. To the old detective Gillian said: "Dan, have you got those five men under twenty-four-hour observation?"

"Yes, sir. And I'll have a report of their movements on your desk every morning by ten o'clock."

"They're sailors," Gillian said, "and sailors ashore have a notorious habit of getting tight. And when any man gets tight, he's inclined to be talkative. The vainest man in the crew is the Negro; he would be inclined to talk more, boast more than the others. Keep an eye on him. And I want a very careful report on Wallaby."

"Sure thing, Mr. Hazeltine; I'll attend to all that. But I think you're on the wrong trail. It ain't the black boy or Wallaby. It's that gorilla. I've got a clever girl on the staff who's gonna scrape an acquaintance with him—and get him to open up. He'll brag, too. I'm bettin' a year's pay he's the guy we want. Anything else I can do?"

"Don't let the Frenchman skip town. I've a hunch he will try it. Go ahead on your theory that the gorilla is the man we want. I'm working along other lines."

"Yes, sir. Anything else?"

"Watch Wallaby."

AT A little after ten o'clock on the third morning following the arrival of the Jula Jungle in the river, Gillian was seated at his desk reading the reports of the trailers of the five sailors, when his secretary brought in to him a card bearing the name of Mr. Chauncey Elsworth Haughton. The card bore in its lower left-hand corner the name of a prominent and highly respected firm of Boston lawyers: Gates, Hanford, Billings, Haughton and Deane.

Gillian was familiar with the distinguished reputation of the firm. He instructed his secretary to show Mr. Haughton in, and while he was waiting, read a summary of the report of Operative Glynn on the previous day's movements of Pete Wallaby and his shipmates.

The cockney's activities were, on the surface at least certainly innocent enough. At a little after eight o'clock in the morning he had left the hotel at which he and his four shipmates had been the guests of the Federal Government, and proceeded with them to a waterfront restaurant for breakfast. After breakfast, he and his companions had gone to a ship chandler's on River Street and purchased a large supply of paints and brushes; thence to a wholesale grocer's, where they had laid in enough provisions, the detective guessed, to last them a month.

The five had then been rowed out to the Jula Jungle, had been searched for weapons by the police guard, and had gone to the fo'c's'le. Ben Carney had established himself once again in the schooner's galley. He and the Frenchman had taken up living quarters in the fo'c's'le; but Wallaby, Larssen and Lester Slick had moved their belongings into the after cabin.

Gillian was interested to learn that Larssen was occupying Carolina's room; Slick, the captain's room; and Wallaby, the first mate's room. These three had spent the day painting these rooms.

The detective guessed that they had thus destroyed what clues might have been left, but this did not trouble Gillian. He had turned loose the cleverest men in the research department at police headquarters on the schooner for two days. Microscopes had gone over that entire after cabin and discerned nothing of interest or value.

After supper the five men went ashore and to a waterfront poolroom and speakeasy. They had played pool, had a few drinks, answered questions of the curious with caution, and returned to their ship before midnight.

THE FIRM clearing of a throat called Gillian's attention from this absorbing document. He laid it down and looked up into the thin, aristocratic face of a man of about fifty-five, modestly attired in a suit of pepper-and-salt gray. He wore a black four-in-hand tie. A conservative gold watch-chain was draped across his vest. His gray muttonchops were neatly trimmed. *Pince-nez* of the bifocal variety rested on his thin, aquiline nose. Through the glasses cool, critical eyes were inspecting Gillian.

Gillian rose with his warm smile and held out his hand. The visitor accepted it with a clasp lacking in warmth and pressure.

"I am Chauncey E. Haughton, Mr. Hazeltine."

"Sit down, Mr. Haughton," Gillian said cordially.

Mr. Haughton cleared his throat as he sat down. His manner made Gillian wonder if there was dust on the chair.

"I am interested," said the lawyer, "in the Roger Pawling case. To be quite honest, I took the liberty of stopping at the jail and seeing young Pawling before I came here."

"I see," said Gillian, a little perplexed.

"The truth is, Mr. Hazeltine," the thin, precise voice went on, "I have been retained by the Pawling family to act as the defense counsel."

"I am quite sure," Gillian said warmly, "that your assistance in this case will be very welcome. It is a difficult case."

"So I had gathered from the newspapers. In fact, it was the newspaper reports of the investigation which brought me here. This talk of a ghost that may have committed those murders— did you authorize that story, Mr. Hazeltine?"

Gillian smiled and nodded.

"It was called to my attention by members of the family," Mr. Haughton went on. Gillian reflected that men like Mr. Haughton always had things called to their attention; they seldom read them for themselves. "I declared that no lawyer in his right mind would have authorized such a ridiculous story."

"Indeed?" said Gillian, looking at the neat little man very keenly.

"Indeed!" repeated Mr. Haughton stiffly. "I have, of course, heard rumors from time to time of the—shall we say—spectacular manner in which you handle murder defenses? I cannot say that I approve of such methods."

"There are many who do not," Gillian amiably agreed. "They are generally the people on the other side of the case. My clients, if I may say so, seldom complain."

"This case," Mr. Haughton asserted, "must be handled with dignity. There is the Pawling family to consider. It is one of the oldest, most respected, most distinguished families, in Boston. Roger Pawling, in our opinion, is guilty of the murders."

"If you are so sure that Roger is guilty," Gillian said ironically, "would it be quite ethical, according to Boston standards, for you to go into court to defend him?"

"It is not a question of his innocence or guilt," the Boston lawyer replied. "It is a question of the honor of his family. He will of course enter a plea of not guilty. I will make every effort to clear him of the charge, with, of course, your assistance."

Gillian smiled. He was beginning to work up a cordial dislike for this supercilious, pompous little man from Back Bay.

"I don't think Roger is guilty," he said.

"Of course you don't! It is your business not to. But your way of doing business is different from ours. However, we will conduct this case on the basis that he did not commit the murders."

"He did not," Gillian said firmly, "commit them."

MR. HAUGHTON lifted his delicate brows, and he seemed to look down his nose at Gillian. Gillian began drumming rapidly on his desk.

"That will, of course, be our attitude," said the visiting lawyer. "He must be cleared of the charge. We will present to the jury the facts of his early life—his gentle upbringing, the loving care fostered on him by his relatives. Unfortunately his mother and father are dead, but his Aunt Priscilla has nobly offered to take the stand and testify to his innocent boyhood. Then I shall produce witnesses who will testify to the purity of his lineage. It may interest you to know that he is a Mayflower descendant. We will drive it home to the jury that a young man with such a distinguished background could not have stooped to so vile a thing as murder."

Mr. Haughton sat back with a complacent smile. But Gillian's expression was rather sour.

"This is a factory town, Mr. Haughton. We aren't very high-brow here. We don't go in much for family tradition. We're more interested in what a man is than what his grandfather was. You're going to be up against a jury of truck drivers, mechanics, shop foremen, steel workers—men who hate bunk"

"Bunk?" repeated Mr. Haughton icily.

"Bunk," said Gillian. "You've got to gear your defense to their way of thinking. No frills. They want their facts straight from the shoulder."

Mr. Haughton's thin, severe face colored with displeasure.

"I disagree with your choice of words. Besides, I possess information about Roger's childhood and his activities as a young man that would convince any jury he is capable of murder. The Federal attorneys will certainly secure those facts. We must combat them."

"What facts?" Gillian growled.

"Roger," Mr. Haughton obliged, "was always a black sheep. As far back as his preparatory school days he was a disgrace to the family. Why was he expelled from Oxton?"

"Well," Gillian growled, "why was he expelled from that sissified place?"

Mr. Haughton sat up even more stiffly. His eyes were flakes of ice. It was only too evident that he considered Gillian as less than the dust.

"Roger was expelled from Oxton for dropping little glass balls full of nitrous sulfide on the floor in his philosophy class! The balls broke open and fumes from the vile-smelling liquid drove the students from the classroom!"

"How fiendish!" Gillian muttered.

"He was expelled from college for driving a roadster, while intoxicated, down the Boston Post Road with a chorus girl and hitting a milk truck!"

"Anybody hurt?"

"Fortunately, no. But in an interview he gave reporters he declared that he had always longed to turn the Post Road into the Milky Way and he had at last satisfied his ambition!"

"The boy has imagination!" Gillian said.

"Imagination!" Mr. Haughton cried. "Can you picture the consternation of his family?"

"Poor Aunt Priscilla!" Gillian said.

"I am glad you are sympathetic, Mr. Hazeltine. I have cited these instances to show you the kind of young man Roger is. He has been arrested innumerable times for speeding. He was fined in New York for punching a night club proprietor in the nose. I could go on and on. Since he was a boy of fifteen he has been a disgrace to his family. But what really broke his poor father's heart was this latest development—refusing to enter business, preferring instead to dress like a hobo and go about the world in filthy little sailboats!"

GILLIAN'S FACE had grown redder and redder, and his eyes had grown brighter and brighter. "You don't mean that," he said huskily. "You aren't asking me to believe that Roger's father died of humiliation because of these escapades you've mentioned!"

"It is the truth," said Mr. Haughton.

"A father as foolish as that," Gillian broke out hotly, "is better off dead. What has the boy done? Nothing that you wouldn't expect a normal, healthy, spirited boy to do! If I ever have a son, I only hope he'll go Roger one better! And let me remind you that, whatever Roger has done, he has paid a bitter price. He has suffered; he has been brutally punished for anything he ever did. In this experience he has lost his boyishness and become a man. He is a man that you and I can well admire."

The Boston attorney was firmly shaking his head. He said:

"Mr. Hazeltine, it is even worse than I had feared. You and I disagree fundamentally. I am afraid that we are not going to get along. I know a great deal about you. That is frankly, why I came. I must tell you that I will not tolerate buffoonery or sensationalism in connection with this case. Ghosts! Beautiful daughters of sea captains! Bah! I know what kind she is—scum of the water fronts!"

He might have gone even further than that, but just then the door opened and Gillian's secretary intruded her face.

"Miss Dawn is in the outer office. Can she come in?"

"Send her right in," said Gillian.

The girl withdrew. The door opened again presently, and Carolina came radiantly in. She was smiling and her eyes were sparkling with excitement.

"Gillian—" she began and paused. Her smile faded. The anger in Gillian's eyes and face had not subsided. She looked startled. She sent a bright, inquiring glance at the severe man in the other chair.

Gillian said: "My dear, this gentleman is Mr. Haughton, of Boston. He has been sent here by Roger's family to handle this case. Mr. Haughton, this is the young lady we were discussing—Caleb Dawn's daughter."

The lawyer did not rise. Perhaps he did not consider that Carolina's social status entitled her to any such act of courtesy. But he did examine her most thoroughly. Putting back his head, he inspected her inch by inch from the top of her charming little hat to the tips of her black slippers. His eyes throughout this process remained cold and aloof. Completing his appraisal, he sniffed ever so faintly.

"Indeed!" he said.

"Does it mean," Carolina panted, "that he and not you will handle Roger's defense?"

"Not at all," said the Boston lawyer. "It means that I will employ Mr. Hazeltine in an advisory capacity."

"But won't Mr. Hazeltine be in the courtroom?"

"He will," grunted Gillian.

"Assisting me," stated Mr. Haughton.

Carolina looked bewildered and disappointed.

Gillian pressed a button. When his secretary appeared he said: "Mr. Haughton is to have an office. Have one prepared for him. And see that he has a competent secretary."

"Yes, Mr. Hazeltine." The girl went out.

CAROLINA WAS completing her investigation of Chauncey F. Haughton. Bright spots of color burned in her cheeks under the velvety brown.

She said in a low voice: "Mr. Houghton, have you talked to Roger?"

"I have talked to my client; yes."

"Don't you think it's outrageous?"

"You mean, outrageous of him to kill those two men?"

The girl's eyes widened. "What are you saying? Not that you think Roger killed my father and Dirk Morton?"

"I am convinced that he did!"

"But how—how can you go into court to save him, if you think that?"

"It is not a question of his innocence or guilt, as I just told Mr. Hazeltine. It is entirely a question of clearing this horrible blot from the decent name of his family."

Carolina looked at Gillian. He made a grimace and shrugged.

Very coldly the girl said: "In that case, I won't have you defend Roger. I retained Mr. Hazeltine. I am in a position to pay Mr. Hazeltine. I don't like you. I think you're a nasty old fussbudget."

Mr. Haughton sprang up. He choked and gasped. He hissed: "Scum of the seas!"

"I?" said Carolina.

"You!" panted Mr. Haughton. "And I knew it. I was prepared for it. Let me tell you: I have come to take charge of Roger's defense. I have taken charge of it. You have utterly nothing to say about it."

"Nothing," snapped Carolina, "except that I won't have you!"

"Perhaps," Gillian broke in, we can compromise. Mr. Haughton will present the case for the defense when the United States attorneys have presented their side. I will cross-examine the Government witnesses. I am suggesting this, Mr. Haughton, because of the character of the prosecution witnesses. They are a tough, hard-boiled, vulgar lot."

"That arrangement will suit me perfectly," stated Mr. Haughton, glaring at Carolina.

She glared back for a while, then turned to Gillian with a little gesture of hopelessness.

"Gillian, it's all wrong. This man will ball everything up for us. Don't be so damned kind! Treat him rough! You know that our only chance to save Roger is to impeach the credibility of every witness the United States puts on the stand."

"I'm sure," Gillian comforted her, "that Mr. Haughton is a very able lawyer."

"But he isn't a criminal lawyer, Gillian!"

"Thank God," breathed Mr. Haughton.

Carolina chose to ignore that.

"Gillian," she said rapidly, "I came here to tell you I'd found what that tattoo mark on those men stands for. A reporter at the jail said his paper had just found out. They're bringing out an extra about it. That mark was the emblem of a Swedish pirate named Larssen back in the days of Captain Kidd and Blackbeard! One of Hans Larssen's ancestors was that pirate! Larssen killed my dad and Dirk Morton, then organized the crew to turn pirate! That's why they were going to Mexico!"

"The day of pirates," Mr. Haughton said coldly, "is past. What chance would a slow schooner have in this day of forty-eight-knot destroyers and two-hundred-mile-an-hour pursuit planes?"

"Innocent-looking old schooners," Gillian pointed out, "are engaged in smuggling booze, dope, and Chinese."

"And they didn't carry out that scheme," Carolina cried, "because I trapped them in the after cabin at the point of a gun—and nailed 'em in!"

"Hmf!" commented Mr. Haughton. "How sensational!"

Carolina's eyes blazed.

"Gillian," she said tensely, "throw me out of here, quick—or you'll have another homicide case on your hands!"

CHAPTER X

AN AMAZING COURTROOM

CAROLINA DAWN SAT in the front row which was reserved for witnesses and visiting attorneys. From where she sat she commanded an excellent view of the backs of the heads of the three men most vitally concerned with her interests: Gillian, Roger, and Mr. Haughton.

"The daughter of the seven seas," as the press of the nation referred to her, had never been in a courtroom before, and she was excited and depressed even by the preliminary processes of the legal machine.

To the right and left of her sat the witnesses; at one end, the live sailors; at the other the Bostonians.

Carolina gazed at them with ill-concealed displeasure. They had disdained, since their arrival in the town, to acknowledge her existence. To them she was nothing but a flaw in the family honor. That a Pawling should condescend to become engaged to such trash of the sea as Carolina Dawn!

But beyond their dislike for them and their haughtiness was the firm belief that they would be of small use to Roger's cause. Roger must come out of this clean and whole. There must not be the slightest shadow of a doubt upon his innocence.

It had amused Carolina to see these haughty Back Bay Bostonians when reporters and news photographers and movie cameramen were around. How they loved the limelight! How willingly they partook of this "disgusting publicity!"

Carolina hoped that Gillian would bring the trial to a smashing end before their time came to testify to Roger's "character," these snobs who had regarded the lively, energetic Roger Pawling as a "black sheep."

She continued her inspection of the courtroom. To her, this shabby, dusty place was a battlefield upon which the forces of justice and the forces of wrong would presently march and come to grips. Lies, truth and legal genius would be the weapons employed. And upon the outcome of the battle hinged her life's happiness. An indomitable spirit would not let her admit that defeat was a possibility.

Roger's golden head was being held high. Once he turned and looked at her; smiled. Her heart fluttered as it always did when he smiled at her.

She studied Gillian as he sat, relaxed, beside Roger. His face was now in profile. He was talking to Mr. Haughton. Now and then Gillian pushed up from his forehead a lock of black hair that was always falling down into his eyes.

Her eyes narrowed as she looked at the lawyer from Boston. She had seen him but once since that memorable meeting, weeks ago, in Gillian's office, and his manner had been even more insulting than on their first meeting. And she had told him that he was nothing but a monkey wrench in the machine Gillian was building to free Roger! How she hated the man!

From him she looked at the two judges. They were severe-looking old men, and there was something ominous about the black robes they wore. They looked as if they were predisposed to think that any man brought before them was guilty. Gillian had told her that they were fair and just men, but harsh.

One was Circuit judge Barlow; the other District judge Marsh. In a lull, she heard their voices. She caught phrases: "I did that eleventh hole in par." Golf! While a man's life was at stake!

From the judges, she looked at the jury. Twelve good men and true, so someone had said. Good men? True? They looked very dumb to Carolina. They were the result of five days of hot quarreling among Gillian, Mr. Yistle, and Mr. Haughton. Landsmen all, she felt uneasy about them. The foreman was smirking at her now. He was a beefy man with piggy eyes and a thick sensuous mouth; a weak chin. He was trying to flirt—ogling her.

IT FLASHED over Carolina that no one, in the courtroom but Gillian was seriously thinking of Roger. She amended that when her roving eyes lighted on Mr. Adelbert Yistle. His mop of iron-gray hair was rumpled. His face was flushed and moist. His eyes were flashing. There was nothing flippant or irrelevant about Mr. Yistle. He was all fight—a gladiator prepared for the fray!

Then as she watched him, a bailiff banged for order. Everyone stopped talking, and Mr. Yistle began.

"... Necessary to inform you gentlemen that a murder case tried before a United States court is entirely different from a murder case tried before a State court. In this court, gentlemen, there are no degrees of murder. The defendant, if found guilty, is not guilty of first or second-degree homicide, or of first or second-degree manslaughter. He is guilty of murder. If he is found guilty, he is hanged. If he is not found guilty, he is freed. There are no halfway measures in a Federal court.

As the representative of the United States district attorney, who is too ill to conduct this prosecution, it is my duty to prove to you beyond a reasonable doubt that that man who is seated over there, that man known as Roger Pawling, is guilty of the deliberate, horrible murders of Captain Caleb Dawn and First Officer Dirk Morton."

Mr. Yistle now went on to define to the jury just what was meant, legally, by the phrase, "a reasonable doubt." His bearing was majestic. His eloquence was fiery. His attitude, as he talked, became that of an inspired avenger.

"I consider it my sacred duty, gentlemen of the jury, to prove to you beyond a reasonable doubt that Roger Pawling did deliberately enter the cabin of Captain Dawn and murder him by severing his head with an ax; that he then entered the cabin of Dirk Morton, and in the same brutal and fiendish manner did bring his life to an abrupt end.

"Before I present witnesses, I wish to introduce as Exhibit A for the United States this drawing of the deck plan of the Jula Jungle, and as Exhibits B, C, and D these detailed drawings of the after house, the saloon, and the rooms occupied by the officers, the passenger, and Miss Dawn. Has the defense objection?"

"The defense has," Gillian said.

Mr. Yistle glared at him. Mr. Haughton stared at his assistant with icy inquiry.

Judge Barlow said: "Mr. Hazeltine, I thought you had approved of these various sketches in a conference with Mr. Yistle yesterday."

"Your honor," Gillian grimly replied, "certain information has just come to me that has caused me to change my mind on using sketches and photographs. I respectfully petition that this trial take place on board the Jula Jungle."

"I emphatically object," Mr. Yistle barked.

Gillian addressed at him a steely blue glance, and quickly shifted his eyes to the two judges.

"If the court please," he said in a voice that seemed to ring, "moving the trial to the schooner would obviate the use of sketches and photographs, and it would eliminate frequent visits by attorneys, jurymen and judges to the schooner. This trial threatens to be a long-drawn-out affair. The United States has upwards of twelve witnesses. The defense will produce more than twenty witnesses. The mass of testimony from this formidable array of witnesses will be materially reduced if testimony is taken at the scene of the murders."

MR. YISTLE burst out: "Your honor, I will admit that adjournment to the schooner would make the task of newsreel cameramen and news photographers easier. May I suggest to your honor that if Mr. Hazeltine's suggestion were followed, there would be great difficulty in controlling the great boatloads of spectators who would hover about. In case of rain, where would we be?"

"In the very spacious dining saloon," Gillian promptly answered. There was great finality in Mr. Yistle's headshake.

"I submit," he claimed, "that such action would be absolutely without precedent."

"I submit," Gillian came back, "that whereas we are submitting evidence on a nautical scene to a jury of landsmen, it would greatly simplify matters if the scene were constantly before their eyes. Lengthy explanations of nautical terms would be eliminated. I submit that this court's calendar is crowded, and that my suggestion, if followed, would greatly reduce the time required for this case."

Judge Barlow beckoned Gillian and Mr. Yistle to the bench. The two attorneys joined with the two justices in a spirited discussion. With Gillian supplying the pros and Mr. Yistle the cons, the argument waxed warm. The courtroom grew restless. A bailiff banged for order.

Judge Barlow at length said: "Mr. Hazeltine's suggestion to adjourn court to the Jula Jungle is, while without precedent, a practical and workable one. The court orders an adjournment. I regret that there will be no room aboard for spectators, but there will be space enough for the press representatives. Gentlemen of the jury, you are admonished to discuss this case with no one on your way to the Jula Jungle. Court is adjourned."

Mr. Yistle irritably gathered up his papers. Mr. Haughton was also displeased. He said to Gillian with his usual frankness:

"You are displaying the cheap showmanship for which you are so notorious. You have something up your sleeve."

"Yes," Gillian agreed. "It's been up there since the day that old hulk came into the river. It became an amazing suspicion only a few minutes ago, but it is too preposterous to discuss."

Mr. Haughton looked skeptical. He still clung, after all this time, to the belief that Roger Pawling was the murderer, and nothing Gillian had said had shaken him. He said now, with biting irony:

"I suppose that, at the scene of the murders, you will be able to pin the guilt on the *real* murderer more easily than you could in this courtroom."

"You've guessed it," Gillian said.

He joined the exodus of jurymen, judges, witnesses, bailiffs, stenographers and newspapermen to taxicabs. Gillian, Roger, a bailiff, Mr. Haughton, and Carolina rode in one cab.

At the waterfront, a police launch was used to transfer the crowd to the deck of the schooner. Reporters perched on the roof of the after house. Benches were procured for judges and jury; more benches for witnesses.

There was no wind, but the sky was overcast. Rain might begin to fall at any moment.

Mr. Yistle, shuffling irritably through a portfolio of papers, snapped: "My first witness will be Miss Carolina Dawn."

CHAPTER XI

"OUR ONLY CHANCE"

A CHAIR ON a box beside the steering wheel was the witness stand. The daughter of Caleb Dawn, looking very slim—and small and young, walked to the chair and raised her right hand. A clerk with a Bible heard her oath to tell the truth, the whole truth, and nothing but the truth.

Turning to the jury, Mr. Yistle said: "Gentlemen, before we can proceed to the taking of material testimony, it is first necessary to prove to the satisfaction of the law that the two men named in the indictment as the victims of Roger Pawling's horrible act are actually dead. I have asked Miss Dawn to take the stand solely to establish the fact.

"Miss Dawn, shortly after two o'clock on the morning of

April 12th, did you, as the result of a certain confusion and outcry, leave your stateroom downstairs—in the after house and make the discovery that your father and Dirk Morton, the chief mate, had summarily met their death?"

"I did," the girl answered in a low voice.

"You knew both men in life well enough so that your inspection of their dead bodies left no doubt in your mind that Captain Caleb Dawn and First Mate Dirk Morton had been murdered, presumably in their sleep?"

"I did."

"That will be all. Does the defense wish to take this witness?"

"No," said Gillian.

"You are excused, Miss Dawn. My next witness will be Ben Carney."

At this juncture a tug chugged by, with a movie photographer on the deck rapidly turning the handle of his camera. Mr. Yistle snorted. Mr. Haughton sniffed. So, audibly, did several of Mr. Haughton's Boston witnesses.

The Negro cook slouched to the stand. He automatically raised his hand and was sworn.

Flatfootedly, Mr. Yistle faced him. "Mr. Carney, on the morning of April 12th, were you called upon to perform a very painful but necessary duty in committing the remains of Captain Caleb Dawn and of Dirk Morton to the sea?"

The Negro rolled his eyes and grinned for a flash.

"Yassuh. Sho' was disagreeable and painful."

"Kindly tell the jury just what you did."

"Ah sewed up de cap'm and de mate in sailcloth lak Misto' Lahssen done tol' me, suh. Dassall. I sewed up each gemman separate, with iron bars 'round 'em, so's the sharks wouldn't bite through the sailcloth and eat 'em. Yassuh."

"Now, Mr. Carney, in performing this very painful but necessary duty, did you chance to examine the torsos of the two dead men?"

It was strange court room for a Federal trial

"The whassos, suh?"

"The bodies from the waist up. Specifically, the necks. Did you examine the necks, or the stubs of necks, of the two dead men?"

"Sho' did, suh."

"What conclusion did you draw as to how those two unfortunate men had met their death? Tell the jury."

The big black man looked owlishly at the jury.

"Yassuh," he said amiably, and rolled his eyes. "De perclusion Ah drawed was dat de cap'm and de mate had had dey heads lopped off neat wid an ax. Yassuh. One wallop—and off came de cap'm's head. One wallop and off came de mate's head. Lak dat—*wham! wham!*"

"They must have been terrific blows," suggested Mr. Yistle.

"You tell 'em, boss. *Wham! Wham!* Dassall! Goo'-by, friends— hello, hebben!"

Mr. Yistle turned to Gillian. "I will recall this witness later to support and confirm certain material testimony. Do you wish to cross-examine him now, or will you wait?"

Gillian waved his hand in dismissal.

HANS LARSSEN was Mr. Yistle's next witness. The big blue-eyed blond, who had been the acting master of this ship until

Carolina Dawn's "mutiny," went to the chair. He was calm, composed. His eyes on the jury were mild and trustful.

Larssen testified that, as acting master, he had performed burial services over the two bodies and consigned them to the sea.

Having legally established that the two dead men were dead and now at the bottom of the Atlantic Ocean, Larssen was excused subject to recall, and Mr. Yistle began his real attack.

He said to the jury: "Because the events of that tragic night were observed by the witnesses I shall produce, I will have the story of the death of Captain Dawn and Dirk Morton told to you from the witness stand in proper time order from beginning to end. First, we will hear from Mr. Peter Wallaby."

Peter Wallaby crossed the deck to the chair. He sniffled as he sat down. He looked dolefully at the jury. He sniffled again. He looked as if he might burst into tears. The tip of his sharp little nose was red. It seemed to twitch.

Mr. Yistle began to fire questions at him.

"Are you the steward of this boat?"

"Yes, sir; I ham, sir."

"Are you personally acquainted with that young man sitting over there on that bench?"

"Yes, sir; that is Mr. Roger Pawling."

"In the course of your duties as steward, was it necessary for you to go in and out of the dining saloon frequently?"

"Yes, sir."

"On these visits did you ever hear Captain Dawn and Mr. Pawling arguing or quarreling?"

"Yes, sir; often, sir. After the first week out, it seemed like the captain and Mr. Pawling were quarreling hall the time, sir."

"What were they quarreling about?"

"They were quarreling about Captain Dawn's daughter—the young lydy a settin' over there, sir. It seems as 'ow Mr. Pawling 'ad took quite a fawncy to the young lydy, sir. And the captain, 'e objected most strenuous, sir. And on the night before the captain was murdered by this young man—"

"Objection!" Gillian snapped.

"Sustained," ruled Judge Barlow.

Mr. Yistle: "It has not yet been proved, Mr. Wallaby, that Mr. Pawling committed the murders. You must not presume that."

The cockney sniffled and smiled. His vampire teeth flashed and became invisible.

"I get you, sir. On the night before the captain was murdered, the two of them almost came to blows, sir. The young man, Mr. Pawling, 'e says to the captain, 'Captain,' 'e says, 'if you think Carolina and I aren't goin' to get married, 'e says, 'you're a crazy old fool. If necess'ry,' e says, 'I will kill any man wot stands between me and 'er.'"

Carolina's nails were biting into her palms. She sent a wan look at Gillian, but he only smiled. His smile said: The lying has only begun.

Mr. Yistle was briskly and capably leading his witness to tell of other quarrels Roger had had with the Captain, and of quarrels he had had the mate.

ON NUMEROUS occasions, Wallaby testified, Roger had threatened to "get" each of the two men.

"'E and the myte, Mr. Morton came to blows, sir, the night before the myte was killed. The myte, 'e knock Mr. Pawling unconscious, sir; when Mr. Pawling came to, the myte says, 'If I catch you 'angin' around that innocent girl again, 'e says, 'I knock your teeth down your dirt throat.'

"And what did Mr. Pawling say to that?"

"'E says, 'Oh, you will, will you?' 'e says. 'Well,' 'e says, 'two can at that game. You may not live,' 'e says, 'to knock my teeth down throat.'"

Mr. Yistle began to review Wallaby's testimony. He refreshed the, witness's memory, and Wallaby, sniffling, recalled further quarrels, and further threats the prisoner had made on the lives of the two men.

When the fact had been firmly established that Roger Pawling had done practically nothing on board the Julia Jungle except to quarrel with the captain and mate and threaten their lives, Mr. Yistle said politely: "Through with this witness."

Gillian did hot move from his bench. He said:

"Do you intend to recall this witness, too?"

"I do," said Mr. Yistle. "Do you waive cross-examination?"

"Not entirely," Gillian answered with a grim smile. "I want to ask Mr. Wallaby one or two questions. They concern Mr. Wallaby's past. Mr. Wallaby, I want you to think this question over, weigh it carefully—and answer it truthfully. Were you ever arrested and tried for murder?"

Mr. Yistle loudly objected, declaring that the question was irrelevant.

"I am merely," Gillian explained, endeavoring to impeach the credibility of this witness."

Judge Barlow said: "The objection is overruled. Proceed."

"Answer the question," Gillian said to the witness.

"Well, wot if I was?" snarled the cockney. "We all myke mistykes, don't we? I myde mine in Sydney, Australia. I was young. I was took in by a crowd of roughs. I was drinkin' and gamblin'. I can explain everything! You listen!" The cockney's voice was going higher and higher. He was making wild gestures with his hands, fluttering his fingers in great arcs, flashing his little vampire teeth. "I killed that blighter in self-defense!"

"Don't lie to me! You stabbed Dan Parker, a British seaman, in the back after a fight in a pub on the night of January ninth, nineteen hundred and twelve. Wasn't there a fight in that pub?"

"There was. Everybody was fightin'—"

"Didn't you follow Dan Parker down an alley afterward and stab him in the back? Didn't you get twenty years for it? And wasn't the case reopened in a higher court and the verdict reversed because of a technical error? Isn't that how you got your freedom after you had deliberately and with premeditation murdered that seaman?"

The cockney was beating on his knees with his fluttering hands.

Mr. Yistle harshly objected. He said that Gillian was bull-dozing his witness.

"I am merely proving that this man's testimony in any court of law is not fit for intelligent men to hear!" Gillian hotly countered.

"Well, what of it?" Mr. Yistle shouted. "You have established in the minds of the jury that the witness made an early mistake. Your honor, I object to this testimony."

"Overruled!"

"Exception!"

"Exception is noted. Mr. Hazeltine, have you finished with this witness?"

"If the court please, I have endeavored to prove that this man's testimony is worthless in any court of law. I submit that his testimony under direct examination be stricken from the record."

"Denied!"

Mr. Yistle grinned savagely at Gillian. He might as well have cried, like a triumphant duelist, *"Touché!"*

"IT WILL be my plan," Gillian addressed the court, "to prove, one at a time, that the five material witnesses are unfit to testify in this or any other court. Each of these men has a criminal record and—"

"Objection!" Mr. Yistle cried, "It is summation."

"Sustained," ruled the court. "Save such remarks for your summing up, Mr. Hazeltine. Are you through with this witness?"

"No, your honor." Gillian turned back to Wallaby:

"Wallaby, do you own a quarter interest in this boat?"

"Yes, sir."

"Does Larssen own another quarter interest?"

"Yes, sir."

"Did you and Larssen ever quarrel with Captain Dawn as to what kind of trading she was to engage in?"

"Oh, no, sir. We just had friendly talks. That's all. We never quarreled."

"If Captain Dawn were out of your way, you and Larssen could do what you wished with the schooner, could you not?"

"Objection!" Mr. Yistle snapped. "The question is inferential."

"Overruled. The witness will answer."

Wallaby looked scared. He said: "What was the question?"

"I'll put it another way," Gillian said. "You and Larssen would have profited by murdering the captain, wouldn't you?"

"No, Sir!" Wallaby shrilled. "Indeed not!"

"But didn't he oppose your plan of taking this schooner to the Gulf of Mexico and putting her in the copra trade, or the booze-running or dope-running racket?"

"We weren't goin' to run booze or dope!" the witness shrilled. "We were goin' to carry copra."

"But the captain opposed you!"

"The captain, 'e 'ated the tropics."

"Answer my question yes or no. Didn't the captain oppose your plan of taking this boat south?"

"Yes!"

"Then, if you had killed him, you could have taken the boat south."

"We didn't kill him!"

"Wallaby, who cut the lifeboat away from these after davits?"

"I don't know, sir."

"Who took the door off Mr. Pawling's room and threw it overside?"

"Mr. Pawling did sir, while Miss Dawn guarded us with a gun."

"This witness is excused for recall," Gillian said.

Mr. Haughton was frowning. He was impatient for the United States to finish presenting its case, so that he could produce the cream of Boston's aristocracy. He said reprovingly to Gillian:

"You are being too antagonistic."

"I haven't even begun," Gillian growled. "Our only chance so far is to plant in the jury's mind the fact that each of these witnesses has a criminal record and that at least two of them would have had something to gain by the captain's death. That's my campaign."

Mr. Haughton sniffed. Mr. Yistle barked: "Ben Carney— recall!"

CHAPTER XII

GORY TESTIMONY

THE LARGE AND powerful black man returned to the witness stand with his wide, clownish grin.

Mr. Yistle: "Mr. Carney, did you keep an ax in the galley of this ship?"

"Yassuh."

"What was its purpose?"

"It come in handy when Ah needed to split firewood fo' de galley stove, suh. Cain't split firewood widout an ax, boss."

"At any time did you observe that the accused—Mr. Pawling—was peculiarly interested in this ax?"

"Ah sho' did, boss. He sho' was interested in dat ol' ax. He used to come back to de galley an' heft it. He used to take it out and split up wood fo' exercise. Ah didn't hab no quarrel wid him about splittin' mah wood. But what got me wonderin' was when he whetted it up. Yassuh. He sho' did whet up dat ole ax."

"You mean, he sharpened it?"

"Dassit! He sho' did sharpen up dat ol' ax. He whetted it an' he whetted it till dat ol' ax was jes' lak a razor. Sho' could split a hair on it when he got through whettin'. Never did see such a fine cuttin' edge on an ax in mah bawn days."

"Well, what was his purpose in sharpening the ax? Tell the jury about that."

"Reckon Ah cain't explain it, suh. Whuffo' does any man want an ax so sharp? Mebby he was fixin' to chop off somebody's haid."

"Objection!" Gillian barked.

"Sustained. Strike out that answer." Judge Barlow bent a severe gaze on the Negro. "You must answer questions directly and without inference or supposition."

The Negro looked puzzled. He said, "Yes, jedge. Sho'. But whuffo' did he sharpen up dat ol' ax dataway? It was lak dis, jedge. When a man splits wood, he wants a dull ax. When he chops wood, he wants a sharp ax. We wasn't choppin' wood, we was splittin' wood. It was already cut to length fo' de galley stove. Whuffo' did he whet up dat ol' ax jes' to split wood? Da's whut Ah wanna know."

"I see," said the judge.

Gillian could not pounce on that testimony, and it was dangerous testimony. He knew that the Negro was lying about the ax, but Carney testified so convincingly that the jury would believe him.

Mr. Yistle asked: "When did this happen? When did Mr. Pawling put such a sharp edge on that ax?"

"De mawnin' ob de day the cap'm and mate was kilt."

The reporters perched on the deck of the after house murmured. A bailiff glared at them.

Mr. Yistle: "Ben, did you ask Mr. Pawling why he was sharpening that ax?"

"Yassuh. I says to him, 'White boy,' I says, 'whuffo' you whettin' up dat ol' ax so sharp?' And he says, 'Mebbe Ah's gwine kill somebuddy, nigga.' Dat's whut he says."

Mr. Yistle bowed to Gillian, and his eyes were sparkling.

"BEN," GILLIAN began his cross-examination, "were you ever convicted on a criminal charge?"

The Negro rolled his eyes. He lifted his big shoulders.

"Boss man, Ah disrecollect."

"Perhaps I can refresh your memory. On the evening of December twenty-fifth—Christmas night—in 1920, did you not attack a washwoman in Daytona, Florida, with a razor, and slash her face and neck so that it was necessary for her to spend two months in a hospital?"

"Ah don' seem to remember."

"I see. You've attacked so many women with a razor that you don't recollect that particular incident. After all, a man who goes around slashing people with razors as you've done wouldn't recall a single little instance like that one. Isn't that the size of it?"

"Listen heah, white man—" the witness indignantly began.

"Objection!" snapped Mr. Yistle.

"Sustained. Reframe your question, Mr. Hazeltine."

"Yes, your honor. Carney, you served seven years for slashing that woman with your razor, didn't you?"

"No, suh! Ah sutny did not! Ah only served fo' yeahs."

"Then you admit slashing that poor, crippled old lady with your razor?"

"She wasn't a po' crippled old lady! She was a pow'ful young wench. We had wu'ds. Dat black gal, she rode me all ragged, she did."

"So you slashed her with your, razor. You're quite an expert on sharp-edged tools aren't you, Carney?"

"Ah knows a cuttin' edge when Ah sees one."

"Your honor," Gillian said, "I submit that this man's testimony under direct examination lacks credibility because of his criminal record. If the court please, it should be stricken from the record."

This request was purely technical. Gillian knew that his wish would be denied. He merely wanted to keep in the forefront of the jury's minds that a witness with a criminal record was unreliable.

"Will this witness be recalled?"

"He will," snapped Mr. Yistle. "Next witness—Lester Slick!"

THE GORILLA man took the stand and testified that he was a deck hand and was personally acquainted with Roger Pawling.

Mr. Yistle: "Mr. Slick, kindly describe to the jury your actions and observations in regard to the accused on the morning of April twelfth at or before two o'clock."

"Well, sir, it was a hot night—so hot that a man couldn't get a wink of sleep in the fo'c's'le. So Pierre Lohac and I drug out our mattresses and laid 'em on the stabbard side o' the deck just for'ard o' the galley, where we could get what breeze was blowin'.

"The Frenchman and I was layin' there, tryin' to get to sleep. The second mate, Mr. Larssen, was at the wheel. He had just struck four bells—two o'clock, that is, in land time—when I see this young feller, this Roger Pawling, come sneakin' along the deck like he didn't want nobody to see him.

"I was lyin' on my back, looking up at the stars beyond the riggin', when I heard the scuff of his foot on the top stair, or the wave check at the top of the stairway leadin' for'ard out o' the after house. When I looked, there he was, dim-like in the light o' the stars. He was actin' so sneaky that I sat right up and looked. But he didn't see me or if he did, he didn't pay no attention. He snuck into the galley, and when he come out he had the cook's ax in his two hands, holdin' it to his chest like this."

Mr. Slick demonstrated how the accused had held the ax.

"He walked back down the deck to the after stairway again, and I give Frenchy a nudge in the ribs. I says, 'Frenchy,' I says, 'there's some dirty, work goin' on here. Wake up. Roger just borried the cook's ax and took it down into the after house.'

"So Frenchy and I, we circled the after house on the port side and we find Ben Carney standin' beside the wheel talkin' to Mr. Larssen.

"I told Mr. Larssen what I had just saw. And the words was hardly out of my mouth when it happened!"

"What happened?" Mr. Yistle barked in the breathless silence. A fine drizzle was falling, but no one gave heed to it.

"I'll have to explain," the witness answered. "Mr. Larssen was standin' there, with one hand on a spoke o' the wheel. Ben was standin' right there with his back to the rail, and Frenchy and I were standing right there.

"From where the four of us was standin', we could see through those portholes there into the cabins."

"Wait a minute," Mr. Yistle stopped him. "Do you mean there were lights in those cabins?"

"I'm gettin' to that," the gorilla man answered. "That porthole there is the porthole of the captain's room. And that one in the middle there is the porthole of Mr. Pawling's room. And that one, over on the port side, is the porthole of the first mate's room."

Mr. Yistle said sharply: "What did you see in those portholes?"

The gorilla slowly shook his head.

"It was terrible, it was. While the four of us was watchin', we saw Mr. Pawling come into the skipper's room with a candle in his left hand and the ax in his right. We wondered what he was up to. Not one of us had the idee that he was up to anything like cold-blooded murder. We just stood and watched, curious-like.

"Mr. Pawling, he set the candle down on that little table under the porthole, then he grabbed the ax in both hands, lifted it up and swung it down with a terrible swing. Up come the ax—and down come the ax! Like that!

"We heard the thump of it, then a gurglin' sound, and a sort of splashin' sound. I figgered that when a man gets his head lopped off like that, clean, the blood squirts out of the neck arteries in a solid stream. It must have been that stream strikin' the bulkhead that I heard."

"NEVER MIND what you thought. What did you do?"

"Do?" Mr. Slick repeated. "We was just struck dumb. It was just like seein' a terrible dream, it was. We just couldn't believe such a thing—goin' in like that and loppin' off a man's head while he was asleep. What would you 'a done?"

"Answer my question. What did you do?"

"I told you—we was froze stiff! We watched Mr. Pawling pick up the candle—"

"Was his hand steady?"

"I don't remember. He picked the candle up—"

"Wait a minute. Let's go back a little. Did you see the ax strike the captain?"

"I don't like to think about it," the witness answered. "Yes, sir. I saw it all. The old man was lyin' face down on his bunk. It was built as a double-decker, but he had the upper bunk took out. On account o' the heat, he didn't have a stitch of anything on him. He was layin' there plumb naked. I saw Mr. Pawling lift up the ax and bring it down smack on the old man's neck. His head come off just as neat and clean—"

"That will do."

Roger had risen from the bench on which he sat beside Gillian. He was pale and his lips were working convulsively. Gillian quickly grasped his arm and pulled him back. "Never mind," he said.

"But don't you see," the young man whispered huskily, "he's making it sound so damned convincing! I'd almost believe it myself! They're building up an absolutely watertight case! No wonder he can describe it in such detail! If Larssen didn't do it, he did!"

The witness was saying: "… Just froze stiff, we was. And before we could snap out of it, we saw him take that candle up and move on past his room into Dirk Morton's room. Dirk was layin' on his bunk like the skipper had been, without a stitch on, only he was lyin' face up, with his head facin' the door. His mouth was open and he was snorin'.

"Mr. Pawling come in, put the candle down on the edge of the washbasin and took two hands to the ax again. We began yelling at him. He looked up, holdin' the ax, but he couldn't see nothin' because the light was on his side o' the porthole. Up come the ax—and down come the ax! And off come Dirk Morton's red head!"

THE WITNESS paused again. Everyone on the after deck, including the two judges, was staring at him with horror. Even Gillian was, for the moment, spellbound by the picture he had drawn. It was vivid and real and it sounded like truth. He was realizing what a tremendous task lay ahead of him, in persuading the jury to disregard the testimony of these men. How carefully they had rehearsed these lies! How beautifully Mr. Yistle had trained them.

Mr. Yistle said: "You saw Mr. Pawling, the accused, strike off Dirk Morton's head with the ax, after he had struck off Captain Dawn's head with the ax. The light afforded by the candle was sufficient in both cases for you to identify the man with the ax as Mr. Pawling, and his victims, respectively, as Captain Dawn and Dirk Morton?"

"Yes, sir. We could see it plain."

"You say he struck each man a single blow?"

"Yes, sir. He had been practicin' on that wood pile and his aim was mighty good."

"Tell the jury what happened after you saw Mr. Pawling strike off Dirk Morton's head."

"Things was pretty confusin', they happened so fast. The first thing, as I rec'lect, was that Mr. Pawling picked up the candle and started out of the mate's room. I remember Mr. Larssen yellin', 'Come on, you guys. We gotta grab that feller! He'll be killin' us next!'

"Well, we hesitated about gone' down into that cabin. Mebbe you can understand why. It was dark down there by then, and nobody wanted their head to come off the way the captain's and Dirk's had come off. We went to the head of the stairs and waited there a minute.

"We heard the sounds of the ax smashin' down below. Later on, we figgered he had gone all around the big room smashin' things. He smashed in a panel on Miss Dawn's door, and he smashed in a panel on his own door. I guess he smashed up a few chairs, too, but I ain't sure."

The witness paused and bared his tobacco-stained fangs. Mr. Yistle continued his examination:

"Let's go back into Dirk's room a moment. Mr. Slick, after you saw Mr. Pawling chop off Dirk Morton's head, did you notice him do anything strange?"

"Well, it was all pretty strange, Mr. Yistle. Just what do you mean, for instance? I don't quite understand what you mean."

"I mean, did you see him do anything strange in connection with Dirk Morton's head?"

"Oh, yes. Yes, sir, that's right. It sure was strange, all right. After he had chopped off his head, he stood and watched the blood squirting out of the mate's neck and the body flopping around the way a chicken's does when you cut off its head.

"Then he stooped over that bloody mess and picked up the head by a handful of red hair. He stood and looked at it a second, then he grinned. Then he went out with the head in one hand and the ax in the other. It was after that that we heard him smashin' things up."

Gillian wondered if the jury had swallowed that. Coming as an afterthought, it sounded unconvincing. But the jurymen were gazing raptly at the witness, with horror written on their faces. They had evidently swallowed it word for word.

MR. YISTLE: "He didn't pick up the candle when he went out?"

"No, sir; he had his hands full as it was. But he knocked the candle over, or it fell over, I forget which. Anyway, there was no light at all. Just those sounds of smashing goin' on down there, and Mr. Larssen tellin' us to go down and grab him.

"All of a sudden, it got quiet again. I know now that Mr. Pawling was running up the for'ard stairway and to the rail and throwing Mr. Morton's head overboard with the ax. He came back down the stairs, and when he got down, we got there just about a second later. We all struck matches, and we grabbed him."

In the tense silence Mr. Yistle walked ponderously over to the witness. He placed the palm of his left hand under the elbow of his right arm. Slowly he shook his right index finger in the gorilla's face.

"How about the captain's daughter? Where was she? What was she doing?"

"When we got down into the cabin, she was in Mr. Pawling's arms. She had fainted. She was comin' to as we crowded around. First thing she says was, 'Oh, Roger, why did you kill them?'"

"There must have been blood on her from his hands."

"Yes, sir; she was all smeared with blood from him. She kept yellin': 'Oh, Roger, why did you kill them?' Then she got hysterics. She laughed and cried and carried on somethin' awful."

"I want you to tell the jury about the blood you saw on Mr. Pawling and elsewhere."

"Well, sir, he was bloody all over. There was blood on his face and on his hands and wrists clear up beyond his elbows. His hands was solid blood. His pajama sleeves was soppin' wet with it. It was terrible. The saloon and the skipper's and mate's cabins was like a slaughterhouse. Blood everywhere and on everything."

"When you seized Mr. Pawling, what did you do with him?"

"We put him in irons."

"Did he resist?"

"I'll tell the cock-eyed world he did! He socked Frenchy in the jaw and Pete Wallaby in the forehead and knocked them cuckoo. We carried him into the chain locker."

"Did he escape from there?"

"You might call it escapin'. Noon the next day, the five of us was settin' in the saloon eatin' lunch when Miss Dawn's door pops open and out she comes with a gun in her hand. She says to stick 'em up. She made Mr. Larssen hand over the keys to Pawling's handcuffs."

"That will be all for the present," Mr. Yistle said.

Gillian arose. The drizzle was increasing. He said:

"Mr. Slick, what was Mr. Pawling wearing that night?"

"A suit of pajamas and a blue bathrobe."

"What became of them?"

"They must have been thrown overboard, sir."

Gillian pointed to the window farthest over on the port side.

"Is that the porthole at which you were standing when you saw Mr. Pawling chop off Dirk Morton's head?"

"Yes, sir; that's the one."

"You saw him place the candle on the washstand, then pick up the ax and chop off Mr. Morton's head?"

"Yes, sir."

"Then you say he stood and watched the blood spurt out of the stump of the dying man's neck and observed the manner in which the body was jerking and twitching?"

"Yes, sir."

"And then you saw him stoop down and pick up Dirk Morton's head?"

"Yes, sir."

"From where you were standing, or crouching, what did that head look like? Try to describe it."

"I don't know if I can, sir. Mr. Morton had, as you know, bright red hair. Mr. Pawling just grabbed a handful of it and held up the head."

"Was the hair long?"

"Yes, sir. Dirk wore his hair pretty long."

"He wasn't inclined to be bald?"

"No, sir; he had real thick hair."

"Was his mouth open—I mean, when Mr. Pawling picked up the head and looked at it?"

"I think it was. And the eyes were open, too. I can remember seeing the light on them. It was terrible."

GILLIAN NODDED. "Mr. Slick, I want you to tell the jury just what was your honest opinion of Dirk Morton. Please answer that question carefully. Take your time. Did you love him like a brother?"

"No, sir; I did not. He was a bully. No one liked him. He was mean to everybody on board. Captain Dawn was a-scared of him half the time. I don't think he realized what a bully Dirk was when he signed him on."

"Did Dirk ever beat you up?"

"There wasn't a man in the crew he didn't beat up sometime or other."

"It didn't break your heart when he was killed, did it?"

Mr. Yistle started to object. He was wearing a puzzled frown. He opened his mouth, reconsidered, and closed it.

The witness bared his yellowed fangs in a leer.

"I didn't bust down and bawl when I knew he was dead!"

Mr. Yistle interrupted: "Your honor, I can't see that this line of questioning is getting us anywhere. It strikes me as being entirely irrelevant."

But judge Barlow would not sustain his objection. He told Gillian to continue. Gillian did so, but he took a new tack.

"Mr. Slick, was Mr. Wallaby on this deck with Mr. Larssen, Ben Carney, Pierre Lohac and you when the murders were committed?"

"No, sir."

"Was he in the cabin when you arrested Mr. Pawling?"

"He was. That is, he came down right after us,"

"Where had he been?"

"I think in the fo'c's'le."

"How long have you been a deck hand in the crew of this schooner?"

"Four years and two months up to the time we anchored here."

"In those four years, Wallaby and Dirk Morton were also members of the crew, were they not?"

"Yes, sir."

"They had been sailing in this schooner before you joined the crew?"

"Yes, sir."

"Did you ever see Dirk Morton beat up Wallaby?"

"Yes, sir; several times."

"Did it ever strike you that Wallaby was under the influence of Dirk Morton? I'll be more specific. Did it strike you that Dirk Morton ordered Wallaby around like a slave?"

"Yes, sir. I noticed that." The gorilla's eyes were narrow now, and glinting with suspicion.

Gillian proceeded more cautiously.

"Did you ever wonder about it?"

"I guess we all wondered about it."

"Didn't you have a conversation once with Mr. Pawling in which you stated that you thought Dirk Morton 'had something on' Wallaby—meaning, a knowledge of some guilty, incident in Wallaby's past?"

"I don't recall any such conversation," said the witness.

"Your memory," Gillian barked, "has been surprisingly fresh on other points. Try to recall that conversation."

"I don't remember it."

"**VERY WELL.** Let's go back a few years," Gillian suggested suavely. "Were you not arrested in Pensacola, Florida, on March 18, 1923, by Coast Guard officers with a gang of rum runners in connection with the murder of Coast Guard Lieutenant Andrew Leslie?"

The gorilla bared his fangs.

"Did I kill him?" he snapped.

"Were you not sentenced to a three-year term for perjury?"

"What if I was?"

"Your honor," Gillian said quickly, "I submit that this man is a perjurer; was convicted of a charge of perjury in a United States court; that his entire testimony is inadmissible."

Judge Barlow denied Gillian's request. The judge then said to the jury:

"Gentlemen, I presume that you are all aware of what Mr. Hazeltine is trying to do. He has every right to bring up the question of these men's criminal pasts, if they have such pasts. Such testimony as they have given in direct examination is admissible to the record. I am sure that Mr. Hazeltine will not object to my making it quite clear that he wishes you to consider the weight of their testimony as influenced by their criminal records. He has a perfect right to cast doubt on the credibility of every witness the United States offers. Do you wish to ask further questions of this witness, Mr. Hazeltine?"

"Yes, your honor." Gillian addressed Slick. "I want you to tell the jury just when you had that mark tattooed on your chest. Kindly open your shirt and show the jury that mark."

The gorilla unbuttoned his shirt.

Gillian: "When was that mark tattooed there?"

"I don't remember."

"Wasn't it done on the forenoon of the day Captain Dawn and Dirk Morton were buried at sea?"

"I don't remember."

"I'll try to refresh your memory," Gillian said grimly. "On the night of May 6, did you go to a nightclub with a girl named Clara Delaney?"

"Here, in this town?"

"Here, in this town."

"Well, what if I did?"

"In the course of the evening, don't you recall telling Miss Delaney that Ben Carney tattooed you, Pierre Lohac and Pete

Wallaby, with a careful and artistic imitation of the mark on Hans Larssen's forearm?"

The gorilla snarled. "So that tomato was one of your spies, eh?"

"I can produce her to corroborate what I am saying."

"Don't bother. Sure! We got tattooed that morning. We didn't have anything else to do. We were killin' time."

MR. YISTLE interrupted. He declared that all of these questions and answers were irrelevant. The two judges looked inquiringly at Gillian.

Gillian said to them: "I am endeavoring, a step at a time, to prove that a conspiracy exists to send the accused to the gallows; that these five men have plotted and planned to foist the guilt of the two murders on him. Each of the five men has this mark tattooed somewhere upon his body. That mark is prima facie evidence that such a conspiracy was and is in effect."

Judge Barlow said quickly. "Can you prove that now, Mr. Hazeltine?"

"My whole defense, your honor, is based on the fact that such a conspiracy exists and that each member of it, because of previous criminal records, is unfit to give testimony in any law court."

"Objection is overruled, You may proceed, Mr. Hazeltine."

"This witness is excused," Gillian said.

"My next witness," Mr. Yistle snapped, "is Hans Larssen."

CHAPTER XIII

A DANGEROUS WITNESS

THE BIG BLOND mate took the stand and was sworn. Very carefully Larssen answered Mr. Yistle's questions. Yes; he had been at the wheel, aft, at the hour of the murders—two o'clock in the morning. Yes; he had looked into the portholes at the rear of the after cabin, and, by the light of Pawling's candle, had seen

He made the jury see the scene of horror he was describing

Roger Pawling dispatch with the ax first the captain, then the big redheaded mate.

"Why," Mr. Yistle asked, "did you not run down into the cabin when you saw Mr. Pawling murder the captain? Why did you not rush down there and overpower him? Why did you permit him to go into Mr. Morton's cabin and murder him? Kindly give the jury your own answers to these questions, Mr. Larssen."

The mild blue eyes of the second mate traveled to the jury.

"We were scared stiff, that's why. After what we had just seen—the way he chopped off the skipper's head—no man alive would have gone down there. He could have blown out that candle and killed any of all of us. The only firearms aboard were down in that cabin."

"When did you go down?"

"It must have been a couple of minutes after he chopped off Dirk Morton's head. We decided to rush him. When we went down there he was in a daze. He was holding Miss Dawn in his arms and—"

"Wait a minute! Did you hear her say, 'Oh, Roger, why did you kill them?'"

"Yes, sir. I heard her say it several times."

"Did you see much blood on him?"

"Yes, sir, he was smeared all over with blood."

"Did he offer resistance when you tried to put him in irons?"

"Yes, sir. He knocked out two of the men and kicked me in the shins."

Mr. Yistle questioned Larssen at length, drawing from him a more detailed picture of the murders and of the arrest of Roger Pawling. Larssen made an excellent witness.

Gillian opened cross-examination by asking the big blond man to tell him something about the unusual influence which Dirk Morton was reputed to have exercised over Pete Wallaby.

"I was not aware of it," Larssen said firmly.

"Do you recall saying on one occasion to Miss Dawn that it struck you as strange that Wallaby would stand for such abuse from Dirk Morton, unless Morton had something pretty serious on Wallaby?"

"No, I don't."

"Didn't you once ask Dirk Morton why he was so abusive to Pete Wallaby?"

"I did not."

Gillian abandoned that line of questioning. He said:

"Mr. Larssen, when I questioned you on the morning when this boat put into port here, I asked you about the weather on the night, or morning, of the murder. You told me that there was no wind, that there was a flat calm."

"Yes, sir."

"It was hot and calm?"

"Yes, sir."

"It must have been very unseasonable weather."

"Yes, sir."

"This boat was not moving at all?"

"No, sir."

"The sails were hanging limp and motionless?"

"Yes, sir."

"When a sailing vessel is becalmed in such a way as you have described, and if there is no indication that a wind is apt to spring up, is it customary for a man to stay at the wheel?"

"It was on this ship, sir. Captain Dawn was very particular."

"But Captain Dawn was in bed and asleep, wasn't he?"

"That makes no difference. He was my superior officer and he had given me orders to stay at the wheel. I was at the wheel."

"You always obey orders without question?"

"I always do!"

"Have you never disobeyed an order that a superior officer has given you?"

"I always obey orders!"

You aren't lying?"

Larssen glared at him. "You heard me. I always obey orders!"

"WHY WERE you discharged from the crew of the schooner Azura in Baltimore on January 5, 1913?" Hazeltine demanded. "Wasn't it because the captain—Captain Black—told you to take charge of the ship while he motored to Philadelphia, and then came back unexpectedly to find you had gone ashore on a spree?"

Larssen did not answer. Judge Barlow said: "The witness will answer!"

"I had forgotten."

"Then you do," Gillian pressed his point, "occasionally disobey orders—when the captain isn't looking?"

"Say," Larssen snapped, "I can see through you like a piece of glass! If I say I wasn't at the wheel, you'll say: I was down in the cabin with that ax!"

"That's where you were, wasn't it?"

"No!" Larssen roared.

"But you've admitted you weren't at the wheel!"

"I do not! I was at the wheel! I tell you, I was at the wheel!"

"In a dead flat calm, with the skipper asleep, and the barometer showing no indication of wind coming?"

"Yes, yes, yes! I was at the wheel!"

"You're going to stick to that story, are you?"

Mr. Yistle objected. He was sustained.

Gillian: "Mr. Larssen, isn't it true that you use cocaine?"

"What if I do?"

"In using cocaine, isn't it customary, using it as you do, to dissolve a cocaine tablet in warm water, fill the needle with this solution and inject the contents into a vein?"

"You seem to know as much about it as I do!"

"You use cocaine, do you not, when your spirits are low—when you have need of reckless courage?"

"Objection!" roared Mr. Yistle.

"Sustained!"

Gillian said rapidly: "Larssen, isn't it true that you left that wheel to fix yourself a shot of cocaine so you'd have enough nerve to go into that cabin and kill those two men?"

"No! No! I didn't kill them! I tell you, I was at the wheel and saw Pawling cut off those men's heads!"

"Where did you take cocaine that night?"

"I don't remember."

Gillian said quickly: "After you took the cocaine, who were the ghosts that you saw?"

"I didn't see any ghosts!"

"Who cut the lifeboats from these after davits?"

"I don't know!"

"Let's go briefly over the events of the morning following the murder. After breakfast, you ordered Ben Carney to sew up the dead men in canvas for burial. When they were properly sewed up, you read the burial services and put them overboard; then you had Slick, Lohac, Wallaby and Barney tattooed. Then what did you do?"

"I didn't have them tattooed. They had themselves tattooed. After that we sat down to eat lunch."

"What did you do after the tattooing and before lunch?"

"Nothing."

"Didn't you throw Mr. Pawling's door overboard?"

"No! He threw it over himself so he could get away with that fishy story about its panel having been smashed and having blood on it!"

"Did you see him?"

"Yes!"

"What do you know about that missing lifeboat?"

Larssen looked at him narrowly. Then he said harshly: "Nothing, mister; not a thing."

"When did you first notice that it had been cut from its falls and was towing astern by its painter?"

"I didn't pay any attention to it. I didn't see it. How could I? There wasn't any wind until an hour or two after we had been nailed up in the after cabin."

"You mean, you weren't on this deck at any time after the murder and the arrest of Mr. Pawling?"

"No.

"Of course; why should you be? There was a flat calm, didn't you say?"

"That's what I said."

"You didn't think it was necessary to be at the wheel or to put a man at the wheel?"

"No."

"Yet, at the time of the murders, it was calm, too, and you were at the wheel. How can you account for that?"

Larssen's eyes had narrowed to slits. His hands were clenched into fists on his knees. He licked his lips repeatedly and blurted:

"I was captain after the murders, wasn't I?"

"Yes!" Gillian said triumphantly. "You could do what you pleased then, couldn't you?"

"I had command of this ship, if that's what you mean."

"And you were also a fourth owner. With the captain out of your way—"

Mr. Yistle shouted an objection. He was sustained.

GILLIAN GRIMLY proceeded, reframing his question: "You were in command, and you had, at the captain's death, acquired the right because of your quarter ownership to dictate where she should go?"

"I did."

"And you decided to take her to Mexico. Why Mexico? Why not the nearest port?"

"Why not the port we were cleared for?" Larssen growled. "What difference did it make? We weren't inside territorial waters, were we? I could decide the best place to go, couldn't I?"

"Why were you going to Mexico?"

"Because I was going to put this boat in the copra trade, as I'd been wanting to do."

"Not dope-running or rum-smuggling?"

"I said copra."

"Didn't you have a conversation in Havana, Cuba, about a year ago with a man named Leon Harmanos, who owns a rum distillery there?"

Larssen did not answer.

"Didn't you tell Leon Harmanos that you were planning to turn this boat into a rum-runner? Didn't you talk to him about shipments?"

Larssen spat out: "What if I did?"

"Then you were lying about the copra."

"I was not. I intended carrying copra."

"To hide the rum? Well, never mind. Let's go on. I suppose, Mr. Larssen, you have been reading the lengthy newspaper accounts of this case since this ship came into port here?"

"I have."

"Then you must have read of the statement given out by Mr. Arnold Blackwood to the effect that that tattoo mark on your forearm is an old secret symbol of your family, and was used by one of your ancestors a Swedish pirate named Johannes Larssen, as a house flag."

"Sure. I read that."

"Do you deny that it is true?"

"I certainly do."

"Your honor," Gillian said, "I should like to read into the record the report that Mr. Arnold Blackwood, the cipher expert, has made on this tattoo mark that these men are wearing."

Mr. Yistle hotly objected, but was overruled. Gillian read the report and another report, this one from a genealogist, who had traced Hans Larssen's pedigree directly back to the old pirate. The report concluded with the statement that Hans Larssen's great-great-great-great-great-great-great-great-great-great-great-grandfather, Johannes Larssen, had been hanged in Maracaibo in the year 1708.

Then Gillian addressed the witness with this question:

"You deny, do you, that you were carefully organizing this crew to stand behind you on a rum-running or dope-running program or any other illegal sort of venture, call it piracy or what you will?"

"I do!"

"Then I ask you once again: Why did you have that old pirate's house flag tattooed on the bodies of these men?"

The Swede stared at Gillian malevolently. Gillian quickly turned to the jury.

"Gentlemen," he said, "you have been listening carefully to all of this evidence. You have heard me prove with reports from authorities that this man is a descendant of a pirate who was hanged; that he is wearing on his forearm the symbol of that old pirate, that he was planning to engage in rum-running, dope-smuggling, or some other illegal venture—perhaps piracy. Now I want you to hear his answer to my question: Why did he have that piratical emblem tattooed on these three men?"

"Objection!" yelled Mr. Yistle.

"Overruled."

"Because," Gillian said with a wide smile, "they thought it was pretty? Is that why they had it tattooed on themselves?"

"They liked the looks of it," Larssen shouted.

Mr. Yistle now moved that all of this testimony be stricken from the record. His request was denied. He drew a deep breath and looked at Gillian. In that look was supreme confidence. Gillian might shake his witnesses on minor points, but he could not budge them an inch from their story of the murders.

CHAPTER XIV

MORE SPECTERS FROM THE PAST

GLLIAN RESUMED: "MR. Larssen, were you ever convicted on a criminal charge? To be exact, did you serve five years in the French penal colony on Devil's Island—1915 to 1920—for beating to death a beggar who asked you for a few centimes on the waterfront at Marseilles?"

"I didn't know I was going to break his neck."

Mr. Yistle groaned.

"Ah," Gillian pounced, "so you didn't know you were going to break his neck! Did you care?"

Mr. Yistle: "Objection!"

"Sustained."

"Mr. Larssen," Gillian pursued, will you kindly tell the jury just how you broke that beggar's neck?"

"It was an accident," the mate growled.

"You mean, he fell off the dock and broke his neck?"

"No," the witness muttered surlily. "I pushed him. He fell. He broke his neck. It was too bad."

"And you served five years on Devil's Island?"

"What if I did?"

"Very well. Let's not go into that. Let's go into another matter. Why did you leave Sweden eighteen years ago?"

"Because I wanted to go to sea."

"No other reasons?"

"No.

"Have you ever been in a town in Sweden near Stockholm, named Norrkoping?"

The witness nodded curtly.

"Where did you spend the years 1911 and 1912?"

"I don't remember— In Sweden."

"Did you not spend those two years in a prison in Stockholm for seducing a fifteen year old girl in Norrkoping?"

The witness's mild blue eyes were dancing now with fury.

"I don't remember!" he snarled.

"You deny seducing the girl?"

"I don't remember!"

"And you don't remember organizing the crew of this schooner to go in for piracy?"

"No! I did not!"

Mr. Yistle wiped moisture from his forehead. The drizzle, which had stopped, had set in again. But the moisture on Mr. Yistle's brow was not entirely bestowed by heaven.

Gillian surrendered the witness to him. And Mr. Yistle tried desperately to restore Larssen to his former stature. But Larssen had lost his temper. Smarting under Gillian's lashing, he snapped at Mr. Yistle. He became a little confused. Mr. Yistle gave it up. Gillian leaped into the breach, in recross-examination, and reduced Larssen to a state of sputtering incoherency.

But the next witness, Pierre Lohac, turned the tide back again under Mr. Yistle's clever questioning.

PIERRE LOHAC told of having been waked up by Lester Slick, as they were lying on deck, shortly after four bells on the morning of the murders; told of seeing Roger Pawling sneak down the forward stairway of the after house with the ax in his hand. With excited gestures, Lohac described the two murders just as Larssen and Slick had described them.

Then Gillian took the witness.

"Mr. Lohac, why did you have that mark tattooed on your body?"

"Because I liked it."

"You admired it?"

"Yes, sir."

"For artistic reasons?"

"Yes, sir."

"You liked it so much that you wanted it copied on your body so that you could admire it at your leisure. That's what you mean, isn't it?"

The Frenchman's eyes were flashing. He may have been thinking of more than one thing at a time. At all events, he fell into the trap.

"Yes, sir. So I could admire it."

Mr. Yistle groaned. Distinctly he said, "Oh, my God!"

And Gillian said rapidly: "Then why, in the name of heaven, did you have it tattooed on your shoulder blade?"

The Frenchman stared at him. He wet his lips. He made several expressive gestures with his hands. Then he grinned foolishly.

"You have me there," he admitted.

Mr. Yistle groaned again. Gillian, having turned the tide once again on this insignificant pebble of a trick, hastened to say:

Mr. Lohac, I suppose you have no criminal record. I suppose you have never been convicted of the crime of murder."

"No, sir. Never!"

"That distinguishes you from the other four members of this conspiracy, doesn't it?"

"Objection!"

"Sustained."

But Gillian plunged on. "Not being a murderer places you on a much higher level than your shipmates, does it not?"

Judge Barlow said sharply: "Mr. Hazeltine, you must confine

yourself to the taking of direct testimony. Your last two questions are inadmissible, as calling for a conclusion."

"I apologize," Gillian said. "We will go back. Mr. Lohac, I want to ask you again: Have you ever been *convicted* of a murder?"

"Objection!" shouted Mr. Yistle.

"Sustained! Mr. Hazeltine—"

"Your honor, I apologize." But Gillian did not look contrite. He said:

"I will reframe the question: Mr. Lohac, have you ever been sentenced on a criminal charge?"

The Frenchman looked pale and worried. He hesitated so long that Gillian helped him.

"Perhaps your memory is bad, too. Did you not serve two years in the Atlanta penitentiary, beginning in 1922, for your participation in smuggling cocaine, heroin and morphine into Louisiana from Cuba?"

"I was framed!"

"But did you serve those two years?"

"No! My time was shortened for good behavior!"

"You're excused."

Several of the jurymen laughed. Even judge Barlow smiled. Then he said:

"Mr. Yistle, how many more witnesses have you?"

"Only one, your honor—Ben Carney. And I wish to recall Peter Wallaby afterward."

Judge Barlow looked at his watch. He said: "I think we'll have time to hear one of them before we recess for luncheon."

"I would suggest, your honor," Gillian said, "that we adjourn to the dining saloon for the remainder of this session. This drizzle of rain is growing worse."

This suggestion was acted upon. Judges, jury, stenographers, witnesses and lawyers descended to the Jula Jungle's spacious dining saloon. Chairs and benches were brought down. Lamps were lighted. Reporters huddled in doorways. A chair in a corner was selected as the witness stand.

Mr. Yistle announced his next witness: "Benjamin Carney—recall!"

CHAPTER XV

A FIGHTING CHANCE

GILLIAN EYED THE big Negro uneasily as he went to the stand. Ben Carney had a quick imagination. His story somehow remained the most credible of any that had been told. His testimony now, as an actual eyewitness, might well be very damaging. But Gillian had other facts of Carney's criminal past with which to combat this.

Mr. Yistle began the examination by asking Carney where he had been at about four bells, or two o'clock, on the morning of April 12.

The Negro rolled his eyes until the white showed. His teeth flashed whitely in the dark room.

"Ah was standin' on de after deck wid Misto' Lahssen. It was too hot fo' sleep; so Ah had come up and walked aft fo' a breath ob air. De mate and Ah was standing there talkin' 'bout Misto' Pawling and de ol' man, and how dey was always wranglin' 'bout Miss Carolina, when Misto' Slick an' Frenchy come hot-footin' it around from de stabbard side an' said dey had jus' saw Misto' Pawling go sneakin' down de for'ard stairway wid an ax—de ax Ah done tol' you he was whettin' dat mawnin'. Yassuh."

"Did you see Mr. Pawling go into the two cabins and chop off the heads of the two men?" Mr. Yistle' encouraged.

"Yassuh. Sho' did. Ah seed dat boy go into de cap'm's room, and den into de mate's room, wid a candle in one hand and de ax in de other. Ah seed him lop off dey heads—jes' lak dat.

Wham! Wham! Boss, Ah means to say Ah was one scairt black boy. Yassuh! It sho' turned mah blood into ribbons ob ice."

"Did you see Mr. Pawling pick up Dirk Morton's head from the floor, after severing it from his body, and stare at it?"

"Yassuh. Ah seed dat, too."

"You saw him carry it out of the room?"

"Yass. Sho' did."

"After you had recovered from the shock of that horrible sight, were you one of the men who rushed into this room and seized Mr. Pawling?"

"Yassuh. Ah was de last one down! We done seized him right ober by dat do'."

"Did you see any blood on the defendant?"

"Boss, ask me where Ah didn't see no blood! Go on and ask me! Wherever Ah looked, dat's all Ah saw. Blood on everything. Blood on his hands. Blood on his face. Blood all ober de flo'. Nebber did see such a mess. No, suh."

Gillian took the witness. Unwrapping a paper parcel, he brought to light a pair of large rubber gloves and a yellow oilskin coat.

"Ben, do you recognize these articles of clothing?"

"Ah sho' do'! Dey's mine!"

"Where'd you get them?"

"I bought the oilskin. A ship doctor made me a gift ob dem gloves."

"Where were they on the night of the murders?"

"In de fo'c's'le—under mah bunk. Yassuh!"

Gillian put the objects down and walked toward the Negro.

"Ben, do you deny that you ever discussed with Mr. Larssen, Pierre Lohac, Lester Slick and Peter Wallaby a proposition of Mr. Larssen's to turn this schooner into a rum boat—or a pirate ship?"

"Yassuh, sho' Ah do. Ah mean, no, suh, Ah nebber did!"

"You mean," Gillian promptly took him up, "they wouldn't let you into the conspiracy because you're a black man?"

"No, suh, Ah don't. Mah color didn't make no difference. Dey—" He stopped, seeming to choke.

"They let you into the conspiracy, did they, to send Mr. Pawling to the gallows and turn pirates?"

"No, suh," the Negro shouted. "No sech a thing. Wasn't no 'spiracy. Ah done tol' you dey wasn't no 'spiracy!"

"Ben," said Gillian, "that sentence you served in Florida for slashing that washwoman wasn't the only time you ever served, was it?"

In the dimness, the Negro's eyes seemed to gleam.

"Ah don't know whut you mean, boss," he said uneasily.

"I SEEM," Gillian said, "to be spending most of my time refreshing your and your shipmates' memories. Didn't you get into a knife fight with a white man named Judson Herrick, in San Francisco, on the afternoon of July 4, 1911?"

"Did Ah?"

"Didn't you? Didn't you stab that man seven times in the chest? Didn't you serve ten months for that?"

"Boss," said the cook earnestly, "lemme explain. Ah did cahve mah 'nitials on dat white man, jes' lak you say. 'Cause why? 'Cause he run in a pair ob loaded dice on me in a crap game. Yassuh! He had it comin'!"

"In other words, whenever you get angry at a man—or a woman—you pull out a razor or a knife, or you pick up an ax—"

"Nebber picked up no ax to hit a man wid!" the Negro shouted.

"How do we know?"

"Ah'm tellin' you. Dat's why!"

"All right! Whenever you get mad, you use some sharp-edged cutting instrument—"

" 'Tain't so! Ah cahved dat black wench, an' I cahved dat crooked gambler. Dassall—ain't it?"

Gillian waved his hand. Mr. Yistle sprang up and attempted to undo the damage Gillian had done. But Ben Carney was resentful. He was rattled and not a little scared. There was dark magic in the way Gillian had resurrected those old affairs of Ben's, and Ben was wary. He was, in fact, overcautious. Mr. Yistle's reexamination was distinctly a failure. The Negro practically refused to talk.

Gillian wished that it was possible to avoid the cooperation Mr. Haughton was so anxious to give. Those Boston society folk with their supercilious airs would antagonize the jury of honest workingmen. He wished it were possible to take up immediately a discussion of the evidence now in.

He had, he believed, an even chance to bring in an acquittal verdict for Roger as things stood now. He was sure he had implanted in the jury's mind a suspicion, which he might fan into a certainty, that the five men had conspired to send Roger to the gallows.

Mr. Yistle was worried. He looked worried. There were creases between his eyes and he was repeatedly running his fingers through his hair—a sure sign.

Judge Barlow said: "Mr. Yistle, have you any more witnesses?"

And Mr. Yistle said: "I want to recall Pete Wallaby, your honor. He is the last."

"Will this examination take long?"

"No, your honor. No longer than ten minutes."

"Very well. We will take recess immediately afterward. Take the stand, Mr. Wallaby."

The cockney went to the chair in the corner and seated himself.

MR. YISTLE: "Mr. Wallaby, at four bells, or two o'clock on the morning of April 12, where, to the best of your recollection, were you?"

"Asleep in the fo'c's'le, sir."

"At what time were you awakened?"

"It must 'ave been just a few minutes after two, sir."

"What awakened you?"

"I 'eard some shouts, sir, or at least I fancied I did. I woke up and I went to the fo'c's'le doorway and listened. I remember that it was a blistering night, sir. I 'eard men yelling and I ran toward them. My first thought was that the ship was on fire.

"When I reached the after 'ouse, I 'eard the yelling down below in this room. I came down the for'ard stairway, and everywhere I looked I saw blood. Mr. Morton was lying dead, with 'is 'ead missing, in 'is cabin; and Captain Dawn, with 'is 'ead off, was lying dead in his cabin. I was absolutely 'orrified, sir. Mr. Pawling was struggling and fighting with Mr. Larssen, Mr. Carney, Mr. Lohac and Mr. Slick. Some one said Mr. Pawling 'ad just murdered the captain and the myte. Mr. Pawling was putting up a terrific fight, but finally 'e was subdued and put in irons."

"During this fight, did he strike you?"

"Yes, sir. He landed a powerful blow on my forehead right 'ere, sir. It fair knocked the daylight out of me, sir."

"Did he knock you unconscious?"

"Yes, sir; I fancy 'e did. And at the same time, I believe 'e knocked Mr. Lohac unconscious."

"Did you see blood on Mr. Pawling?"

"Yes, sir. 'Is 'ands were bloody and 'is face was bloody. And there was blood all down the front of 'is pajamas and bathrobe."

"Do you know what became of these pajamas and bathrobe?"

"Yes, sir; they were thrown overboard that same day."

"By whom?"

"By myself, sir."

Mr. Yistle asked a few more questions pertaining to the scene in the dining saloon when Wallaby entered it that fateful night, then dismissed him. He said curtly:

"The United States rests."

Judge Barlow asked Gillian if he intended to cross-examine the witness on his recent testimony.

"Yes, your honor."

"It had better go over until this afternoon. Gentlemen of the jury, we are about to take a recess until two thirty o'clock this afternoon. The Court admonishes you not to speak about this case among yourselves or permit anyone to speak to you about it. You will keep your minds open until the case is finally submitted to you.

"Bailiff, if you will have the police launch come alongside, we will go ashore. You will take charge of the prisoner now, and the other bailiff will accompany the jury to the nearest restaurant. I believe there is a good restaurant located nearby on Water Street."

The few newspapermen who remained filed out. Since they had come aboard, their number had thinned considerably. In ones and twos they had been hastening ashore, to file their running stories.

CAROLINA WAITED until no one remained but Gillian and herself.

"Gillian," she said, "how do things stand?"

The lawyer shrugged. "If Yistle and I could start arguing the case immediately after recess, there might be a fighting chance, I am worried about Haughton. He will befog the issue. If I only had a clean deck, I might succeed in convincing the jury what liars these five witnesses are. But I'll frankly admit that, as things stand, the odds are against us."

"But, Gillian, with what you brought out about that tattoo mark, you've proved there was a conspiracy! And what about these amazing disclosures you've been hinting at? Aren't you convinced it's Larssen?"

"I've run into blind alleys," Gillian said wearily.

"But even if you get Roger off with clever arguments, there'll still be a horrible cloud over him. You've got to find the guilty man!"

"If I can get him off at all, I'll be satisfied. Run along now, Carolina. I've got some terrific concentrating to do."

She looked at him for some hope, but there was none to be found in his face.

When she was gone, Gillian sat down at the table, opened a leather dispatch case and removed from it a thick pile of documents. These represented only a small part of the data he had been securing through agents from various corners of the world. Much of this data was worthless, but he had industriously and tirelessly sifted through it all.

Drawing a pad of paper before him and uncapping his fountain pen, Gillian compiled a list of the clues which had led him eventually into a blind alley.

The list he had compiled was as follows:

1. Had the rubber gloves and yellow slicker been worn by the murderer and washed in the sea afterward?

2. How otherwise was it possible for the five suspects to appear in the dining saloon within five minutes of the time the murders were committed without blood being seen on any of them?

3. Why were the head and ax thrown overboard?

4. Where was Larssen when the murders were committed? (Gillian had interviewed some twenty-odd sailing men on the question of whether or not a man would be at the helm during a flat calm which had persisted for hours and showed no sign of ending. Their almost unanimous answer had been that the helm would have been deserted.)

5. Why do Larssen and Wallaby turn pale when ghosts are mentioned?

6. Who removed the door from Roger's room and threw it overboard?

7. Who cut the lifeboat falls and tied the boat to the stern rail by the painter?

8. Wallaby and Dirk Morton sailed together for fifteen years in this ship.

9. Dick Morton exerted some powerful influence over Wallaby. What was behind that influence?

GILLIAN PUSHED the pad aside and opened a bound record

of the Jula Jungle's career. The old schooner had engaged in almost every known trade, from pearling to filibustering. Gillian made a note of the filibustering, and picked up the several bound volumes of typed sheets which represented the detailed reports of several operatives on the activities of the schooner's crew.

All of these reports were fundamentally the same as the first that had reached his desk. Except for a few mildly drunken shore parties, the five men had conducted themselves beyond reproach. Perhaps they were too conscious of being shadowed. They had done considerable painting and caulking on the schooner.

Generally, they spent their evenings shooting pool or at a movie. Dan Murphy had seen to it that plenty of girls were thrown in their way; but the only piece of information of real value that the girls had secured had been that which pertained to the tattooing.

Lester Slick, the human gorilla, had said nothing more of importance to the Delaney girl. The five men had for the most part, lived simply and quietly aboard the boat.

Gillian smoked and pondered these simple, straight, innocent facts—and got nowhere.

Filibustering! The word tapped at Gillian's imagination. Filibustering! Eleven years ago, so the record ran, the Jula Jungle had successfully run a number of machine guns through the United States blockade into Nicaragua. One night a destroyer had stopped the Jula Jungle, but her captain had somehow bluffed his way through and landed the machine guns.

Gillian sat back in the chair and smoked and scowled. Suddenly his mouth opened and the cigar slid out of it and fell. He jumped up and ran up the forward stairs and into the rain.

His subsequent actions were comparable to those of a man suddenly bereft of reason. He opened hatch covers' and scrambled down into cargo holds. He returned to the deck and raced forward to the fo'c's'le, only to turn about again and start madly aft. When he was amidships, he saw the police launch putting out from the dock. He would not have time to give full play to his inspiration. But wait till he had Wallaby on the stand!

Gillian went into the bathroom and washed the cobwebs and grime from his face and hands. He went out on deck and paced up and down with a long blue plume of fragrant cigar smoke trailing him while the two judges, the jury, the prisoner and the witnesses came aboard and went below. He called to Carolina, but she did not hear him. As she disappeared into the cabin, he started aft.

Gillian threw his cigar overboard and went down the stairs with the light of battle in his eyes.

"Filibustering." A word packed with adventurous possibilities!

CHAPTER XVI

STARTLING EVIDENCE

JUDGE BARLOW, DECLARING court open, requested Peter Wallaby to take the stand. Gillian watched the cockney as he walked to the chair as a cat might watch a rat on which it will presently pounce.

Mr. Wallaby," he began, "I want to go over once more some of your testimony. How long have you been steward of this schooner?"

"For fifteen years, sir," said Wallaby, showing his little sharp vampire teeth.

"All of that period, until the night of April 12, you served with Dirk Morton, did you not?"

"Yes, sir; all of it."

"Will you kindly tell the jury in what business this schooner was engaged during the summer of 1919?"

"Eleven years ago, sir? Let me think. In the summer of 1919, she was engaged in carrying lumber, I believe, from Charleston to Nova Scotia—'Alifax, to be exact, sir."

"Let me refresh your memory, Mr. Wallaby. Wasn't it the summer of 1920 that she was in the lumber trade? On the previous summer, wasn't she engaged in filibustering—carrying machine guns and ammunition into Nicaragua?"

The witness wet his lips. He shot a glance at Mr. Yistle. But Mr. Yistle could give him no help.

Wallaby nodded. "Yes, sir; I believe she was, sir."

"Did she not, on the night of August twenty-fourth, successfully land in Nicaragua, on a beach near the town of Prinzipolca, about a hundred machine guns and ten thousand rounds of ammunition?"

Again Wallaby glanced in distress at Mr. Yistle. And Mr. Yistle acted.

"I object, your honor. I cannot see how incidents which may or may not have taken place eleven years ago have any bearing on the guilt or innocence of the man charged with these murders."

"What I have in mind, if the court please," Gillian replied, "has a direct bearing on the murderer."

"You may proceed, Mr. Hazeltine."

"On this August night, eleven years ago," Gillian resumed, "was not this schooner overhauled by a United States destroyer?"

Even in the dim light of the room, the cockney's pallor was noticeable. His eyes began to glitter with fright.

"Yes, sir," he mumbled.

"Did officers from the destroyer come aboard this schooner?"

"Yes, sir. They came aboard to see our papers, sir."

"And when they saw your papers, didn't they search this ship for machine guns and ammunition?"

Wallaby started to shake his head. His color was now almost green.

He stammered: "Y-yes, sir!"

"Did they find any?" Gillian shot at him.

"N-no, sir! You see—"

"Why didn't they find them?"

"They only looked 'astily, sir!"

"And when the destroyer officers went back to their own ship, this schooner proceeded to shore, did it not, and landed those machine guns and ten thousand rounds of ammunition on the beach near Prinzipolca?"

"Ye-yes, sir!"

"WHERE," GILLIAN roared, "were those machine guns hidden?"

The cockney cowered back. He licked his lips. He rubbed his hands together. He fluttered them in futility.

"I—I don't know, sir!"

"You were on board this ship, were you not, when those machine guns were loaded?"

"Yes, sir!"

"You were on board this ship, were you not, when they were unloaded?"

"Y-yes, sir!"—a hoarse whisper.

"Where were they hidden?"

"I tell you," the cockney cried, almost squealing, "I don't know. I never knew. I never asked."

"They were so well hidden that the naval officers did not find them. Weren't they? Answer me!"

"Ye-yes, sir."

"Where were they hidden?"

"I tell you, I don't know!"

Gillian turned to the jury. "Gentlemen," he said, "it has been obvious to you throughout this trial that I do not subscribe to the proposition stated at the outset by the United States acting district attorney. In short, I have been convinced that the accused is not guilty of the murder of Captain Dawn and Dirk Morton. Before going on with the present witness, I must ask your tolerance while I give you my picture of what happened aboard this schooner on the fateful morning of April twelfth."

Mr. Yistle said promptly: "Objected to as summation."

Gillian said: "I beg to submit that it is not summation. It takes the form of a detailed question which is being put to this witness. Will the court give a ruling on this point?"

After a brief discussion, Gillian was instructed to proceed.

"In considering the murders which took place on this schooner," he went on, "and in the course of my investigations, I came upon a number of puzzling and enlightening clues or signposts which pointed the way, in my mind, to the solution to this problem. The problem is, simply: Who killed the two men?

"As they arranged themselves in my mind, there were about a dozen points to be considered and analyzed. They were:

"What was, or is, the significance of the tattooed mark on the bodies of these men? Why had it been placed there, at Larssen's instigation, shortly following the murders?

"Had the rubber gloves and yellow slicker found by a policeman under Ben Carney's bunk been worn by the murderer and washed in the sea afterward?

"How otherwise was it possible for the five men in the crew—bearing in mind my contention that Roger Pawling is innocent and that one of them had an easy opportunity to commit the murders—manage to appear in the dining saloon within five minutes after the murders were committed without blood being seen on any of them?

"Why were the head and the ax thrown overboard?

"Where was Larssen when the murders were committed?

"Where were the other members of the crew?

"Was there a stowaway aboard?

"Why do Larssen and Wallaby turn pale when ghosts are mentioned?

"Who removed the door from Roger Pawling's room and threw it overboard? Why was this done? Who cut the lifeboat falls and tied the boat to the stern rail by its painter?

"What value to us is the fact that Wallaby and Dirk Morton sailed together in this ship for fifteen years?

"What was behind the powerful influence that Dirk Morton is known to have exerted over Wallaby?"

Gillian paused. There was no sound in the cabin but the steady drumming of rain on the roof.

"LET ME take up these points separately," the lawyer continued.

"Let me give you my answers, in order that I can compound a single vitally important question to ask this witness.

"Was Larssen at the wheel before or after those murders took place, or while they were taking place? He certainly was not!

"Had the gloves and slicker been worn by the murderer? They had not. They were under Ben Carney's bunk at the time.

"Why do Larssen and Wallaby turn pale when ghosts are mentioned? Because they know that I have guessed the truth. I will return to this point again in a moment.

"Why and when was Roger Pawling's door thrown overboard? Because it was battered in and covered with blood and proved that he did not commit the murders. It was thrown overboard next morning. By whom? That is not important. Probably Wallaby."

Wallaby was staring at him with terror and fascination.

Gillian went grimly on: "Who cut the lifeboat from the falls and tied it to the stern rail? Wallaby! When? Within an hour after the murder! Why? To permit the murderer to escape!

"Was there a stowaway aboard? There was!"

"Wait a minute," Mr. Yistle expostulated. "Are you trying to tell us that a stowaway committed these murders and made his get-away?"

"Nothing of the kind," Gillian answered. "I will discuss that stowaway in a moment. Let us consider the tattoo marks. Why did Larssen have them put there? I will admit that the tattoo mark was my first real clue, because it meant conspiracy. By whom? Why, Larssen, of course! Why should Larssen organize this conspiracy? To make absolutely sure that the murders would not be fastened upon him! He was going to put this boat into the rum trade or the dope trade or the hijacking racket—all so close to piracy that it was easy for him to persuade these adventurous cutthroats that they could profitably organize under his banner! United, they were a pirate band and would reap riches in Southern waters with this schooner disguised as a copra boat! United, and if they cooked up a plausible story, Roger Pawling instead of one of them would be hanged for the murders!"

Mr. Yistle barked: "What you're doing is accusing Larssen of committing the murders!"

"Let's put it this way," Gillian said. "Let's say that Larssen went to all these pains so that suspicion, even if placed upon him, would be cast off by the clever story he and his shipmates concocted with Roger Pawling as the victim!"

Gillian mopped his forehead with a snowy handkerchief. He stuffed the handkerchief into a side pocket of his coat, took a deep breath and faced the jury again.

"Gentlemen, I am not summing up this case. In a moment I am going to ask this witness if what I say is not true—every detail of it. But there are other questions: What possible connection is there between these murders and the successful attempt of this schooner to smuggle machine guns and ammunition into Nicaragua eleven years ago? Where was Larssen when the murders were committed? Where were his shipmates? How was it possible for the five men, any of whom might have committed the murders, to appear in this room without a spot of blood on any of them so soon afterward?

"I'll answer those questions briefly. Larssen's shipmates were taking cocaine. It makes no difference where he was or what he was doing. He was not at the wheel! It was possible for the five men to appear in the cabin shortly after the murders because none of them is the murderer!"

Mr. Yistle sank back with a relieved and contemptuous, smile.

GILLIAN WENT on, in a tense voice: "Let's follow Larssen! He leaves the paint locker—or wherever he went—and returns

to the after deck. Through the portholes he sees Roger Pawling with Miss Dawn unconscious on his arm. Roger Pawling
is holding a match in his free hand. By the light of that match,
Larssen sees that the captain and Dirk Morton have had their
heads chopped off! He rushes to the fo'c's'le and wakens the
crew. None of them knows who committed the murders. What
they do know is that, with their criminal records, suspicion must
not be fastened on any of them. Hence, the conspiracy; hence
the general tattooing the next morning, symbolizing it!"

Mr. Yistle said impatiently: "But who do you claim committed the murders?"

"Wallaby," Gillian said; "you can answer that. And you can tell
us why, for fifteen years, you were Dirk Morton's slave! And you
can tell us where that secret hiding-place is! Will you tell us?"

The cockney stared at Gillian with glazed eyes. His color was
green. His lips were like ashes.

Gillian smashed his fist into the palm of his hand. "Where,"
he roared, "is he hiding?"

Mr. Yistle angrily broke in: "If the court please, this witness
is being bulldozed. I respectfully submit that Mr. Hazeltine is
endeavoring deliberately and with his familiar melodramatic
methods to befog the issue, to confuse the jury. With his array
of startling facts, what has he proved? Missing lifeboats! Tattoo
marks! Criminal records! Stowaways! Doors thrown overboard!
Filibustering! Secret hiding-places!

"Hiding! Where is who hiding? This schooner has been under
guard from the moment she dropped anchor in this stream. It is
inconceivable that any man hiding on her could escape detection
over all these weeks. Let's get down to brass tacks. Let's discuss
a few of these startling facts. Let's discuss that missing lifeboat."

"Very well," Gillian agreed. He turned to the witness.
"Wallaby, did you not cut down that lifeboat so that the
murderer could escape? And did not Miss Dawn's unexpected
arrest of you and your shipmates prevent you from helping the
murderer escape?"

Wallaby stared at him stupidly.

Gillian roared: "Answer my questions! Isn't it true that *Dirk Morton is still alive?* Isn't it true that, on the morning of the murders, he somehow got in touch with you and enlisted your help? Isn't it true that you had to help, because he has something on you? Isn't it true that you are the only man in the crew who knows that Morton committed those murders? Isn't it true that Morton is still hiding on this boat?"

Mr. Yistle stared at Gillian, then burst into harsh laughter.

A startling crash occurred in the small room behind Mr. Yistle. It was Dirk Morton's old room—the room that Wallaby had been occupying since the murders. The dirty old carpet had been violently pushed up and aside, revealing a square hole in the floor from which a trap door had been thrown back. A man was climbing out of that hole—a gaunt, redheaded man in rags, with shocking eyes staring from cavernous sockets.

Mr. Yistle gasped, stared, backed away from the doorway in such haste that he all but fell over a chair.

Dirk Morton plunged through the doorway!

BEFORE ANYONE could prevent him, the man whose headless corpse was supposed to be on the bottom of the Atlantic Ocean dashed toward the forward stairway. A bailiff tried to reach him and failed.

Dirk Morton rushed up the stairway with a bailiff at his heels. A police whistle blew.

Gillian was halfway up the stairs in pursuit when Dirk Morton, with a policeman firmly grasping either arm, was brought back into the cabin. Handcuffs were snapped on his wrists.

Panting, he glared at Gillian.

"I'll get you," he said.

Gillian grinned. "Morton, they always say that. Where you're going, you won't get anything but flowers, and I doubt if you'll get those. Who was the man who stowed away in New York, down in that secret hold, and came up that night and tried to murder you?"

Dirk Morton sneered: "Try and find out!"

"Wasn't his name Jake Harper, the same Jake Harper who sailed as second mate on this schooner eleven years ago when she was filibustering?"

"What if it was?"

"Didn't you run off to Atlantic City with Jake Harper's wife one week-end last winter, when this schooner was in dry dock—and didn't Jake Harper say he'd kill you if he had to follow you all over the world?"

Dirk Morton stared at him and made no answer. Gillian went on:

"Wasn't it Jake Harper who came out of that hole at about two o'clock on the morning of April twelfth?"

"What if it was?" the red-haired man snarled.

"The point that puzzles me," Gillian said, "is, who ran and got the ax? Did he slip out and get the ax while you slept? Or did you get it? Never mind. It isn't important. After your fight with him, in which you chopped off his head—very unfortunately for you, Captain Dawn saw you. Isn't that so? You had to kill him, didn't you, to be rid of witnesses? Then you stripped Jake Harper, laid his body on your bunk and threw his head and clothes and the ax overboard, before going back to hide.

"You got away with it because no one saw you. And then, somehow, you got in touch with Wallaby, but before Wallaby could help you escape in the lifeboat, Miss Dawn had nailed him in this cabin with the rest of the crew. And you couldn't get away all the time you've been in port, because of the police guard. What I want to know is: What have you got on Wallaby?"

"I'll never squeal on Wallaby!" the red-haired giant spat out.

GILLIAN FACED the judges. "If this court please, I wish to lodge a formal charge of murder against this man. And I wish to lodge a charge of perjury and conspiracy against Hans Larssen,

Pierre Lohac, Ben Carney, and Lester Slick. The charge against Wallaby will be more serious: perjury, conspiracy, and aiding and abetting a criminal to escape justice."

It was impossible for Gillian to make himself heard above the rising roar of voices. Everyone was talking at once. Over tossing heads, Gillian saw Roger hugging Carolina. His attention was then distracted by Mr. Haughton.

The Boston lawyer was pale, perspiring and puffing.

"I knew you had something like this up your sleeve, Hazeltine!" he panted. "I knew it from the very beginning! Humiliating me! Humiliating my witnesses! You were perfectly aware that this would make me the laughingstock of Boston—a brutal and heartless jest that I will never live down!"

Gillian looked at him coldly and inquiringly. "I'm afraid," he said, "I don't quite follow you, Mr. Haughton."

"You knew all along," Mr. Haughton angrily declared, "that that man was hiding down there! You held it out as a last-minute surprise—a bid for notoriety! As if you needed notoriety! As if you aren't sufficiently notorious already, with the sensational methods you always employ!"

Gillian looked at him for a long time before he answered that charge. Then he didn't answer it. All he said was:

"It's queer, but the only people who really do approve of my methods are the ones I manage to save from the gallows or the electric chair."

THE DIAMOND BULLET

*Never had Gillian Hazeltine defended a man he
knew was guilty—and much as the strangeness and
pathos of this murder case tugged at his mind and his
heartstrings, he was determined to keep out of it.*

CHAPTER I

A FRIGHTENED
"MYSTERY WOMAN"

THE WHITENESS OF the girl's face was so startling that Gillian Hazeltine almost dropped his newspaper. The express elevator was slowing for the floor where his law offices were located. The girl's eyes, as black as two spots of night, were staring at him as if some shutter behind them had been tripped, letting him see her naked, terrified soul.

Gillian thought she was ill, perhaps on the verge of fainting. Then he recognized her as the girl who had been following him. It had been going on for days. He had first seen her in his waiting room; white and tense and terrified, sitting stiffly in a chair with her hands clasped and pressed between her knees in a fold of her dress.

It was a cheap blue dress and showed signs of wear. Her small black hat looked cheap. So did her shoes. And Gillian had noticed that her silk stockings were darned and that a run in the back of one of them had been painstakingly studied.

The mysterious, frightened unknown had sat in his outer office for two hours. Gillian's secretary, questioning her, had reported that the girl said she wanted to see no one, but merely wanted to rest. She wasn't feeling well. At the end of two hours, the girl went away.

Gillian had seen her again, later the same day he had almost collided with her when he had left the building for the night. The white-faced girl was standing on the sidewalk, just around the turn of the wall. She had flattened herself against the wall and stared up at him with trembling lips.

Two evenings later, Gillian saw a white face at one of his dining room windows as he sat dining alone. Vee, his wife, was visiting some friends in Chicago. Glancing up, he had seen the white face, the terrified eyes, of someone staring in at him. But the afternoon light had faded. It was dusk. He could not be sure that it had been this girl.

It was altogether very disturbing. Gillian had countless enemies. Plots had been laid against his life. Unscrupulous women had tried to blackmail him. But he could not believe that this girl was bent upon such an enterprise.

She did not look like the blackmailing kind. She looked to him like a country girl—her hat, dress, stockings, shoes— all carried out that impression. He concluded that she was in some kind of difficulty, but for certain reasons, was reluctant to approach him.

As the elevator stopped and the heavy bronze doors silently shot open, Gillian thrust the Greenfield *Times* under one arm and, on the point of leaving the car, turned quickly to the girl.

"You were in my office the other morning," he said. "Did you have something to say to me?"

The girl looked up at him with terror and dismay. She shrank back against the side of the elevator. He had evidently taken her so by surprise that she was speechless. A small, work roughened hand flew to her trembling mouth. The fingers opened and moved down her chin to her throat. She gulped, choked, shrank away. Her eyes were glittering with fright.

Gillian sniffed faintly. He was more than ever convinced that she had some problem to lay before him, but was afraid to talk about it.

He walked out into the corridor. From the tail of his eye he saw the girl's hand dart out in a fluttering gesture to detain him. Then the doors clanged.

GILLIAN PROCEEDED thoughtfully through his outer

Gillian saw a white face at his dining room window

offices and on through his law library into his private office. He was disturbed by the girl's obvious terror. And he was curious to know why she was following him.

He opened the golden humidor on his desk—a gift from a grateful client whom Gillian had saved from the electric chair—extracted a long blond perfecto and, walking to the window which overlooked a reach of the Sangamo River, lighted it.

His brisk and efficient secretary, Miss Walsh, came in with an open notebook and a determined air. It was her private opinion that, without her, her famous employer would never get a stroke of work done, but would devote all of his time to gazing dreamily out that window, pondering heaven only knew what attractive but unproductive visions.

"Come back in an hour," Gillian said, without turning from the view. "I want to do some thinking."

"But you promised Mr. Kelly—"

"Kelly can wait. Miss Walsh," Gillian turned to look at her, "do you remember that little derelict who sat in the waiting room for two hours the other morning, looking as if she were scared to death?"

"Yes, Mr. Hazeltine."

"That girl has been on my trail for days. I'll swear she was staring through the window at me the other night at dinner. I bump into her on the street. I find her staring at me from the sidewalk when I get out of my car. Just now she rode up in the elevator with me, staring as if I were something in a zoo. I asked her if she had something on her mind. She said she hadn't. What do you make of that girl, Miss Walsh?"

His competent secretary lifted her expressive eyebrows. She uttered what sounded like a sniff.

"Mr. Hazeltine, if I showed you a fraction of the letters that come to you from hero-worshiping girls you'd be positively ill. You are the idol of the masses. These silly girls must have some hero to worship. And you," added Miss Walsh, with an impish twinkle in her eyes, "are the romantic type—strong, handsome, fearless."

"Rubbish," Gillian snorted. "Do you think this girl is one of—um—those?"

"I shovel them off the doorstep every morning, Mr. Hazeltine! Have you forgotten the girl who used to bake a chocolate layer cake every week and send it to you? Have you forgotten the flapper who sent you the platinum cigar lighter with your initials and hers woven together in a diamond monogram?"

Gillian was blushing.

Miss Walsh said, "If you'll dictate the rough draft of that brief for Mr. Kelly—"

"Damn Kelly," Gillian barked. "I want to know more about this girl."

Miss Walsh groaned. "Won't you rely on my feminine intuition?"

"No! Why is she so terrified?"

"Because she adores you and must be near you, but is terrified at the thought of your discovering it."

"Bunk," Gillian grunted. "You would never make a detective. I'll give you that brief for Kelly in an hour," he said with finality.

MISS WALSH briskly withdrew. Gillian sat down at his desk and opened his *Times*. His real reason for dismissing Miss Walsh was not to reflect at his leisure upon the mystery of the girl with terrified eyes, but to give that agile mind of his the recreation of probing about in an absorbing murder mystery.

It was known to the newspapers as the Diamond Bullet Murder Case.

The press, with its propensity for summing up any situation in capsule form, had so described an absorbing tragedy that had occurred near the agricultural community of Clinton, about forty miles north of Greenfield.

Gillian loved a good mystery, and this promised to be an exciting and absorbing one—the kind that brings forth some fresh and shocking development each day.

It had begun modestly, as most good mysteries do, with a small item on the back page which briefly mentioned that a wealthy farmer named Amos Grundle had mysteriously vanished and that his wife, Sarah, had committed suicide by cutting her wrist arteries, both events coinciding with the disappearance of the Grundle servant, a girl named Nellie Hearthstone.

Gillian had at first drawn the obvious conclusion. The wealthy farmer had run off with Nellie Hearthstone, and his wife, rather than face public humiliation, had committed suicide.

That had been about a week ago. The next development had taken the story to the front pages. Several people had seen the Hearthstone girl board an interurban street car for Greenfield—alone. She had been seen in Greenfield twice since—always alone. Foul play was hinted at.

A search was instituted for Farmer Grundle. In the course of the search, the flooded pit of an old quarry a half mile from his house cooperated with certain laws of nature and gave up Farmer Grundle's swollen body. A rifle was found in the bushes nearby.

The Grundle case now acquired a sensational note. The

tabloid press, always hungry for lurid details, pieced together a story of a strong man's lust and a helpless girl's revenge.

Nellie Hearthstone was, it appeared, an orphan. She had been found one bitter winter morning eighteen years ago bundled up in a ragged old blanket on the hearthstone in the parlor of the Clinton Orphan Asylum. That was how she had come by her name. She had been taken from the asylum a year ago and employed as a maid of all work in the Grundle household, which consisted only of her and Mrs. Grundle.

The girl was said to be very pretty and a hard little worker. Prominent men in the village vigorously denied that Amos Grundle had tired of his aging wife to become infatuated with the lovely orphan.

They pointed out that Amos Grundle was a man of flawless character; was a prominent churchgoer and a power for good in the civic life of the township. They condemned as vicious gossip the theory that a love-making scene between Grundle and the girl on the edge of the old rock quarry had resulted in the murder. And they hotly resented the implication that Mrs. Grundle, aware of impending scandal, had committed suicide. She had committed suicide, they declared, because of ill health. She had been a sick woman for years.

THESE VARIOUS explanations were slightly complicated by the discovery that the rifle, which was identified as Grundle's, was a modern United States Army rifle—loaded with *blank* cartridges.

The case was given an exotic touch by the statement of an elderly spinster named Nettie Jarvis, who declared she had seen a tall man with a black beard follow Grundle into the woods toward the old quarry on the morning of his disappearance. Nettie Jarvis was a seamstress.

Gillian accepted this with a grunt of skepticism. Old women were always seeing tall men with black beards at or near the scene of murders. A murder would be incomplete without a mysterious stranger.

A new batch of rumors next brought a handsome young farmer, one James Truman, into the spotlight. Truman's farm adjoined Amos Grundle's. It was asserted by village gossips that young Truman was himself infatuated with the lovely orphan and had been seen kissing her in a motion picture theater.

James Truman, Gillian guessed, knew more about the murder than he was admitting.

This morning's development capped the climax—sent the story shrieking to the front pages of the press of the nation and made the sleepy town of Clinton the Mecca of long lines of automobiles.

Even the sedate *Times* gave the new development a seven-column screamer:

DIAMOND FOUND IN GRUNDLE'S HEART!

A diamond weighing approximately four and one-half carats had been found by the Clinton coroner embedded in Amos Grundle's heart. The leading jeweler of Clinton gave his testimony. Diamond, said he was nothing but white coal, and, given the opportunity, would burn like coal. The flash of rifle powder had started to ignite the diamond, as its scorched edges proved, but before it could burn, the diamond had plunged into Amos Grundle's astonished heart.

Who owned a diamond of such value? Why had it been used as a bullet? What connection could there possibly be between such a fine stone and a poor but beautiful orphan? The old woman who had seen the blackbearded stranger was interviewed again. She stuck to her story. He was a giant of a man with a sinister, foreign air.

Further down the pages was another sensational development. The county prosecutor, a man named Elton Dawbridge, had brought charges against the elderly superintendent of the Clinton Orphan Asylum, accusing him of flagrant misuse of his office; charging him, in so many words, with nothing less than white slavery.

The asylum superintendent, declared the county prosecutor, was empowered to let his orphans, go to work in respectable homes as servants when they were old enough; but it was now unearthed that he was disposing of the most beautiful of the orphans to those farmers who paid him the highest premium.

A fiery denunciation of this distressing practice was quoted in the *Times* in Mr. Dawbridge's eloquent words. And Gillian, who seldom believed what he read, was of the opinion that Mr. Dawbridge had selected this opportunity to thrust himself into the limelight with a bright and eager eye on political advancement.

Mr. Dawbridge promised startling disclosures in the Grundle mystery before to-morrow morning. It was now tomorrow morning, and Gillian's interest in the Diamond Bullet Murder Case was so feverish that he was tempted to drop all work and drive out to Clinton and do a little investigating for the fun of it.

GILLIAN'S EFFICIENT secretary drove this whimsical notion from his mind. She was standing before him now, with an opened notebook, a poised pencil, a grim expression about her pretty lips and the word Kelly fairly snapping in her eyes.

And Miss Walsh saw to it that Gillian was so busy the rest of the day that his lunch had to be sent in. He did not have another moment to spare for the Grundle Diamond Case until it was time to go home for dinner.

His favorite newsboy met him with a copy of the *Evening Bulletin*. Gillian, seating himself in his coupé, glanced at the headline.

TRUMAN HELD AS GRUN-
DLE DIAMOND OWNER!

A glance at the opening lines of the story assured him that his yesterday's guess was correct—James Truman had been arrested. It had been proved beyond doubt that he was the diamond's owner.

There was still another startling disclosure. On the afternoon of the murder he and Nellie Hearthstone had applied for a marriage license at the county clerk's office. The State law required that an avowal of matrimonial intentions be filed a week prior to the marriage.

Gillian read no further. He wanted to digest the story at his leisure, while he was digesting his dinner.

He drove to his home on the hill overlooking the river, and drove on into the garage. He opened the newspaper to steal another glance at the Grundle story before going into the house.

Now the Hazeltine garage was a somewhat spacious affair, with ample room for Gillian's coupé, his wife's roadster and her limousine. It was a two-story building. Upstairs was a loft for the storage of odds and ends—gardening tools, discarded furniture and the miscellany which will be found in such a catch-all.

As Gillian glanced again at the headline, he distinctly heard a thump overhead. He knew that today was the gardener's day off, so he presumed that the thump had been caused by his Japanese servant, Toro.

"Toro?" he called.

There was no answer. Gillian, listening, heard further sounds, as of someone moving about.

He climbed out of his coupé and called firmly: "Who is up there?"

Still no answer.

A little irritated at receiving no answer, Gillian shouted: "Come down out of there!"

A pair of slim, silk-clad legs appeared at the top of the narrow stairs. Gillian next saw the hem of a blue serge dress. The feet began to descend. He now observed that the stockings were darned in several places.

He waited, with suddenly accelerating pulses.

The white-faced girl, who had so mystified him during the past few days, climbed down and into the light of the opened garage doors.

Her eyes, as she stared at him, were dark with terror. Her

mouth was quivering. For some unaccountable reason, she selected this moment to snatch off her small black hat, and her hair came tumbling out and down almost to her shoulders. It was thick, rich, curly, brown hair. Her eyes seemed to swim.

In the cool light of evening, her face was beautiful. It had the pallor of some martyred saint, and considerably more beauty.

There was a newspaper in her hand—a copy of the same edition that Gillian had been reading a moment before.

"What," Gillian asked in astonishment, "were you doing up there?" The girl caught her hand to her heart.

"Please," she whimpered; "don't you know who I am—now?"

Gillian's eyes grew suddenly dark with understanding.

"One guess," he said crisply. "Nellie Hearthstone."

The girl pitched forward unconscious; would have fallen on the cement floor if Gillian had not swooped down and caught her by the elbows.

CHAPTER II

IN HOT WATER

HAZELTINE LIFTED THE limp orphan in his arms, dismayed at her lightness—the poor little thing was hardly more than bones—and carried her into the house, fervently wishing that his wife were at home. Fainting women terrified him. He never could remember whether you elevated the head or the feet.

He transported Miss Hearthstone into the comfortable living room, arranged her on a settee and shouted for Toro. As he had come in by the side door, he had missed Toro, who was busy in the kitchen preparing his master's dinner.

Toro came noiselessly in, gazed with Buddhist gravity at the tableau, and inquired in his impeccable English:

"Did you call, Mr. Hazeltine?"

"Bring some water!" Gillian said hoarsely. "Bring some brandy! Bring a bowl of ice! Bring a towel! Bring some smelling salts! Do something Get busy! Act! Don't stand there like a stalled car!"

Toro fled, to return promptly with a decanter of brandy and a liqueur glass. Gillian filled the glass and forced its contents between Nellie Hearthstone's gray lips.

She quickly revived. Eyelids trembled and lifted. Gillian pulled up a chair and began to rub her hands.

The beautiful orphan gazed up at him with the dim, vague eyes of semiconsciousness; then intelligence fully returned and, with it, the black, stark look of terror. She shrank away from him.

"You're better now, Miss Hearthstone?"

She gasped: "You—you aren't going to have me arrested?"

"Have you done anything for which I should have you arrested?"

"No!"

"Then stop worrying."

She looked at him gratefully. Some of the terror in her eyes vanished.

"I'm glad it's over," she said faintly. "I couldn't have stood another hour of it. I couldn't have endured another night with those rats."

"What rats?"

"The ones in your garage. One of them ran across my face last night. I thought I'd die. And the night before—"

"I'll get a cat to look after those rats," Gillian interrupted. "Have you been living in my garage?"

"Yes. I didn't know where else to go. I was afraid they'd find me."

"How long have you been there?"

"Almost a week. I came right here. I wanted to talk to you. Then I lost my nerve. I—I didn't dare. Every day since I've tried to work up enough courage. I went to your office. I waited for you outside. Every night I tried to make myself come in and tell you. This morning I intended following you into your office. But when you spoke to me—I almost fainted."

"What," Gillian asked, "have you been doing about food?"

"Oh, I'm not hungry. I can't stand the sight of food. I'm too nervous to eat."

Gillian glanced up at Toro. "Dinner for two," he said. "Hurry it."

"Yes, sir."

"I can't eat here," the girl said.

"Nonsense. We'll talk while we eat. Or would you like to talk now—get some of it off our mind?"

She looked at him dubiously. "I didn't kill Amos Grundle," she blurted.

"Of course you didn't. You came to me because you thought they would accuse you."

"No. I thought they would accuse Jim Truman."

"They finally did. They arrested him this morning. It's in tonight's papers."

The girl nodded. "I knew they would. I knew they'd find that diamond. That's why I've been hiding here. That's what I wanted to talk to you about."

"**ARE YOU** in love with Jim Truman?" Gillian asked gently.

The girl began beating on the edge of the settee with one small clenched fist. She burst out hysterically:

"I can't explain it. It goes deeper than that. I'd do anything for him, I love him so. He's the only man I've ever known who's been kind and decent to me, and respected me. All the others have tried to take advantage of the fact that I'm an orphanage girl—a nameless nobody. They don't care how hard I've worked to improve myself.

"Until I met Jim Truman I hated the very word love. It meant nothing but men pawing me and saying ugly things. Jim was the first decent man I knew. If anything happened to him, I'd die. I mean it. I wouldn't want to live. I'd kill myself. If I could save him by confessing that I'd killed Mr. Grundle I would. But *I can't lie.*"

"I understand," Gillian said.

"You don't understand," she said fiercely. "Nobody understands. I literally cannot tell a lie."

Gillian was frowning. "You mean you have certain standards which won't permit your telling lies?"

"No. You don't understand. You can't understand."

The criminal lawyer shook his head.

"I'm afraid it's too deep for me, Miss Hearthstone. I've never met a person like you in my life. My dealings are chiefly, with men and women who literally cannot tell the truth. They will take the witness stand and lie about the most unimportant details—where a lie or truth wouldn't make the slightest difference. Most crooks are congenital liars. If the sun was shining yesterday, they will say it rained hard. They can't help lying."

"I can't help telling the truth," the girl said. "Lies simply won't come out of my mouth. It may have something to do with pride. Perhaps you don't appreciate what a foundling, a supposedly illegitimate child, faces in this world. I've known girls to kill themselves because they didn't know who their fathers and mothers were. They could not stand the shame. Heaven only knows who my parents were. And even when I was a little girl I was jealous of other little girls who were regular orphans—not foundlings. I was terribly ashamed for years.

"I made up my mind that I would be so good, so decent, so honest that people would have to respect me. I wouldn't steal. I wouldn't be a sneak. I wouldn't lie; I thought lying for any reason was weak and cowardly. I wouldn't be a coward. I wouldn't lie. Now, I can't lie—not even to save the man I'd willingly give my life for. Even when I think of lying, I feel faint and sick. Something horrible happens inside of me. I can't lie."

Gillian was beginning to understand, and he was beginning to have the greatest admiration and respect for this shabby girl.

"This Jim Truman," he said thoughtfully, "must be an exceptional young man. Tell me something about him."

"He is a farmer," said the beautiful orphan. "He has the most successful farm in this part of the State. He is the only scientific farmer in the region. A great many of the neighboring farmers are jealous of him. They disapprove of what they call his newfangled notions. They envy him; therefore they hate him.

"For example, Jim has been planning for some time to install a small hydroelectric plant so that electricity will cost him nothing. He built an artificial lake for water storage. It happened that this lake was full at the beginning of the recent drought. When the drought became really serious Jim simply used his storage water for irrigation—and saved practically all of his crops. He was the only farmer in that district who had the forethought—or the luck.

"Naturally, the others were jealous. They had all been telling him what a fool he was to waste his time on these newfangled notions—and Jim calmly went ahead and showed them they were wrong. People don't like being shown they're wrong. They don't like his quietness, either. They call it secretiveness. He isn't secretive; he simply minds his own business, works hard—and makes good. He is the most modest man I ever knew, and very unselfish and kind."

"How old is Jim?"

"Twenty-seven."

"Parents living?"

"No. He's an orphan, too. He met me at a party where a young farmer—Tom Lenk—was trying to make love to me. I asked Jim to make Tom stop. The two men had a quarrel about it, and Jim knocked Tom down, then he said to me, 'We orphans have got to stick together.' We've been sticking together ever since."

NELLIE HEARTHSTONE was smiling. It seemed to brighten her whole being. Watching her, Gillian wondered how any orphanage could produce a young woman of such refinement. If it had not been for her toil-roughened hands and her shabby clothing she might easily have been mistaken for one of the season's prettiest débutantes.

"How did Amos Grundle like the attachment of you and Jim?"

"Mr. Grundle hated Jim."

"How about Jim?"

The blackness of terror returned to the girl's eyes.

"He—" She hesitated.

Gillian bent closer. "You can talk to me in perfect confidence, Miss Hearthstone. Let's face the truth about this. Did Jim Truman kill Amos Grundle?"

The answer came from her lips as though she were an automaton.

"Yes."

"Did you see the murder?"

"Yes."

"Any other witnesses?"

"No." Her voice was no louder than a whisper.

Gillian looked thoughtful. He was beginning to realize why this girl had been too terrified to come to him.

"There were extenuating circumstances, of course," he suggested.

"Grundle attacked your lover, and he killed Grundle in self-defense."

"No. Mr. Grundle didn't attack Jim."

"I see. Grundle was shot by your lover because your honor was involved—the so-called unwritten law."

"No. He did hate Mr. Grundle because Mr. Grundle was constantly making improper proposals to me. But Mr. Grundle never did anything more than kiss me. No man ever has."

"But there was a quarrel which led up to the killing," Gillian said desperately. "In the course of the quarrel, Grundle made threatening remarks to Jim?"

"No," the girl said dully. "Nothing of any kind happened

that would make a case for Jim in a courtroom. He killed Mr. Grundle as you would kill a snake."

There was no longer any question in Gillian's mind that this unfortunate girl was telling the truth. And there was no longer any question that the young farmer she loved was in very hot water indeed.

"Tell me the story from the beginning," he requested.

CHAPTER III

THE WHITED SEPULCHRE

THE GIRL'S MOUTH was trembling. She made a helpless little gesture with her hands, and began to talk in a low but clear voice.

"The newspapers have told only one side of it," she said. "I went to work a little over a year ago for the Grundles, and the first night I was there he came into the kitchen and tried to kiss me. His wife was in the next room. It made me so mad I cried and it made me sick, too. I was glad to be working at the Grundles,' because it was so near Jim's farm. I hadn't given Grundle himself a thought, except that when he came to the orphanage, I didn't like his looks.

"He was a big, heavy man—the kind that looks fat but isn't. He had heavy shoulders, and heavy hands and large feet. His hands were thick and ugly and covered with reddish hair. He had mean eyes, too. One of them was injured when he was a boy, and had a cast in it. It made him look just as mean as he was.

"Mrs. Grundle was an invalid. For years she had done all the housework, including all the washing, wood chopping and water pumping. There was no running water in the house—no conveniences. Grundle was one of the farmers who hated newfangled ideas. His nearest approach to a modern convenience was an old, broken-down Ford he had bought for thirty dollars.

"I thought, naturally that he had taken me from the orphanage because Mrs. Grundle was rheumatic and really needed help. That wasn't the idea at all. He had seen me and, according to what he whispered in the kitchen that first night, had fallen in love with me.

"He was going to get rid of his wife somehow and marry me. But he wanted me to show him first that I really loved him. I told him I loathed him. I told him I was in love with Jim Truman and that we were going to marry when I was nineteen.

"When I told him I loathed him, he hit me with his fist across the muscles of my upper arm—here—and the pain was so great that I bawled. I couldn't help it. My arm was almost paralyzed all the next day. Mrs. Grundle came hobbling out into the kitchen, and he told her he had just given me a little disciplining so I'd know my place.

That was what he always called it—'disciplining.' He was cruel to people and animals. I've seen him beat a horse that was too tired to do any more work. He kicked one dog, an old setter, in the stomach for no reason whatever. It caused some internal injury, for the setter died a few days later."

"How often did he have these rages?" Gillian asked.

"He didn't have rages at all. I mean he never got red-faced. His eyes would narrow—and he would reach out and strike. He reached across the supper table once and struck Mrs. Grundle because she didn't answer a question quickly enough. And whenever he tried to paw me or kiss me, and I told him how I detested him, he would strike me.

"Once he kicked me in the knee. I limped for a week. Another time, when I was milking, he came behind me and grabbed me and kissed me. I told him if he did it again I'd hit him with the nearest thing handy. He went away and came back in a moment with an old buggy whip. He brought it down just once across my shoulders. I can still hear that whip whistle. It was so painful and I was so furious that I cried all night."

"WHY DIDN'T you report him?" Gillian indignantly asked.

The girl's eyes narrowed. "No one would believe me. I never knew what a real hypocrite was before I knew Amos Grundle. He saved his meanness for his home. In Clinton, he was a pillar of the community—prominent in charity work and in politics— a big talker."

"Why didn't you tell Jim—or did you?"

"At first my pride wouldn't let me. I'd always fought my own battles. Jim likes people who are self-reliant. He hates women who are clinging vines. We were going to be married when I was nineteen—"

"Whose idea was that?"

"Mine. I wanted those two years for studying and improving myself. I wanted to be worthy of Jim. He is a college graduate. I wanted him to be proud of me. You see, in marrying him, I wanted to be able to face people who would say that I married him to elevate myself. Jim didn't want to wait. But I insisted. I wanted to give him plenty of time to think it over."

"So you didn't tell Jim about Grundle?"

"Not until the night before he killed Grundle. I had to tell him then. I was frantic. Mrs. Grundle had had one of her sick attacks and had gone to bed. That was just before supper. While Mr. Grundle and I were eating supper, he pulled his chair around close to mine and took both my hands and held them. He said he had made a new will that afternoon, bequeathing everything he owned to me. And he said we were going to get married as soon as his wife was dead.

"It was horrible. There she was, sick in bed at the top of the stairs and he was pawing me and telling me we'd be married soon—as soon as she was dead. He made some reference to the fact that if she didn't die soon, he knew ways to hasten it. I can't recall his exact words. He was trying to kiss me when he said them, and I was fighting him off.

"It scared me stiff. I could stand his pawing and clumsy love-making and his cruelty, but this was serious. I didn't want him to will his estate to me, and I was terrified at what he had muttered about hastening his wife's death. I had to tell someone. And I knew no one but Jim would believe me.

"After supper, I hurried over to Jim's house and told him. Everything. I wanted him to advise me. At first he said he would go down and tell the sheriff, or Judge Lindley. He acted awful queer. He was so white that I was scared stiff. I didn't know what he was going to do, but I made him promise he wouldn't do anything drastic. And he said he would do nothing until the next morning. He wanted to think it over. He told me to meet him at the old quarry at ten o'clock the next morning. He wanted to show me something he had for me, he said, and we would talk over what we had better do."

Nellie Hearthstone paused. Her eyes had the soft glow of one who sees a vividly remembered scene.

"Jim kissed me good night and I hurried back home. I event to bed and locked my door. But I couldn't sleep. I heard Mrs. Grundle breathing in the next room, and I heard Mr. Grundle walking about downstairs. He didn't go to bed until long after midnight.

"Next morning, Mrs. Grundle was well enough to get up and have breakfast, but she looked at me strangely. Every few minutes I'd find her eyes on me, with that queer, probing look. But she didn't say anything. And Mr. Grundle kept looking at her in a queer way, too. His eyes ran over her coldly. I can't describe it. It was something in his face. I knew he was thinking of ways to kill her.

"When I had my work done, I was so glad to be out of that house that I ran all the way to the quarry. Now before I go on, are there any questions you'd like to ask?"

"I'm very curious to know," Gillian replied, "if any one except you and Mrs. Grundle was ever present when Grundle was striking you, his wife or any of the animals?"

One man," the girl said. "A farmer named Jeff Pavlitch. He is an old man, a Lithuanian, and speaks rather broken English. He owed Mr. Grundle some money, and he often came over to the house to do odd jobs. He was so meek and cowering that Mr. Grundle hardly noticed him."

"Was this Jeff Pavlitch present when Grundle struck you or his wife?"

"Often. Why?"

"If he will testify in court, it will be helpful. He will make a very valuable witness. Now, tell me about the diamond bullet."

CHAPTER IV

"WHAT CASE IS THERE?"

NELLIE HEARTHSTONE RAN her hand nervously through her thick dark hair. Gillian, waiting for her to begin, could understand why men lost their senses over her.

"Jim was waiting for me at the quarry. We sat down on a log and he took a little square white box out of his pocket and showed me the diamond. It had been his mother's. It was an heirloom. I don't know how many generations it had been in his family. It had been set in a brooch of gold filigree. Jim had had Mr. Beckwith, the Clinton jeweler, take it out of the brooch. He was going to have it set in a ring for me—my engagement ring.

"He put the diamond in my hand and I held it up on the tips of my fingers. It flashed and sparkled like a little ball of white fire. We didn't hear Mr. Grundle walk up behind us. We didn't know we weren't alone until a hand reached down and took the diamond.

"Jim turned and looked up at him. Mr. Grundle had a rifle in one hand—an army rifle he had bought from a soldier. I suppose the soldier had stolen it. Mr. Grundle never used it until last year. After the Memorial Day exercises at Evergreen Cemetery, he found a case of blank cartridges which the soldiers had brought, but hadn't used. He loaded the case into his car.

"After that, he used the cartridges in his rifle for shooting small game. He carried birdshot in his pocket. When he wanted to shoot anything, he would pour some of this shot down the barrel. He loved to kill. I've seen him kill robins and wild canaries and orioles. He pretended he was only shooting crows and hawks."

"Didn't he threaten Jim in any way with that rifle?" Gillian asked hopefully.

"No. He stood there, scowling, with the diamond in his hand. He looked at it and then at Jim. Finally he said, 'This stone would make a good bullet, Truman. How far do you s'pose it would go into that tree over there?' He pointed to a tall pine tree. 'I've a good mind to try and see,' he said. It wouldn't hurt the diamond, because a diamond is harder than flint. You could dig out the diamond and it would still be as good as ever."

"What did Jim say to that?"

"Nothing. He just looked up at Mr. Grundle. He was white and there was the same funny look about his mouth that had scared me the night before. But he didn't say a word. He looked up at Mr. Grundle. Mr. Grundle put a cartridge into the chamber and dropped the diamond down the barrel. Jim stood up slowly, took the rifle out of his hands and shot him."

"Grundle had pointed the rifle at him and Jim thought he meant to kill him," Gillian said.

"No. Mr. Grundle wasn't pointing the rifle anywhere near him. He hadn't threatened Jim in any way. Jim just took the rifle away from him and killed him."

"What happened then?"

"Mr. Grundle slumped down and rolled over the edge of the pit into the water and sank out of sight."

"What did Jim say then?"

"He said, 'I couldn't help it, honey.' He said it over and over. He said they would electrocute him for doing it, but that he couldn't help it. He said that he would do the same thing to any other man who laid a hand on me. But that he had spoiled everything. He said I should go away, start life some place else.

Then he went all to pieces. He put his head in my lap and cried like a baby. He said over and over he couldn't help it. No man had ever lived who laid a hand on a Truman woman—and I was the same as a Truman woman. And he said that it had been his mother's diamond that Grundle was defiling.

"I told him I loved him as much as ever. I made him go with me to the county clerk's office for an application for marriage. Of course, we can't get married. I took a streetcar to Greenfield. I made him promise to say nothing until he heard from me. I haven't been in touch with him."

GILLIAN STOOD up and began stalking up and down the room. He turned suddenly and said: "But what can I do?"

Nellie Hearthstone's large eyes seemed to shine in the growing dusk.

"You're famous for helping people out of trouble," she said simply. "Certainly no two people were ever in greater trouble than Jim and I are."

"Are you sure," Gillian asked, that you've omitted nothing important?"

"Quite sure. And—you'll take the case, won't you?"

"What case is there, my dear?" Gillian asked. "Your lover hated a man and killed him. We admit his hatred was justifiable. We admit it was excusable for him to kill Grundle, who was pawing you and robbing him. Jim was almost out of his mind. But can you make a jury of Grundle's friends believe that? We all hate people, but we don't go around murdering them, do we?"

"I've got to save him," said the girl simply. "I love him. There must be some way. I'll do anything."

"There is a way," Gillian told her. "Go on the witness stand and swear you saw Grundle murderously attack Jim. If you told such a story, with plenty of realistic embroidery, you would sway a jury. Your beauty would help. It's a slim chance, the only one."

The dark eyes were staining at him hopelessly. "I can't tell that story. No matter how hard I tried, I couldn't. The truth would come out in spite of me."

"If you can't lie," Gillian said, you can't save him."

The telephone at the other end of the room rang. Gillian answered it. A reporter on the *Bulletin*, a tabloid, wanted to know if he was interested in the Grundle murder case.

"Why should I be?" Gillian cautiously answered.

"A girl, whose description tallies pretty closely with the Hearthstone girl has been seen coming out of your office," the reporter informed him. "Grundle's will has just been read and that foxy little jane comes into an estate of over a hundred thousand bucks in farm lands, real estate and bank bonds. The county prosecutor says it was her sweetie's motive for killing Grundle. He has a warrant out for her as a material witness. What can you tell me about it, Mr. Hazeltine?"

"Not a thing," Gillian replied.

"Will you take the case if they ask you to?"

"No." Gillian hung up the receiver.

Toro came in to announce dinner. Nellie Hearthstone was looking expectantly at the criminal lawyer.

"We'll have dinner," he said, "then I'll drive you out to Clinton." He waited until Toro was gone, then added: "Dawbridge has a warrant out for your arrest. It always looks better to give yourself up than to be captured. Grundle's will leaves you an estate of a hundred thousand."

"I won't touch a penny of it!" the girl exclaimed; then: "Yes, I will!" she cried. "I'll give you all of it for defending Jim."

"I don't want it," Gillian said. "I'm not taking the case, because there isn't a case. If you were a congenital liar like Nettie Jarvis, the seamstress, and could invent black-bearded strangers with an exotic air, there might be hope. As things stand, Jim Truman must pay for making a foolish mistake."

Nellie Hearthstone stood up. Her mouth was firm with determination.

"Mr. Hazeltine, I know how hopeless the case is. But I also know how brilliant you are. You've used amazing tricks to save men from the electric chair. You could save Jim if you would."

"I've never yet defended a man," Gillian answered, "guilty of deliberate murder. I'll talk to Jim if you wish. Have you told this story to anyone else?"

"Not a soul. Only three of us know—you, Jim, and I."

"Don't let Dawbridge trap you into talking," Gillian advised her. "He will try to make you talk. He will realize that you are his star witness."

"I won't say a word or answer a question."

"Has Jim a lawyer?"

Yes. His name is Seth Peters. He has been out of college only a couple of years."

"Is Peters in with the Clinton political gang?"

"No. He won't go in with them. They've all but driven him out of town."

"Is he a fighter?"

"Yes, but not at all clever."

"I'll talk to Peters, too," Gillian promised.

CHAPTER V

IN THE NEWSREEL SPOTLIGHT

CLINTON, A TOWN of some five thousand population, had the air of a town which has successfully resisted the inroads of modern civilization. Its streets were narrow and badly lighted. The Randaman River which threaded its way through the town was flanked on both sides by old-fashioned red brick buildings.

The county jail was one of these. Its small windows were thickly barred. It was a grim and somehow sinister structure.

Gillian entered the town by way of a covered bridge and drove into a lot beside the jail. The lot was packed with cars. A large talking picture truck was parked in front of the jail entrance.

Cables as thick as pythons went from the truck, up the steps and into the entrance ball.

The large entrance hall was crowded with men and glaring with high-powered lights. For a moment, no one took notice of Gillian or the pale girl with him.

A tall, dark-eyed man with wavy black hair and the look of an actor—a ham actor, Gillian had always thought, was addressing remarks to a microphone held on a pole. He was waving his arms. His eyes were flashing.

"I would like to say to the great American motion picture audiences," he was saying, "that the man who sent that strange missile, that diamond bullet, into the heart of my fellow townsman, is safely behind the bars of this jail. I have dropped all other work and shall prosecute this case without rest until that monster has paid the penalty he so richly deserves!"

They sounded to Gillian like the words of a cheap politician; but Gillian knew that Elton Dawbridge was more than a cheap politician; he was ambitious and clever and vicious. This was the county prosecutor's golden opportunity. A diamond bullet had shot him to the front pages of the nation and onto the screens of fifty thousand motion picture houses—and he was going to stay there.

A thick-set man with small blue eyes and carrot-colored hair who stood beside the county prosecutor with a hard grin was presumably Sheriff Ranse.

A reporter cried: "Hey! Here's Gillian Hazeltine!" And another yelled: "There's Hearthstone!"

The next moment a flashlight powder went off with a soft boom and a puff of smoke mushroomed against the ceiling. The sheriff and the county prosecutor were fighting their way through the newspapermen who crowded about Gillian and the frightened girl.

Gillian felt uncomfortable. He hadn't wanted to step into the limelight, and he wanted to avoid Elton Dawbridge. They were political enemies, and nothing was to be gained by a public quarrel. A tabloid reporter was plucking at his sleeve.

"Are you taking Truman's case, Mr. Hazeltine?" he eagerly asked.

"No," Gillian said.

The county prosecutor did not hear this question and answer. He made his way to Gillian and said dramatically:

"So you've decided to stick your finger into this pie!"

Nellie Hearthstone was clinging to Gillian's arm and was staring at the ring of men as a mouse might stare at a pack of yapping fox terriers.

"I haven't," Gillian made himself heard, "the slightest interest in your pie, Elton. Miss Hearthstone came to me for advice. I advised her to surrender herself. I promised her to have a talk with Truman. Can it be arranged?"

Elton Dawbridge laughed. It was a very irritating laugh. It did something to the hair at the back of Gillian's neck.

The reporters were silent now. Here was news.

"HAZELTINE," THE county prosecutor said loudly, "I've been wondering if you'd horn into this case. It's just your type, isn't it? Premeditated murder—beautiful orphan. Let me tell you that the citizens of this county want none of your trickery. Oh, we know how you've bought judges and bribed juries and employed perjured witnesses. But we don't want anything of that kind in Clinton. A decent, fine, kindly member of this community has been foully murdered by a jealous man, a dangerous, vicious man. As the representative of the people, I am going to see that this murderer receives his just deserts."

Gillian remained calm. His enemies had been throwing such insults his way for a good many years. He looked at Elton Dawbridge gravely. A motion picture man said:

"Will you give us your opinion of the case, Mr. Hazeltine? The American public will be interested in knowing how you feel about it.

Lights glared into Gillian's eyes. A microphone was held before him. A camera began to grind.

Gillian had never overcome his original feeling of microphone fright. He didn't like the idea of his words going bellowing out into fifty thousand theaters. But he spoke now, as he always did, directly and crisply.

"I have no interest in this case except as a private citizen. As a private citizen, I always feel that it is unsafe to leap at conclusions or to permit mob madness to influence intelligent decisions. My hope is that mob madness will not result in an innocent man being sent to the electric chair. That is all I have to say."

A nervous-looking man inquired, "Do you say positively that you will not defend James Truman?"

Gillian glanced at the county prosecutor, and said: "My present intentions are not to touch this case. If circumstances arise which cause me to change my mind, I will change my mind."

Elton Dawbridge now intruded himself into the picture. He came forward with an upraised fist, but he did not strike. It was only a dramatic gesture.

"We don't want you to change your mind," he declared oratorically. "This is a decent, clean community. We can wash our dirty linen without help from legal tricksters.

He did not look at Gillian when he said this, but into the twinkling lens of the camera.

The cameraman said, apologetically: "I'm sorry, Mr. Dawbridge, but I ran out of film just before you started. Do you want to say it over again, after I reload?"

Gillian looked at the county prosecutor and grinned. It looked very much like his fighting grin.

"It's too bad, Elton," he said wickedly, "that fifty million motion picture fans are going to be deprived of that gem."

Reporters again crowded about and shot questions. They wanted to know how the Hearthstone girl had got in touch with him, what she had said to him, and what he had said to her.

"She came to my office for advice," he answered. "After Mr. Grundle disappeared, she grew worried. A man with a black beard had been hanging around—"

"That's bunk!" Mr. Dawbridge shouted. "That's a fairy tale!"

"I have nothing more to say," Gillian smiled.

Over against the wall, he saw news photographers posing Nellie Hearthstone. A battery of cameras, suggestive of a firing squad, was clicking away to the blaze of flash light powders.

The lovely orphan had been snatched up by the greedy machinery of publicity, and the equally greedy machinery of the law—as practiced in Clinton.

Gillian, as he fought his way to the door, wondered if they would grind and tear her to destruction.

THERE WAS no question in Gillian's mind as he left the jail and climbed into his roadster that a special grand jury would rush through an indictment and remand James Truman to the superior court for trial. He would be tried, Gillian guessed, before Judge Lindley.

Shaking off the reporters who had followed him to his car, Gillian drove to a filling station, made inquiries pertaining to Judge Lindley's whereabouts, and was presently parking in the judge's driveway.

Ushered into the study, Gillian found his honor eagerly reading newspaper accounts of the Diamond Bullet murder case.

Judge Lindley was a man of about fifty with moody blue eyes, a thin, cruel mouth and a predatory nose. He was, Gillian well knew, a power not alone in county, but in State politics.

The reception the judge gave Gillian was exceedingly cold. He did not rise or offer his hand. Behind his desk he sat and stared frostily at his visitor.

"I dropped in," Gillian cheerfully explained himself, "to see if you mightn't arrange to let me see Jim Truman."

The judge's eyes narrowed.

"Is Truman retaining you?" he snapped.

"No, judge. I am interested in the case merely as a bystander. It has stirred my curiosity. A man who kills another by shooting him with a four and a half carat diamond is unique."

The cold eyes stared at him. "Has that Hearthstone girl been in communication with you?"

"She has, judge."

"What did she say?"

"Supposing we make a deal," Gillian suggested.

"Supposing you promise to let me see Truman in exchange for the amazing inside facts she gave me."

"What did she say?"

"She said she ran away because a big, tall man with a black beard had been hanging around—"

"That's poppycock! You know what happened, Hazeltine. Her lover, Truman, was jealous of Amos Grundle and shot him. Those are the simple facts of the case, and I'm warning you if you come into my court with any tricks, you'll be disappointed."

"But if Truman is guilty, how could a trick save him?"

"It can't!" the judge snapped. "I suppose," he said with heavy irony, "you can produce a man with a black beard."

"I leave him concealed in my sleeve," Gillian chuckled.

Judge Lindley turned red. He stood up.

"Hazeltine, I don't want you in this town and I don't want you in this house. You are my enemy politically—and you will be my enemy if you go into court. Don't forget that. Stay out of Clinton. Keep your hands off this affair. If you interfere, you'll be sorry."

Gillian looked at him gravely. "That sounds like a threat."

"Construe it as you wish."

"It sounds," Gillian murmured, "like taking men for rides, guns in the dark, knives in the back. Judge, you almost tempt me to stay. It sounds like a poker game. I am strongly inclined to stick around and call your bluff."

"You'll regret it," the judge snapped.

"My hole card," Gillian returned, "might prove, at that, to be a knave of diamonds."

Judge Lindley's eyes went narrower still. He pressed a button. The man who had admitted Gillian came in.

"Show this man the door," his honor snapped.

"I may see you in court, judge," Gillian said as he went out.

But Gillian had no real intention of taking the case. He was merely following the dictates of his curiosity. His curiosity led him now to the door of Seth Peters, attorney-at-law.

CHAPTER VI

IN THE STEAM ROLLER'S PATH

SETH PETERS, TRUMAN'S lawyer, had offices over a grocery store, the windows of which were now dark. But there was a light burning in the offices above them. Parking at the curb, Gillian climbed a flight of steps and knocked at a door with a frosted glass panel.

The door was swung open violently and Gillian found himself looking eye to eye into the pale, haggard face of a young man with curly yellow hair, broad shoulders, and a fighter's jaw.

Behind the young man, on a desk, an electric light burned and cast its rays upon a number of opened law books.

Seth Peters stared at Gillian and, slowly, a wave of red crept up from his neck to his hair. He grinned with astonishment.

"Why!" he said. "You're Gillian Hazeltine!"

"I came in behind a tall man with a black beard," Gillian said, smiling.

The young lawyer was trying to conceal his embarrassment and astonishment. He looked about the shabbily furnished room. He said:

"Gee whiz, this certainly is an honor, Mr. Hazeltine. I've

"I go to the movies," Miss Jarvis snapped.
"I guess I know how Indians creep!"

gone to court to listen to you a lot of times but I certainly never thought you'd walk into this room. I was just reading up on some of your cases—wondering how I'd handle this one. Did they tell you Jim Truman has retained me?"

Gillian nodded. "While they weren't telling me that I'd get a knife in the back if I stayed in this spotless town they were saving that you were Truman's lawyer. I dropped impurely out of curiosity."

"Please have a chair. I've been reading up on your defense of Compton MacArthur and—"

"You won't find the solution to this riddle in any book," Gillian gently interrupted. "MacArthur was not guilty, and my job was merely to find who was. In this case, we know that Truman killed Grundle and your only hope is to prove that he had a sufficient motive. My personal inclination," Gillian said with a chuckle, "is to pin the job on Elton Dawbridge or Judge Lindley."

Seth Peters grinned, then sobered. "I guess you don't have to be told what's going on in this town, Mr. Hazeltine. Clinton is rotting with political corruption. Dawbridge is the big boss. Even Lindley takes orders from him."

"How do you stand with them?"

The young man growled, "Hell's bells, I'm nothing but an insect in the triumphant course of the steam roller. I'm slated to be squashed flat. They've even made threats on my life. You see, I've been delving into records. They've covered themselves pretty thoroughly, but the smell of dead rats is strong in the wind. I annoy them the way a horsefly annoys a horse. But I don't worry them."

"Have they ever taken a shot at you?" Gillian asked.

"Not yet. And I'm safe for the immediate present. I'm elected to be the goat in this murder trial. Dawbridge knows he'll mash me flat. This is his golden chance. He's using Jim Truman and the Hearthstone kid as a springboard for a leap into the big political puddle. He has his eye on Washington. Look at him grabbing publicity! Doesn't it make you physically sick? When he's sent Jim to the chair, he'll be famous. And he'll send him there!"

"HOW WELL," Gillian inquired, "do you know Truman?"

"He's the only pal I have. He's a great guy—hard working, a real scientific farmer, and as decent and square as they make 'em. The only trouble with Jim is, he has too damned much pride. Dawbridge hates him, like poison. Jim got up on a soapbox at the last city election and told people what jellyfish they were if they elected Dawbridge's gang. He has told Dawbridge to his face that he's a crook a sneak-thief and a liar. Now Dawbridge has him where he wants him. Have you seen the Hearthstone girl?"

Gillian told him of meeting the lovely orphan, of her story of the murder, and of delivering her to the jail.

"She might lie Truman out of this," Gillian said, "except that she can't lie. What do you know about her?"

"Finest kid that ever breathed," said the young lawyer. "She's as game as she's good-looking, and clever to boot. Jim and I used to play games with her, trying to make her tell lies. It's a funny kink. She literally can't tell a lie. She gets all red and chokes up if she tries. She would have made a fine wife for Jim. She has the finest principles of any girl I ever knew. I wish she'd fallen for me instead of Jim."

The voting man paused and looked anxiously at Gillian.

"Mr. Hazeltine, if it was anybody but Jim, I wouldn't touch this case. I know he was a damned fool to kill that man, but he did it, and I'd give anything to help him out of the jam he's in. He and Nellie are simply crazy about each other. I feel he had just as much moral right to kill Grundle as one would to kill a rattlesnake that was getting ready to strike in a minute or two. I certainly do wish you'd take this case."

"I'm no miracle worker," Gillian said. "I have no more idea how that boy could be saved than you have."

Seth Peters grinned. "Yeah? Well, I'd lay a bet that you'd have some sweet ideas before many hours had passed. I'd match you against a dozen Elton Dawbridges. This is my first murder case and I don't know what to do. I'm not very clever. All I know how to do is put my head down and my fists up, and slam into 'em."

"Tell me about Grundle," Gillian said.

"I never knew the truth about that skunk," the young man replied, "until they arrested Jim. Then Jim spilled the works— told me what he'd learned from Nellie the night before he shot Grundle. Grundle was a regular *Dr. Jekyll* and *Mr. Hyde*—a model citizen in the city, a wife beater in the home. He was on the board of education and the board of charities, taking orders from Dawbridge. They were a pair of fine thieves. Only one man knows the truth about Grundle's home life—the truth about the real man."

"Jeff Pavlitch?" Gillian said.

"Yes, sir. Pavlitch knows."

"IF YOU could put the farm hand on the stand and draw a story out of him of Grundle's brutality, it might make a jury disagree," Gillian offered.

"But what would my case be?"

"Proving that Grundle was a *Jekyll* and *Hyde*—prove that Grundle was infatuated with Nellie and intended to kill his wife and marry her. The will is proof enough of that. Dawbridge will try to convince the jury that the girl is little better than a woman of the streets—that she somehow cajoled Grundle into making her his heiress. He will have to ruin her reputation to put his case over—unless he relies on her true story."

"Would you like to drive out and see Pavlitch?" the young lawyer asked.

"Yes. We might see how reliable he is. There's one more question. This morning's papers carried the story that Dawbridge had accused the Clinton orphanage superintendent of gross misuse of office—it amounted to an indictment for white slavery. Is that story true?"

"No, sir!" Seth Peters indignantly exclaimed. "It is another of Dawbridge's filthy lies. Old Pete Wardell has been the orphanage superintendent for twenty-seven years, and a finer, more decent old man doesn't live. Dawbridge had his ax out for Pete because the old man once told several people that Dawbridge was a crook. Dawbridge has a worthless, drunken brother he wants to put in Pete's job.

"Old Mr. Wardell was up to see me this afternoon. He'd had a heart attack. The scandal has just about killed him. He's been proud of his record at the orphanage and proud of the decent boys and girls to whom he was practically a father. Dawbridge's rotten lies cast a cloud of suspicion on every girl who ever lived in the orphanage. That was what hurt Mr. Wardell. I certainly do wish, Mr. Hazeltine, that you'd jump into this situation and roll up your sleeves and—"

He stopped as a sharp knock occurred at the door.

"Come in!" he shouted.

The door opened. A tall, thin woman with sharp, black eyes came in and closed the door firmly behind her. Her hair, which was black, was obviously dyed, for her face had the sharpness and the lines which hair dyeing somehow brings out.

She glared at Gillian.

"Are you Gillian Hazeltine?"

He nodded. "Yes, madam."

"My name is Nettie Jarvis. You're just the man I want to see."

CHAPTER VII

THAT MYSTERIOUS STRANGER

A MUFFLED EXCLAMATION of impatience escaped the younger lawyer.

"Miss Jarvis," he said, "I told you this afternoon that I simply cannot make use of your testimony. Mr. Hazeltine and I are very busy and—"

"Not too busy to talk to me," Miss Jarvis said grimly. She looked searchingly at Gillian. "So you're Gillian Hazeltine, the great criminal lawyer. My, but this is certainly a pleasure, Mr. Hazeltine! I've read about all your trials. When I heard the rumor that you were in Clinton, I wore myself out trying to find you."

Gillian's eyes were sparkling with secret amusement.

"I understand, Miss Jarvis," he said, "that on the morning of Amos Grundle's murder, you saw a tall black bearded man follow him from his house and into the woods."

The seamstress's black eyes glittered.

"That's true, Mr. Hazeltine. I was riding along the road on my bicycle. What's funny about that?" she demanded, glaring at Gillian. "I'm a poor woman. I can't afford a car. I've ridden a bicycle since I was a girl years before you were born. It's much pleasanter than walking."

"And very good exercise," Gillian said in a subdued voice.

"Elegant exercise!" Miss Jarvis cried. "Look how slim I am! I don't have to take Hollywood diets and drink prune juice by the gallon to reduce. It's bicycling that does it. If these modern girls would only—"

"You were saying," Gillian gently broke in, "that you were riding past Grundle's house on your bicycle the morning he was shot."

The black eyes glowed. "Yes, sir. It was a little before ten in the morning. I should say it was approximately nine forty-three. I was on my way to Mrs. Brubaker's, five miles farther along the road, to help make the clothes for her new baby. Mrs. Brubaker will testify to this.

"As I was passing the Grundles' front yard—their house is close to the road, you know—I saw Mr. Grundle walk out of the back door with a rifle under his arm. Then I saw a face peering out at him from the bushes."

"Was this the man with the black beard?" Gillian asked. Seth Peters softly groaned, as one might who has heard a story for the fifth time, and an absurdly false story at that.

"Yes, Mr. Hazeltine. He was a great tall man. He wore a black slouch hat and had a long tangled black beard. And as Mr. Grundle started off in the direction of the quarry, this tall, mysterious man stepped out from the bushes and stealthily followed him. He crept from tree to tree like an Indian."

"Did you ever," Seth Peters growled, "see an Indian creep from tree to tree?"

"I go to the movies!" Miss Jarvis snapped. "I guess I know how Indians creep!"

"Go on with your story, Miss Jarvis," Gillian encouraged her.

"Mr. Grundle vanished into the woods," she obliged, "with this tall, sinister-looking man dodging around behind. That is all I saw except that there was a mysterious bulge in the man's hip pocket."

"Such as a revolver might make?"

"Exactly!"

"Then how do you account for the fact that Grundle was shot with a diamond?"

"The stranger stole the diamond the night before from Mr. Truman's house."

"But why did he waste a perfectly good diamond on killing a man when an ordinary bullet would have sufficed?"

"He wanted to cast suspicion on Mr. Truman."

"Why?"

"How do I know who Mr. Truman's enemies are?" the old lady testily answered. "It was probably some enemy out of his Past."

"Mr. Truman is rather a young man to have much of a—past. From what I've gathered, his 'past' was devoted mostly to getting an agricultural school education—and working his farm."

"I DON'T say," Miss Jarvis answered, "that I know who the man was. If I did, I'd shout it from the housetops. All I say is that it is a wicked shame for Mr. Truman, who is a fine young man, to be locked up for a murder he did not commit."

"How was this black-bearded stranger dressed, Miss Jarvis?"

That was an easy one for the seamstress. She took it in her stride:

"He wore a black slouch hat, a black sateen shirt, a vivid red bandanna handkerchief, blue serge pants and a pair of scuffed brown oxfords. As I told you, that is what I saw—"

"While you were bicycling past the Grundle farm?"

"Yes, sir. I wanted you to know this." She started for the door. "If you want to use my testimony I'll gladly take the witness stand and tell in detail what I saw. I have withheld a certain amount of detail to use in the courtroom scene."

"Scene?" Gillian said, as if baffled.

"I mean, in the courtroom. I will gladly sacrifice my time. And I must say it's an honor to meet you. I knew you would be courtly and gallant and considerate." She shot a sour glance at Seth Peters. "Which is more," she added acidly, "than I can say for some of the younger members of your glorious profession."

Gillian gave her his courtliest, his most gallant bow. And

when the door was closed and she was safely out of earshot, he sat down and covered his face with his hands.

But Seth Peters did not see the humor of it.

"She's nothing but a damned old pest," the young man said.

Gillian feebly waved his hand.

"I know, I know," he said weakly. "The poor old girl is in an awful predicament. Her pride is involved. She has told this lie and she has to stick to it."

"She's the worst old liar in town. She's notorious."

"Yes. She's a congenital liar—just as Nellie Hearthstone is a congenital, truth-teller. Miss Jarvis has doubtless led a dry, dull, uneventful life. Who knows what glorious adventures she lives through as she bicycles about the county? This lie—this romance she told us about a man got up like something out of an old-fashioned stage melodrama—is like the bear that had a man holding its tail. The man didn't dare let go. Miss Jarvis must stand by her lie. She must nourish it along. It is already so real to her that she believes it herself. Do you know who that black-bearded man really is?"

Seth Peters looked perplexed, "What do you mean, Mr. Hazeltine—who is he?"

"I'll tell you," Gillian laughed. "That man is our old friend—the bogey man. He is the mysterious, invisible bad man we think about as kids. We think we forget about him when we grow up, but we never do. He always bobs up at murder trials. There was a black-bearded, mysterious stranger mentioned in the Hall-Mills case. When Ruth Snyder and Judd Gray killed Albert Snyder, she told the police that a black-bearded giant of a man had come to the bedside, bent over her husband and bashed in his skull with sash weight—or was it a hammer? We hate to admit it, but most of us still believe in the bogeyman. Who else is it that makes us scared to walk into a black room?"

"I suppose you're right," Seth Peters politely agreed, "but it's pretty obvious that we can't save Jim Truman with a bogey man alibi."

Gillian shrugged. "You never know who or what you may use in a case as tough as this one," he said. "Shall we drive out and see how Jeff Pavlitch stacks up as the one and only witness for the defense? How old is he?"

"About forty-seven."

"Married?"

"Yes, sir; to an American woman. I talked to them yesterday. As a matter of fact, Pavlitch has been talking pretty freely. He hated Grundle."

"If I were you, Peters, I'd send him away until the: very day you want his testimony. Don't let Dawbridge know about him. Don't even let him appear at the grand jury inquiry. He is your table card."

CHAPTER VIII

STARK TRAGEDY

TWO REPORTERS WERE lounging in Gillian's coupé, and three more were making themselves at home on the running board when the two lawyers crossed the sidewalk.

One of the five was Josh Hammersley of the *Times*—an old and trusted friend of Gillian's. Josh threw away a cigarette and said:

"Yeah, I expected to run into you out here, Gill. A good wholesome murder can't take place anywhere these days without your being in it up to your ears."

"I'm not in this one, Josh."

"You will be, sooner or later. If I were a lawyer, I would climb aboard if only to annoy Dawbridge. We ornaments of the press have developed acute cases of tin-ear-itis from listening to the roar of bouquets hurled by Mr. Elton Dawbridge at Mr. Elton Dawbridge."

A reporter seized Gillian roughly by the arm. "Say," he barked, "who killed Amos Grundle?"

"Cock Robin," Gillian answered.

"The bogey man," Seth Peters sourly added. "He has long black whiskers, he creeps from tree to tree like an Indian, he shoots his victims with diamonds, and he can be seen only from a bicycle."

"There's your story," Gillian said. "Go and interview Nettie Jarvis, the seamstress."

The reporters collectively groaned. Josh Hammersley said, plaintively: "Interview her! We can't get away from her. She asked me an hour ago if I would like to run the story of her life in serial form. Gill, be a good egg and let us have the exclusive story that you are taking this case."

Gillian shook his head. "When I go back to town tonight, I'm washed up."

"You mean," Josh guessed, "Truman hasn't a chance. He is sewed up in a bag and the bag is dangling from Dawbridge's scalp belt. Well—give us some dope on the Hearthstone girl. What is she—the sweetheart of Clinton County?"

"Nope. I talked to her for four hours. She's decent, cultured, refined—a wonderful girl."

"Can Dawbridge make her testify against Truman?"

"Yes."

One of the reporters grinned. "You're saying, Mr. Hazeltine, that the Hearthstone girl saw Truman murder Amos Grundle. That's great! Now, tell us how he happened to use that damned diamond."

Gillian looked at him coldly, then at Josh Hammersley.

"Josh," he said, "this young man is evidently new and overambitious. You might take him aside and tell him how it distresses me when I am misquoted. I'll give you boys an interesting sidelight on the Hearthstone girl. She is a psychological rarity. She literally cannot tell a lie. Because of her obscure origin, she has a tremendous amount of pride. This excessive pride has made her so honest, so truthful that the normal man or woman could not grasp it."

"Is this straight?" Josh demanded. Gillian nodded.

"Wait a minute!" Seth Peters interrupted. "Aren't you apt to hurt the case, Mr. Hazeltine, by letting that out?"

"Not a bit of it. What the case most needs is public sympathy. When the public learns that Nellie Hearthstone is a decent, high-principled girl, sentiment will swing to her. Public sentiment is the most powerful weapon a lawyer can use."

"How about that will?" a reporter asked.

"Miss Hearthstone told me flatly that she will not touch a cent of Grundle's money."

"What's the defense going to be?"

"Ask Mr. Peters. He is Truman's lawyer."

Several of the reporters grinned. One of them told Peters, "You'd better kidnap Mr. Hazeltine, buddy. If you don't, when Elton Dawbridge gets through with you, you'll ride out of this town with a lily in your hand."

Gillian said quickly, "Let's go, Peters." He climbed behind the wheel. Peters got in beside him.

IT WAS beginning to sprinkle. Lightning flickered in the west, and the faraway rumbling of thunder rolled through the streets like the sound of distant drums.

Following Seth Peters' directions, Gillian drove rapidly out of town along a badly rutted dirt road. At the Grundle farmhouse, which was in total darkness, Gillian slowed but did not stop. Several cars were parked in the ditches. Flashlights gleamed like fireflies. Curiosity-seekers were evidently swarming over the premises. Gillian drove on.

"There's a car following us," Peters said presently. "I think those reporters are after us."

"We'll have to duck them. Where is Pavlitch's house?"

"Up a side road a half mile on. Step on it!"

Gillian stepped on it. As they neared the side road, he

switched off his lights and drove slowly around the corner. After an interval, two cars went flying past on the main road. Gillian waited until they were well past, then switched on the dimmers and drove on.

Rain was now falling heavily. It made of the small structure, which Seth Peters designated as the Pavlitch farmhouse, a somewhat ghostly residence. It was unpainted, and the weather had blackened it. Oil lamps at curtainless windows added to its air of desolation.

Even before Gillian had turned off the ignition, he heard the muffled wailing of a woman. It was a shivery sound. He ran across the yard and into the house. The room he entered showed various evidences of poverty. There were no rugs or carpets on the scrubbed floor. The furniture was poor and shabby.

A man was lying on a couch against one wall. Beside the couch a woman was huddled in a chair, wailing.

She was unaware of Gillian's presence until he spoke; then she sprang up with a scream.

Gillian felt more than a little faint. Accustomed as he was to murders, the sight of a dead man always affected him. And one glance at the figure on the couch was sufficient to tell him that Jeff Pavlitch was dead.

The woman was too hysterical to do more than babble, and wail. But Gillian, gently questioning her, gathered that it had all happened within the last two hours. A man had come to the door and asked Jeff to step outside. He had been gone about an hour. Mrs. Pavlitch, worried over the sinister developments of the past week, had gone out to look for him.

She had found him, lying in the ditch at the fork, with his skull crushed in, as if he had been struck with terrific force by some heavy object—a club, perhaps. She had run back for a wheelbarrow and brought him home in that.

Seth Peters, almost as white as the man on the couch, was staring past Gillian.

"The coroner," he said shakily, "will find that he was struck by a passing car—driver unknown. Page Elton Dawbridge!"

Gillian led him outside. As they returned to the coupé through the rain, the young lawyer said savagely: "It gives me a choked, strangled feeling, as if everything was closing in. Vollmer, the coroner, is Dawbridge's brother-in-law. You know as well as I do that Dawbridge put Pavlitch on the spot. He isn't going to leave the smallest stone unturned. He has killed the only witness I could possibly count on for help. What'll I do now?"

Peters cursed in his half-hysterical horror.

CHAPTER IX

THE RULER'S COMMAND

BACK IN SETH PETERS'S office, Gillian took a cigar from his pocket, lighted it and began pacing slowly up and down the small room, with a vertical groove between his eyes, a pale banner of smoke trailing after him.

Seth Peters sat hunched on the edge of his desk, his smoldering blue eyes following Gillian's strides, his face haggard, his air one of hopeless defeat. He had seen, in the past few days, the crumbling of his hopes to get a foothold in Clinton and to deal summarily with the rascals who ran Clinton.

He was whipped by ruthless might before he had a chance to fight. If the truth were known, he was more than a little disappointed in Gillian Hazeltine. He had heard so much about this slender, keen-eyed man. His enemies called him the Silver Fox—and not because Hazeltine's black hair was prematurely sprinkled with silver. He was supposed to be so brilliant, so resourceful. Well, if he was so damned clever, why didn't he do something? Why did he talk so childishly about bogey men?

Gillian now and then halted his stroll, removed the cigar from his mouth, and gazed thoughtfully, almost hopefully, at the ash. Then, with an imperceptible headshake, he strolled on.

Ideas were coming to Gillian from the thin air or, perhaps, the cigar ash, but he discarded them as rapidly as they presented themselves.

On one of his turns, feet were heard on the stairs. The flimsy building vibrated with the heavy footfalls.

Gillian stopped in his tracks and owlishly gazed at the door. Seth Peters swung about and glared at the frosted glass panel.

"More reporters," Gillian guessed.

"Nettie Jarvis," Seth Peters said cynically, "about to divulge further details on the bogey man."

The door opened. It was Elton Dawbridge. His theatrical black eyes seemed to snap. His wavy black hair was disordered. He stepped over the threshold and firmly closed the door behind him. His eyes danced from Seth Peters to Gillian.

The county prosecutor placed his back against the door. He looked dangerous. There was somehow in his appearance and air a suggestion of a panther crouched to spring.

"I want to know," he said coldly, "what you are doing in this town, Hazeltine."

Gillian leisurely replaced the cigar in his mouth and puffed at it. The question seemed to puzzle him. It was as if he were asking himself just what he was doing in this town.

"I'll tell you," Gillian drawled. "I'm curious to find out how you're going to launder Clinton's dirty linen. There's so much of it to wash that I'm anxious to know where you're going to begin."

"Now it's my turn to ask one," Seth Peters whipped out as he rose from the desk. "You dirty rat, who invited you to come into my office?"

The county prosecutor glanced at him and smiled. It was a thin, contemptuous smile. He wasn't afraid of this cocky youngster. His eyes, when he swung them back to Gillian, were, however, hard and measuring.

"Are you coming into this, Hazeltine, as his associate counsel?"

"No!" Seth Peters snapped. "And I'd give my right arm if he were! We'd give you a run for your money—you rat!"

ELTON DAWBRIDGE ignored him. Gillian blew three perfect smoke rings at the ceiling. The county prosecutor smiled.

"You've made a very wise decision, Hazeltine. I don't have to tell you what this case represents to me. I'll come clean, because I want you to realize that this case is dynamite. This case is an opportunity for which I've been waiting for years. It means I'm through being a hick town lawyer. I'm going to be the next attorney general of this State."

Seth Peters was breathing hard through dilating nostrils.

"That isn't news," he said hotly. "This isn't a question of whether Jim Truman goes to the chair rightly or wrongly, to you. His electrocution is nothing to you but a peg to hang publicity on."

The county prosecutor continued to ignore him. "You see what I mean, don't you, Hazeltine?"

"Yes," Gillian said, "I see what you mean."

"And you see that there's no room here, don't you, for your clever tricks—courtroom surprises, lying witnesses, bought judges."

"It's funny," Gillian remarked, "the way you harp on my tricks. How could any trick—any kind of trick—possibly save that Truman boy from the chair, with you prosecuting, Lindley presiding, and a handpicked jury with a verdict decided before the show starts?"

Elton Dawbridge grinned.

"You have the situation nicely sized up, haven't you? I'd be willing to bet you that all the tricks in your bag wouldn't upset that scheme."

Gillian lifted his heavy black eyebrows. "Really, Elton? I didn't know you were a gambler. I thought you never laid money on anything but fixed fights."

"This fight is fixed."

"But just how much of a bet did you have in mind?"

"I'd bet everything I own!"

"Let's get this straight. You would bet everything you own that I could not spring any surprise, or trick, to knock this beautiful scheme of yours into a cocked hat?"

The county prosecutor was looking at him with narrowed eyes.

"That's what I said!" he snapped. I'd bet everything I own including the shirt on my back that my scheme is going through as I've stated."

"How much," Gillian inquired, "is everything you own, converted into cold cash?"

Elton Dawbridge laughed harshly. It sounded like a bark.

"A hundred and fifty thousand dollars!"

Gillian looked astonished. "You really mean, Elton, that you'd bet that sum that I could not spring a surprise that would ruin your little scheme?"

"Every dollar of it! That's how sure I am. That puts a cash value on the risk you'd run in touching this case. You can consider it, if you wish, a warning."

Gillian was studying his cigar ash. He looked at Dawbridge gravely.

"Elton," he said, "you aren't being fair. You know you're taking advantage of my worst weakness. You know how I love to gamble. You know I can't resist a sporting proposition."

THE COUNTY prosecutor reached for the doorknob. "This joke's gone far enough. Get out of this town, Hazeltine, and stay out."

"But I'm taking your bet!" Gillian answered. "I'm betting you a hundred and fifty thousand that I can upset your little scheme. Supposing we each deposit one hundred and fifty thousand cash in any bank you name—in escrow. Winner takes all. If you land Jim Truman in the hot seat—you get it all. If I get him an unconditional verdict—the pot's mine."

The county prosecutor was glaring at him.

"You can't do it honestly!" he barked.

"My dear man," Gillian smiled coldly, "when was I ever accused of being honest?"

"All right!" Dawbridge shouted. "I say you can't do it honestly or dishonestly."

"Does that mean—the bet stands?"

"You're damned right it does! Bring out your tricks! Trot out your surprises! I've got this case right here!" He extended a clenched fist. "Right in here! This is my town. The case will be tried by my judge. You're getting weak-minded, Hazeltine. You're a fool!"

"I've been called worse names than that by rank amateurs," Gillian cheerfully returned. "It's too bad about poor old Jeff Pavlitch, isn't it?"

The county prosecutor's eyes narrowed and hardened.

"What do you mean?"

"Haven't you heard? He was run down and killed by an automobile just a couple of hours ago."

"By an automobile?"

Gillian smiled. "You didn't think, did you, Elton, that someone called him out of the house and led him down to the fork where a gang was waiting to bash his skull in?"

Elton Dawbridge licked his lips.

"I don't know what you're talking about."

"I'm talking," Gillian said calmly, "about the only witness who could take the stand and tell the real truth about your sidekick Amos Grundle. Pavlitch is dead."

DAWBRIDGE SHOOK his head with a thin smile.

"Isn't that too bad? It's really a pity. Poor Pavlitch! You know, Hazeltine, it's a queer thing, but I've noticed around here, in

Clinton, that people who talk too much often do get hit by passing automobiles. They suddenly seem to grow careless with their
lives, as it were. You might bear that in mind."

"Thank you," Gillian said, "I will. And I want to tell you a
queer thing, too. There is a gang of young fellers back home who
seem to have the strangest respect for my life—and a positive
dislike for any one who takes liberties with it. A man who didn't
seem to like me tried to kill me one time by putting dynamite
under the hood of my car. When I turned on the ignition, an
electrical connection was to be made that would set the dynamite off. But one of this gang of young fellers caught him as he
was attaching this to my car. I know it sounds incredible, but
when that man's body was found in the river a week later, there
were two hundred and seven bullet holes in him by actual count."

The county prosecutor was grinning.

"I understand. You think you can bluff me, don't you, Hazeltine? You think you're going to lick me with one hand tied
behind you."

"Not at all," Gillian protested. "I am a very modest man. I
expect to use both hands and both feet."

"And strike below the belt—plenty!"

"When in Rome," Gillian answered. "I always conduct myself
in accordance with the standards set by the Romans. In Clinton,
I will naturally stoop to anything. One of the reasons for my
success is my adaptability. I never hesitate a moment in adopt-
ing the methods of my opponents regardless of their question-
ability."

Dawbridge nodded, still smiling. "I think we understand
each other perfectly. Are there any details we haven't discussed?"

Gillian was suddenly hard of lip and eye.

"We will have to have one ironclad agreement before you
leave this office. There is to be absolutely no third-degree stuff
pulled on the Hearthstone girl."

"I wouldn't dream of such a thing!" Dawbridge exclaimed.

"No clever little tortures," Gillian said. "No dope in her food.

No keeping her awake hour after hour. If you or any of your pups lay a hand on that girl—fireworks! With machine guns and anything else available. The same goes for Truman. Question them within legal limits—no more. I'm going to keep in touch with those two babes in the wood. If they say you're getting rough—I'm just as apt as not to bring that gang here. And if any attempts are made to prevent me from having access at any hour to them—I'll blast. Got that?"

The county prosecutor opened the door.

"My!" he breathed. "But aren't you hard! You send cold chills all over me, *Mr.* Hazeltine. I'm almost afraid of my own shadow. I've got it. And what I said before still goes, you're weak-minded."

CHAPTER X

THE OPENING SHOT

WHEN DAWBRIDGE WAS gone, Gillian resumed his pacing. He walked up and down the little office, puffing at his cigar. Seth Peters followed his movements now with wide-eyed amazement verging on bewilderment.

"Gee whiz, Mr. Hazeltine," he said in an awed voice, "you must have had a swell idea all of a sudden."

The Silver Fox stopped and looked at him. "What do you mean?"

"Well, a minute ago, you didn't have the slightest idea what Jim's defense would be. You must have struck a dandy!"

Gillian folded his arms and looked at the pale young lawyer as if he were puzzled.

"I struck a dandy idea hours ago. It's just beginning to grow up. In a little more time, it's going to be ripe and husky—with whiskers."

"Whiskers?"

"Black ones."

"You're back to the bogeyman," Peters groaned.

"My dear boy, I've never let the bogey man out of my sight."

"You don't mean to tell me you are going to put Nettie Jarvis on the stand and try to make a jury believe in the black-bearded stranger? Gee, Mr. Hazeltine, everybody in town knows she's a terrible old liar. You'll be laughed out of court."

Gillian's eyes were twinkling. "Think so, kid?"

"There isn't any question about it. How can that old liar have any weight against Dawbridge's case? There's the jeweler who knows the diamond was Jim's. And there's the coroner who found the diamond in Grundle's heart. Even if Nellie doesn't take the stand and spill everything with her story, Dawbridge has an airtight circumstantial case, hasn't he?"

No case is airtight until the last rivet is in."

"You're going to lose that, bet, Mr. Hazeltine."

"How," Gillian asked, "would you like to lay a little side bet?"

The young man laughed. "I haven't even paid my last week's board bill. Besides, I—I know you're going to win." He didn't say this very decisively. Seth Peters was, in fact, more than doubtful that Gillian had a chance to win that bet. But he realized that, if Gillian won the case, his own future was assured.

These reflections were interrupted by a gentle knock at the door. The youngster called out: "Come in!"

The door opened to admit a white-haired old man. Through thick, gold rimmed glasses he peered at Seth Peters, then at Gillian.

"Excuse me, Seth," he said. "I thought you were alone."

"It's all right. Come in, Pete. This is Gillian Hazeltine. Mr. Hazeltine, this is Pete Wardell, the orphanage superintendent. Pete, Mr. Hazeltine is taking the case. How's that for good news?"

The old man peered at Gillian.

"That is, indeed, good news. I am delighted to know you, Mr.

Hazeltine; and I do hope you can do something for that poor boy—and Nellie. She is a splendid girl. She was like my own daughter."

"I TAKE it," Gillian said, "that you did not know the kind of man Grundle was when she went to work in his house."

"I certainly did not, sir. It came as a shocking surprise. And the accusations made by Dawbridge—that filthy-minded, despicable—" The old man's voice was shaking so with emotion he could not go on. He cleared his throat and said: "I am sure that you will put that rascal where he belongs, Mr. Hazeltine."

"I'm going to do my best."

The orphanage superintendent turned to Seth. "You are still on the case?"

"Yes. Mr. Hazeltine is, nominally, my associate counsel, but actually I am his office boy. I'm going to learn something about criminal law. It will be a wonderful chance for me."

"I came up here," Pete Wardell said, "to tell you a rather curious thing I just learned, Seth. It may be of no value—it may be useful. I just found Jumbo Waller, lying drunk in a doorway, and I took him home. Jumbo," the old man explained to Gillian, "is a sort of assistant to Dr. Vollmer, the coroner. The coroner has an undertaking establishment which serves, in times like this, as the city morgue. The body of Amos Grundle is there now. It is to be taken to the crematory tomorrow morning."

"I read about that in the papers," Gillian said. "Grundle once stated that he wished to be cremated. He had some curious superstition about being buried."

"Yes, sir. And this Jumbo Waller told me a mighty curious thing. He said that Dr. Vollmer did not find that diamond in Grundle's heart at all."

"Really?"

"Yes, sir. It was embedded in a rib above the heart—the third rib down."

Seth Peters grunted. "Well, it served its purpose just the same. The shock of the impact killed him."

"I suppose so. But I thought you might like to know about it."

"Thanks, Pete," the young lawyer said, "but the status of the case remains the same as it was. Truman killed him somehow by firing the diamond into him. That's all the law cares about. Isn't that so, Mr. Hazeltine?"

Gillian was looking at the orphanage superintendent.

"Do you know, Mr. Wardell, how much of an autopsy Vollmer performed?"

"According to jumbo, he only probed for the bullet—and found the diamond stuck in that third rib."

"Didn't he cut into his heart?"

"No, sir. He found the diamond and quit with that."

"That's curious."

"Of course, Mr. Hazeltine, the body had been in the water several days. It must be a sickening job to work on a body that's as far gone as that."

"True."

"Why bother with going further with an autopsy?" Seth Peters impatiently asked. "The diamond killed him—and they found that."

Gillian was pale. "I want to take a look at that body," he said. His aversion to dead bodies made him feel ill already.

"I don't see what's to be gained," Seth Peters protested.

"You don't have to go."

"Oh, I'll go. But it strikes me as being a waste of time—and emotion. I hate dead men."

But he accompanied Gillian to Vollmer's Undertaking Parlors.

TWO MEN were lounging in the entrance—two large, tough, grim looking men with police clubs. One of them said, gruffly, "No one's allowed in here."

"But," Seth Peters protested, "we are Jim Truman's lawyers. We want to inspect Amos Grundle's body."

"Nothing doing. The coroner's inquest was held this mornin'. No one's allowed in here."

"Whose orders?" Gillian asked.

"The county prosecutor's."

Gillian looked past him into the dimly lighted interior of the undertaking establishment. He saw four men lounging in there, armed as were these two, with clubs.

The watchdog growled: "Yeah and there's four more lookin' after the back door."

"Amos Grundle, up there in heaven," Gillian said dryly, "strumming away on his golden harp, must feel very much flattered at such protection."

"Yeah—and maybe you two guys can mooch."

Out of the guards' earshot, Gillian said, in perplexed tones, "Now, just what is there so precious about the mortal remains of Amos Grundle?"

"I think the diamond is locked up in the coroner's safe," the young lawyer answered. "It's had a lot of publicity. Dawbridge is probably afraid some yegg will take it."

"A four and a half carat diamond would interest no yegg," Gillian pointed out.

"Then he may be afraid we'll steal it, to rob him of evidence."

"I'd question that," Gillian said. "If the diamond is so precious, why hasn't he stored it in a bank vault? Peters," he went on briskly, "I'm going back to Greenfield to look up a couple of my friends. While I'm gone, drop in at the jail and tell Nellie and Jim that I am going to do all I can for them, and that they are under no conditions to say a word about the murder to any one—not even to you. Dawbridge will move heaven and earth to get a confession out of them. So far, neither of them has admitted the slightest knowledge of the murder. Tell them I said to keep mum."

"Yes, sir. Will you be back tonight?"

"As fast as I can burn up the roads. When you have delivered my message to Nellie and Jim, go to your office and stay there. Don't let any excitement which may occur on the street attract you out. Understand?"

"No, sir; but I'll do what you say."

They parted at Gillian's car. The rain had stopped. Gillian climbed in and raised the side windows of his coupé, although the night was not cold.

He drove under the covered bridge. A black Packard roadster followed him. It was without lights. It tailed him for five miles, along winding roads up through the hills. When Gillian reached the wider, straight concrete stretch which went through bogs and thickets to the village of Chester, he opened the throttle.

So did the driver of the black roadster. At a four corners, the roadster swept up beside him. He had no warning of its presence until headlights flashed along the road beside him. Then it was abreast.

He saw dimly a man bending over the wheel; another man crouching down in the rumble seat.

There was a spurting of blue-red flame. A savage shattering sound occurred at the window beside which Gillian sat. The coupé slewed away, and the roadster swerved off into the left branch of the intersecting road. Its ruby taillight dwindled, vanished completely.

Gillian drove on. A glance had told him that the bulletproof window was ruined. He was angry. Bulletproof windows were expensive. But he was relieved, too. Elton Dawbridge had fired the opening shot in the war, and missed. Gillian only hoped that the following ones would leave him unscathed. At all events, the fight was on—and it was Gillian's next move.

CHAPTER XI

OUTSIDE THE LAW

WITH HIS ACCELERATOR flat on the floor, except for curves, crossings and villages, Gillian drove the forty miles in less than fifty minutes. It was midnight when he reached Greenfield.

He drove past his own house and along the exclusive residential parkway above the Sangamo, to turn with shrieking tires into a crushed-stone driveway. He stopped under the *porte-cochère* of a spacious colonial house in which one window alone was alight. He ran up the steps and pressed the bell.

His summons was answered presently by a tall, middle-aged man with iron-gray hair, a pair of cool, steady blue eyes, who wore a black dressing gown over pajamas. There was a book under his arm and a pipe in his mouth.

"Good evening, Hank," Gillian said. "It's a shame to disturb you, but how would you like to do me a great favor?"

Dr. Henry Hoffman's cool, steady blue eyes narrowed. Then he smiled whimsically.

"It's nice of you to put it that way," he said. "When you snap your fingers, I jump—as who doesn't?"

Gillian looked displeased. "Let's not put things on that basis," he said. "You make it sound like blackmail—a word I particularly detest."

"Very well, Gillian. What can I do?"

"Take some X-ray photographs of a corpse. Have you a portable X-ray outfit here or will we have to go to your laboratory?"

"I have one here. Tell me, how long has this corpse been a corpse?"

"About a week."

"Hm. What are the circumstances?"

"I'll tell you as we drive along. Don't bother changing your clothes. There will be no ladies."

The Roentgenologist, despite his eyes, made no objections to this informal suggestion. But his mouth tightened peculiarly. The X-ray expert did not know whether Gillian had made that reference to ladies pointedly or not. Ladies had been responsible for a certain painful predicament from which Gillian had extricated Dr. Hoffman and earned his lifelong gratitude—and obedience.

The two men loaded several heavy black boxes into the rear deck of Gillian's coupés and started off.

"This corpse," Gillian explained, as, he headed the car toward the business section, "reached its present distressing condition because of a murderous attack by an assailant or assailants unknown."

"Where is it, Gillian?"

"Clinton."

"Ah! Not the farmer the papers have been so full about!"

"Yep. Amos Grundle."

"He was killed in an amazing way, wasn't he? A diamond in the heart. It stirs the imagination."

"An odor of rats has been detected," Gillian informed him. "The diamond did not reach his heart. It was found embedded in the third rib from the top—above the heart."

"The shock might have caused death."

"How do I know," Gillian inquired, "that a ruby, sapphire, emerald or even a pearl does not exist in some other part of the anatomy?"

"Each of those stones shows up nicely on a fluoroscopic screen," the doctor said.

"My dear Hank," Gillian laughed, "one of the delightful things about you is your ability to grasp any idea with a minimum of explanation. You have that rare quality, intuition. No wonder women are mad about you."

"I have taken some remarkably sharp photographs of bullets lodged in backbones," the doctor grimly retorted. "A farmer named Truman, I understand, is charged with sowing diamonds not wisely but too well. Is there another suspect?"

"A black-bearded stranger."

"John Doe?"

"In my simple lexicon, he is the bogey man."

"The bogey man exists," Dr. Hoffman said gravely. "I have encountered him under beds."

Gillian laughed. "Do all husbands wear black beards?" He quickly added: "Our corpse is to be cremated to-morrow morning."

"That explains the urgency. Am I to take the stand for the defense?"

Gillian sighed. "If I only knew who would take the witness stand for the defense! A case like this is similar to opening a safe. You can try hundreds of combinations, but only one will work. I am still looking for the right combination."

THEY HAD drawn up before a poolroom which masked one of Greenfield's most notorious speakeasies.

"I'll be back in minutes," Gillian said, and went in.

He walked to the rear end of the poolroom, which was full of men and thick with smoke, opened a door and walked down a hall to another door. On this he rapped three times, then twice.

He waited, knowing that he was being inspected by an ingenious system of mirrors.

The door opened. A sallow-faced man of forty grinned nervously. "Good evening, Mr. Hazeltine. Something up?"

"Where's Silky?"

"He's right here, Mr. Hazeltine."

Gillian found Silky Davis at the bar, nursing a highball: a slim, elegant, white-faced young man with black marbles for eyes.

"Busy?" Gillian asked him.

"Not too busy to do anything I can for you, Mr. Hazeltine. What's up?"

"Come outside."

The elegant young man followed Gillian out to the street. With his thumb, Gillian indicated the splintered bulletproof window.

Silky Davis whistled softly. "Browning," he said. "Where'd that happen?"

"This side of Clinton."

"Oh, yeah? You mixin' into that mess, Mr. Hazeltine?"

Gillian nodded. The elegant young man shook his head.

"They've got a hard mob up there, Mr. Hazeltine. It's a small town, but it's a halfway point, as you know, for a lot of Canadian booze—a kind of a bottleneck, you might say. They don't care who they shoot."

"Afraid of 'em?" Gillian quietly asked.

"Who? Me? Say, listen, Mr. Hazeltine, if you have a little job you want my boys to do for you up in Clinton, say it, Mr. Hazeltine, and the job is done."

"This has to be done immediately."

"Sure thing! We do everything immediately, and sometimes even sooner. Now, just what is this job?"

Gillian told him briefly. Silky made no comments. All he said was, "K.O., Mr. Hazeltine, K.O. You know where the bridge is by that green roadhouse five miles outside of town?"

"Yes."

"We'll be there three minutes after you are. Just leave it to me. Leave all the details to me. See you in church, Mr. Hazeltine."

That was the way Silky Davis did business. Gillian drove out of town on the road toward Clinton and waited at the bridge by the green roadhouse. He had not waited five minutes when three expensive sedans rolled up. Silky, behind the wheel of the foremost, was smoking an opulent cigar. He leaned out and called:

"Trail us, Mr. Hazeltine. When you get to Clinton, the job will be done and everything will be ready for you."

A sputtering on the right became louder, and a motorcycle policeman came up and stopped between Gillian's coupé and Silky's sedan. He looked from one to the other; touched his cap to Gillian and said:

"What's goin' on here, Silky?"

"Why, we're going out and kill a lot o' guys, Mike. Want to come long?"

Mike glanced, puzzled, at Gillian. "What is going on here, Mr. Hazleton?"

"Just what Silky says, Mike. We may kill a lot of guys. Want to come along?"

"Where?"

"Clinton."

"No, thanks," Mike said fervently.

He wheeled about and sputtered off. Silky started down the road for Clinton. The other two sedans fell into line at approximately seventy miles an hour. Gillian tried to keep up.

DR. HOFFMAN said nervously: "Gillian, this is dangerous business, isn't it?"

And Gillian, laughing, answered: "Not if we slow down for intersections."

They shot across the covered bridge into Clinton five minutes after the arrival of Silky Davis's expedition.

That elegant young man had the situation well in hand. When Gillian, stopped his car before Vollmer's Undertaking Parlors, Prosecutor Elton Dawbridge's sentinels were nowhere to be seen. Well-dressed young men lounged in the entrance.

Silky Davis was standing in the doorway, smoking a fresh cigar and softly brushing his hands one against the other.

"It's all set, Mr. Hazeltine."

"What happened?"

"Nothing, Mr. Hazeltine. Nothing at all. We just drove up,

unloaded, and showed 'em a little hardware. We corralled 'em in the back yard, and they're there now—just like lambs."

"Anybody hurt?"

"Only one of them, who has a little sick headache, because his chin fell against something made of brass."

Gillian helped the doctor unload the black boxes. But he did not accompany him into the back room. The very thought of that back room made him feel ill.

He paced up and down until Dr. Hoffman came out, carrying the black boxes. The doctor's face was slightly green. He looked at Gillian, narrowed his eyes and nodded.

"How about the diamond?" Gillian asked.

"It was stopped by that third rib."

"How about the heart?"

"It was untouched."

"I'll see you to-morrow," Gillian said. "Silky will take you home."

"Are you staying here?"

Gillian nodded.

"Will I have to go into court?"

"Certainly." Gillian turned to Silky. "A thousand thanks, Silky."

The gunman made a nonchalant gesture with his cigar.

"It was a pleasure, Mr. Hazeltine. I tossed it off with my left hand. Ask me to do something hard, some time!"

Gillian entered his car and drove to the jail. Five reporters were dozing in chairs. A photographer was holding his camera lovingly in his arms.

Tiptoeing through a hall and into the jail, Gillian found a turnkey. The turnkey said that Mr. Dawbridge had given him orders to admit Mr. Hazeltine at any hour.

"Do you want to see them both?"

Gillian said that he did. The turnkey led him down a corridor to a cell where a young man sat on the edge of a cot with his face in his hands. His sandy hair was rumpled. He looked up. His features were clean-cut. He had a good chin, firm lips and direct eyes.

He sprang up. "Are you Mr. Hazeltine?"

"Yes."

"This is Jim Truman," the turnkey said. "The girl has got the next cell. They're the only guests we've got right now. We thought the poor young things might be lonesome, so we put them as close together as the law allows."

THE TURNKEY walked away. Gillian looked into the adjoining cell. Nellie Hearthstone, standing at the door, resembled a ghost. Her large dark eyes stared at him without expression. He turned and read tragedy in the eyes of James Truman.

"You two kids," he said, "are going to have to snap out of this. Things are never as black as they are painted. Truman, did Seth Peters, deliver my message?"

"Yes, sir. Before they moved us."

"They gave you new cells, eh?"

"Yes, sir; about an hour ago."

"Nice clean, new cells," Gillian said dryly. "You can thank Mr. Dawbridge for that. He knew you would like being close together. Have you engaged in any conversation since this happened?"

"No, sir; we haven't said a word."

"You realize, of course," Gillian said pleasantly," that the able and distinguished county prosecutor has a Dictaphone hooked up so that he can hear every word you say, or so a stenographer can make a record for him. You see, Mr. Dawbridge has had very little love in his life, and is very curious to know what a pair of devoted lovers might say to each other."

Jim Truman was smiling grimly, and Gillian realized that here was a young man with courage. And the thought of permitting Elton Dawbridge to send him to the electric chair became even more distasteful to Gillian.

He asked Jim Truman if the county prosecutor had questioned him.

"Yes, sir; he's been questioning me all day."

"How about you, Nellie?"

"They asked me questions when they arrested me. But they haven't bothered me since."

"You have just one answer to all their future questions: 'My lawyers will answer that.' When the grand jury meets, you will answer no questions. You will be indicted, anyway. Try not to worry. Things may not look so black in a few days."

Gillian said good night and left them. On the sidewalk outside the jail he encountered the county prosecutor, an ugly light in his eyes.

"What," he clipped out, "was the big idea of that?"

"Of what?" Gillian gently asked.

"Bringing in Silky Davis's mob to stick up Vollmer's."

"The answer to that," Gillian replied, "is, what was the big idea of stationing your gang there to prevent my seeing that corpse?" Dawbridge ignored the question and said, "I could have you arrested for that."

"Well, why don't you?"

THE COUNTY prosecutor was pale and nervous. "It may interest you to know that the coroner gave out a statement an hour ago to the press, that the earlier report of the diamond being found in Grundle's heart was erroneous."

"Why didn't he say that in the first place?"

"The sooner you learn," Dawbridge answered, "that I am running this show, and that I am going to keep on running this show, the better. Why did you want to see that corpse?"

"Because corpses never lie."

The county prosecutor glared at him. Gillian said: "Not upset, are you, Elton? Not worried about anything, are you?"

Dawbridge, with an effort, grinned. "Hazeltine," he exclaimed, "the keys of the city are yours. Welcome to Clinton! Pardon me if there aren't fireworks and a brass band. You'll just have to excuse our informality. I want to retract all my harsh words. I want you to know that nothing could suit me better than having you here!"

"I feel flattered," Gillian said dryly. "Am I supposed to ask why you are so delighted?"

"That's right! Why am I so delighted? Because you are going to keep this case on the front page. Hazeltine, the courtroom wizard, is handling the defense. Hooray! Pardon my enthusiasm, but I need publicity. The more I get, the farther I go."

"I know what you mean," Gillian said. "The more dynamite you put under a rotten old stump, the higher it blows."

Dawbridge chuckled. "With you in the case, I realize I was a piker to want the State attorney generalship. I'm going to play leapfrog right over that job."

"I'm glad we're so harmonious," Gillian answered. "But don't forget our little bet."

"Forget it!" the other cried. "I've already spent it!"

"I hope," Gillian said, "on something worthy."

"A trip to Washington!"

"The White House?" Gillian asked in an awed voice.

"Not yet. Only the Senate this time. But wait!"

Gillian made a mocking bow.

"Good night, Senator!"

CHAPTER XII

POLITICAL WARFARE

TWO OF THE Greenfield newspapers made some reference next morning to what they humorously hailed as "Hazeltine's Bogey Man." One tabloid printed a "synthetic photograph" on the front page, showing Gillian Hazeltine chasing a black

The prosecutor flashed the gem at Gillian

bearded dwarf with a butterfly net. In the synthetic photograph, the dwarf had the wings of a wasp.

Editorial comment was inclined generally to the opinion that Mr. Hazeltine was turning the Grundle murder case into a three-ring circus.

Gillian remained in his office all day long. He refused to see reporters. His switchboard operator refused to connect any calls to him except a long distance one from his wife in Chicago.

Vee had read, in the Chicago *Tribune,* that Gillian was defending James Truman, and she wanted to know what it was all about.

"A couple of nice kids in hot water," he told her, "and I have a hundred and fifty-thousand-dollar bet on with the black-hearted crook who will prosecute Truman that I can get him out of it."

"I'll charter a plane and be home in two hours," Vee said. "Love and kisses, darling."

"I need plenty," Gillian said. It was like Vee to come when needed.

He didn't like the way the newspapers were acting. They weren't giving Nellie Hearthstone the sympathy he had hoped for. The afternoon *Bulletin* carried a half page photograph of her, with great black type above it inquiring:

GOOD OR CLEVER?

And Elton Dawbridge was quoted in a lengthy interview as saying:

"We do not want men of Gillian Hazeltine's caliber interfering in this tragedy which has plunged our county into sorrow and thrust it on the front pages of the press of the nation as the scene of a sensational and deplorable crime. We want to get at the bottom of this case by honest, honorable methods. We don't want golden-mouthed law-twisters clogging up the machinery of our courts. We don't want smart Alec city lawyers whose sole ability is to obscure the issue with vaudeville tricks. We don't want a courtroom Barnum, a legal clown, to mock at our grief. We don't want trickery in our courts. We want justice!"

Gillian softly announced to himself that Elton Dawbridge was the world's most mealy-mouthed hypocrite; and read on:

"A pillar of our community, a decent, upright citizen has been murdered—foully murdered. I intend to send the black-guard who murdered him to the electric chair. I have no hope of rewards. In my humble way, I wish but to do my duty and to keep faith with my people, my State, and my God."

Gillian could read no more of that. His stomach was rebelling. He smoked twenty-two cigars that day, and devoted most of his time to gazing dreamily down the river.

ONCE, WHEN Miss Walsh came in and looked at him anxiously, he said: "Tell me how you like working for a smart-Alec city lawyer, a courtroom clown?"

The girl went white. She banged on his desk with a small clenched fist.

"Mr. Hazeltine," she said venomously, "if you don't put that crook where he belongs, I'm going to quit! I'm going to start a farm and grow sour crabapples! I've been with you a good many years, but I've never known you to take a case which smelled so to high heaven. Those hypocrites! I've never met Jim Truman and I've only had a glimpse of the Hearthstone girl, but I'd bet a month's salary they're both fine young people. And I'd bet a year's salary that Amos Grundle was a brute and a beast."

"Did I say so?" Gillian murmured.

"Everybody knows it. They say he was a *Dr. Jekyll* and *Mr. Hyde*—a model citizen in public and a wife beater at home. Isn't it true?"

"Yes, it's true."

"I knew it!" Miss Walsh cried. "I'd kill a man like that myself!"

Gillian smiled. "A nice girl like you?"

"A nice girl like me!"

Miss Walsh was glaring at him. Gillian laughed.

"What's going to happen to those two kids?" she demanded. "As things stand, won't she have to testify against Truman?"

"Yes."

"If she doesn't talk, won't she be sent to prison for contempt of court?"

"Or worse," Gillian affirmed.

"Is it true that she's a psychological freak—can't tell a lie?"

The lawyer nodded. His efficient secretary spread out her fingers in an imploring gesture.

"Well, what are you going to do? You don't dare let her take the stand. The minute she goes on the stand. Your case is lost. Isn't it?"

"Yes," Gillian answered.

"What are you going to do?"

"That's what I'm working on now," he said. "You're right. She must not take the stand. She must not even testify at the grand jury inquiry. Truman must lie. He must say he did not leave his farm the night or morning of Grundle's murder. At his trial, I will not let him take the stand."

"But how about the girl? If you don't let her testify, and if you plant the idea that Truman was on his farm—isn't the conclusion obvious that the girl is guilty?"

Gillian nodded. "You have summed up the problem perfectly," he said.

"Is there a solution?" Miss Walsh asked.

He turned from her and looked down the river. He took several puffs at his cigar. He blew several smoke rings at the ceiling.

"You've heard a great deal lately, haven't you," he asked, "about my trickery?"

"Yes, Mr. Hazeltine."

"It comes down to this," he said. "Give a dog a bad name often enough and long enough and, pretty soon, the dog gets it into his head that he's a pretty wicked pup—I'm that dog."

Miss Walsh gave him a radiant smile.

"That's a relief," she said. "You can't be tricky enough to please me. I want you to make them change it from 'Courtroom 'Barnum' to 'Courtroom Houdini.' Smash 'em!" Her eyes sparkled. "I meant what I said about quitting. You know very well that, if it weren't for me snapping the whip over you, you'd never get a stroke of work done. You lose this case—and I start that sour crabapple farm!"

"I'll do my best," Gillian promised.

GOVERNOR JUDSON WITHROW, calling from the State capitol, telephoned Gillian at his house that night. He wanted to know what was going on in Clinton.

"What's behind the curtain, Gill?"

Gillian told him bluntly. "It's a rats' nest. All I'm trying to do is put a bell on the leading rat."

"If you can bell that rat," the Governor said, "you'll earn my everlasting gratitude. If you need help—holler."

"Thanks, Judson."

In the following days, Elton Dawbridge did his best, his worst, and his utmost to plug whatever guns Gillian might be preparing to wheel into the fray. A clever man, this Dawbridge. He worked on public sympathy until public sympathy wavered and fell his way. Gillian felt his steel more than once in those exciting weeks.

The mystery, meanwhile, remained a mystery. The picturesqueness of the missile used to kill Amos Grundle tantalized the public. There were newspaper rumors that the diamond was losing its popularity as an engagement stone.

The newspapers were very much interested in knowing why Jim Truman maintained such a grim silence. And why did the Hearthstone girl stubbornly refuse to answer all questions?

The logical answer was summed up succinctly in the single word: *Guilty.*

A quickly summoned grand jury tried to question them. Jim Truman was indicted after a hearing lasting no more than an hour. The testimony of the coroner and John Beckwith, Clinton's leading jeweler, established a circumstantial chain which was damning.

Jim Truman was remanded to the superior court, Clinton County, Judge Lindley presiding, for trial.

CHAPTER XIII

A LIFE AT STAKE

THE JURY BOX was slow to fill. Gillian Hazeltine suspected that the panels were handpicked. His only effort was to fill the box with men who resided in remote parts of the county—men who might not be directly under Dawbridge's dominance. Gillian used up his last peremptory challenge on juror Number 10. Twenty minutes later, the trial was under way.

Gillian looked pale and haggard, as he always did at the outset of a trial. But Elton Dawbridge looked triumphant. His face was flushed. His eyes glowed and sparkled. He had the air of a man fighting his way to a triumphant victory.

At Gillian's table sat Seth Peters, Nellie Hearthstone and Jim Truman. Nellie was all in black, which contrasted sharply with her pallor, and gave her spiritual beauty.

The State's first witness was Dr. Adam Vollmer, the coroner. He was a horse-faced man of forty-five, with ink-black hair and very blue eyes under thick black brows.

He testified that he had been called to the flooded quarry on the afternoon of September fourth to examine a body which had come to the surface.

"Did you identify the body as the remains of Amos Grundle, of Blue Hill Road?" Dawbridge asked.

"I did," the coroner answered.

"How long would you say, in your expert opinion, the body had been in the water?"

"About a week."

"What did you do with the body?"

"I had it removed to my establishment on Main Street for a thorough examination."

"Did you perform an autopsy?"

"I examined the body superficially. Later, I performed an autopsy."

"What did you find, doctor?"

"I found that Amos Grundle had met his death as the result of a diamond that had been fired into his body, presumably from the rifle found lying under a bush near the quarry."

"Do you identify this as the rifle?"

The county prosecutor picked up a rusty Army rifle from his table. It was a late model Springfield, with bolt action and telescopic sights—a sniper's arm. The coroner examined the rifle and stated that it was the one found under the bush. It was admitted as material evidence, Exhibit A, for the State.

"Now, doctor, will you kindly tell the jury in what part of Amos Grundle's body you found the diamond?"

"It was lodged in the third rib down on the left side, just above the heart."

"Not in the heart?"

"No, sir."

"Didn't you make the statement that you had found the diamond lodged in the heart?"

"I did. That was before I made a thorough examination."

Dawbridge flashed a gleam at Gillian. He was making sure that Gillian could not make a point of this in his cross-examination.

"Will you tell the jury, doctor, just why you made that statement? To be explicit, why did you first say that the diamond was in the heart, and later change your statement?"

"I hardly need to say that it is extremely unpleasant to handle bodies which are in the advanced state of decomposition in which Amos Grundle's body was when I took charge of it. My superficial impression was that the diamond had gone into Grundle's heart, causing instantaneous death. I packed the body in ice for several days, to arrest further decomposition processes. When it was possible—a couple of days later—I made the thorough autopsy."

"Would you recognize the diamond if you saw it?"

"I believe so."

ELTON DAWBRIDGE opened a small black box and removed from it a white pebble that glittered and sparkled. "Is this the diamond?"

The coroner examined it. "Yes, sir."

"How do you identify it?"

"By its old-fashioned cut and the scorched appearance at the edges."

The county prosecutor introduced the diamond as Exhibit

B for the State. It was admitted as such, and the diamond was handed to the jury.

Dawbridge walked slowly toward the witness stand with his hands in his pockets.

"Dr. Vollmer," he asked in a clear, strong voice, "would you say that the shock of that diamond striking Amos Grundle in the rib was responsible for Amos Grundle's death?"

"I would indeed."

"Kindly elaborate on this point to the jury."

The coroner complied: "The shock of the diamond striking a man so close to the heart might readily result in such a shock to the vasomotor system that death would almost instantly follow."

Gillian objected. "Your honor," he said, "it has not been established that that diamond was fired at Amos Grundle at close range."

Dawbridge said: "Your honor, let me put a question to the witness which will, I believe, clear up this point. Why, Dr. Vollmer, do you state that the rifle from which the diamond was discharged was fired at close range?"

"Because the dead man's shirt was considerably scorched about the hole where the diamond entered."

"In that case," Gillian said, "the shirt in question should be submitted to this court as material evidence. I want to see that shirt."

The coroner was looking at him with hard, narrowed eyes.

"The shirt was lying on a chair with the dead man's outer clothing the evening of the inquest. That night, a grind of men forcibly entered my establishment and made off with that clothing. They were identified as Silky Davis's gang. Perhaps you know something about it."

"Your honor," Gillian said indignantly, "I humbly request that the witness's last sentence be stricken from the record. It is self-evidently an assumption, impossible to prove."

Judge Lindley looked at him coldly. "I will reserve decision until this discussion is settled," he ruled.

"I want to see that shirt," Gillian insisted. "It either proves or disproves a vital point. Was that hole scorched or wasn't it?"

"I submit, your honor," said Dawbridge dramatically, "that the witness is credible, a man of established reputation, and under oath. He says he saw the scorched hole. Will you give us a ruling?"

"Objection is overruled," said his honor.

"But where's the shirt?" Gillian asked plaintively. Several people laughed.

The judge glared. "There will be no horseplay in this court," he snapped. "The State will continue."

"I will repeat a previous question," the prosecutor obliged. "You say, do you, doctor, that the diamond struck Amos Grundle in the rib with sufficient force to result in instant death?"

"I do."

"That will be all," Dawbridge said.

GILLIAN BEGAN his cross-examination. He walked toward the witness and did not stop until he was six feet away. His eyes went to grips with the coroner's.

"You said a moment ago, doctor, that your official duty in examining the corpse was extremely distasteful?"

"I did!" the doctor snapped.

"It was so distasteful, in fact, that you postponed a thorough autopsy for several days."

"It was very distasteful."

"How did you find that diamond in the first place

"By probing!"

"Was the diamond embedded in the rib?"

"It may have been when it killed Mr. Grundle. It came out easily enough."

"Kindly explain yourself."

"I mean that, after death, decomposition set in. The shattered section of the bone became practically jellylike."

Gillian frowned. "I can't understand, if the diamond was in a rib, why you stated it was in the heart."

"My first assumption happened to be incorrect. It took considerable probing to bring out the diamond. I merely assumed that it had got into the heart. I later ascertained it had not entered the heart."

"Did you examine the heart?"

"Yes."

"Did you examine the lungs?"

"I did not consider it necessary."

"You did not consider it necessary," Gillian said, with angry surprise, "to ascertain whether Amos Grundle had perhaps not met his death by drowning?"

"No," the coroner answered. "If Mr. Grundle had died by drowning the legal status of the case would have been the same as if he had died instantly when the diamond struck him. He would have drowned as a direct result of a murderous assault. Am I right?"

"You are quite right, doctor. Let us sum this thing up, then. When you finished your very distasteful task of probing for the diamond and, later, of examining the heart, you considered you had performed your duty sufficiently? I mean, you had discovered what was, in your expert opinion, ample cause of death?"

Elton Dawbridge was looking at Hazeltine suspiciously, but he did not suspect how cunningly Gillian was laying the plans for a trap to be sprung later.

"That's right," the coroner answered.

"In other words, your autopsy was complete when you had removed the diamond, and, later, examined the heart. As an expert, you saw no need of examining lungs or other vital organs or other parts of the body, naturally. In your opinion, the diamond did it. You had the burned hole in the shirt to prove it. Am I right on these various points?"

The coroner was now suspicious, but he nodded and said, "Yes, that's right."

"You're excused," Gillian said, and sat down, mopping his face. No one in that courtroom would know how relieved he was. He saw, at last, the faint glimmering of possible success in the far distance. He had, at least, a fighting chance.

NEXT WITNESS for the State: John Beckwith, jeweler—a pale, obviously frightened man of sixty, who peered about the crowded courtroom as if his eyesight were bad.

"How long have you been a jeweler in this city, Mr. Beckwith?" asked Dawbridge suavely.

"Forty one years and three months," was the faltering answer.

"In that time, you have handled countless precious stones, have you not?"

"Yes, sir—countless."

"Isn't it a fact, Mr. Beckwith, that you are so familiar with precious stones that when you have seen one you can never forget it? Let me elaborate. Isn't it a fact that every precious stone of any size has, to you, a definite personality—as much of a personality as any human being has?"

"That is so—yes."

"Will you tell the jury something about this?"

The uneasy witness faced the jury. "A precious stone," he explained, "has a certain color, certain defects or flaws. An expert who has seen a stone once will recognize it again."

"Isn't it true, Mr. Beckwith, that, about a week before the murder of Amos Grundle, a stone weighing about four and one half carats was brought to you; that it was set in an old-fashioned gold brooch, and that its owner wanted you to remove it from its mount for him?"

"Yes, sir," the old man faltered.

"Who was this man?"

"James Truman."

"Do you see him in this courtroom?"

"Yes, sir. He is sitting at that table, there."

"You say that this man, this James Truman, came to you about a week previous to the murder of Amos Grundle and asked you to remove for him a diamond weighing about four and one half carats from a brooch?"

"Yes, sir. That's right."The witness was now staring unhappily at the floor. This was, obviously, no pleasure to him.

"Did James Truman take that unset diamond away?"

"Yes, sir. He called for it about six days later and took it and the brooch."

"Was that the day before Amos Grundle's murder?"

"I—I think it was."

"Mr. Beckwith, did you ever see that diamond afterward?"

The witness nodded. "Yes, sir," he muttered.

"Kindly describe to the jury the circumstances."

"The day after Mr. Grundle's body had been found in the quarry, I was called to Dr. Vollmer's place and asked to examine a diamond that had been found in Mr. Grundle's body. To my amazement, it was the diamond that I had removed from the brooch for Mr. Truman."

"Was there any question about this in your mind?"

"No, sir; absolutely none. The diamond was an old-fashioned cut—what we call a rose cut, as compared to the modern brilliant or emerald cut, which is sometimes called a baguette. It had two carbon spots and a very small grain flaw. But it was of a very clear blue-white color—a beautiful stone indeed."

"Would you recognize that diamond now?"

"Of course!"

"Is this the diamond?"

The jeweler removed from his vest pocket an optician's loupe and, screwing it into his eye, examined the stone. He looked up, removed the magnifying glass and nodded.

"Yes, sir; this is the diamond."

"That will be all."

Dawbridge glanced at Gillian. It was a scornful glance. With that tiny flashing blue-white pebble, a chain of circumstantial

evidence had been forged which was sufficient in itself to drag
James Truman to the electric chair. Of this there was no doubt.
What trick of Gillian's could possibly crack that mighty chain?
What could Gillian possibly say to the jeweler that would upset
his testimony?

The courtroom buzzed when Gillian waved his hand in
dismissal. He didn't wish to cross-examine!

Even Dawbridge looked at him with astonishment. It
remained now for the county prosecutor to drive in his final
rivets. He placed lying witnesses on the stand who declared
that they had heard the defendant making threats against
Amos Grundle. They had been carefully selected and carefully
rehearsed-henchmen of Dawbridge's. In his cross-examination,
Gillian confused them and ridiculed them. Any lying witness
would regret the hour Gillian cast eyes on him.

Dawbridge roared objections. Judge Lindley stretched the
law to the cracking point in sustaining them all. But Gillian
proved they were liars.

When this was over, Elton Dawbridge played his trump card.

In his dramatic voice, he cried: "Miss Nellie Hearthstone will
take the stand!"

CHAPTER XIV

"TRICKERY!"

THE COURTROOM HUMMED. A bailiff banged with his
gavel. All eyes were fixed on Nellie. This was the moment for
which every one of those morbidly curious men and women
in that court had been thirsting. It was the great moment for
which the press of the nation had been waiting. In every city of
importance in the country, an extra would soon be on the streets:

NELLIE HEARTHSTONE TAKES STAND!

There is no question about it: the great mass of people enjoy scenes of torture. The public knew that the Hearthstone girl would undergo the most exquisite torture when she took the stand.

The savage political machine of the Dawbridge gang would strip the clothes from her, so to speak. Dawbridge would take pains to reveal her ancestry—or legal lack of ancestry. And would force from her lips the story that would send to his death the man she loved.

There appeared to be no way to save her from this ordeal. Dawbridge was staring at her greedily, as a wolf might stare at a lamb. Judge Lindley, staring at her, was all but licking his chops.

She sat at the counsel table, with her lovely head up, her eyes serene. She was so pale that reporters commented on it in their dispatches. And they commented on the fact that she looked a thoroughbred. She had that indefinable something which is described, in modern slang, as "class."

At a word from Gillian, she arose and walked to the witness chair. Elton Dawbridge was rubbing his hands, in anticipation, as he strode toward her.

To the surprise of everyone, the county prosecutor, after she had been sworn, made no reference to her early life—her legal lack of parents. He would, presumably, come back to that later.

Dawbridge licked his lips and said:

"Miss Hearthstone, at the time of Amos Grundle's death, is it not true that you were employed in his household as a servant?

"It is true," she answered.

"Is it true that on the morning of Amos Grundle's death, you left the house shortly before ten o'clock to meet James Truman on the edge of the old quarry which lies between the Grundle and Truman farms?"

"Objection!" Gillian barked.

Dawbridge and the judge looked at him with hard inquiry.

The judge snapped: "On what grounds?"

"According to the laws of this State," Gillian quickly

answered, "a married woman cannot be called upon in any court to give testimony which might be in any way prejudicial to the interests of her husband!"

Judge Lindley's jaw dropped. Elton Dawbridge only glared at him.

"This girl is not married to the defendant!" he shouted.

"I beg to differ with my esteemed colleague," Gillian said gently. "Intentions of marriage were filed by the defendant and the witness on the afternoon of Mr. Grundle's regrettable death. The marriage ceremony was performed yesterday by the Rev. Josiah Minkin, of Greenfield. Dr. Minkin is not present, but he will testify if it is necessary."

Elton Dawbridge looked dazedly at the judge, and the judge continued to glare at Gillian.

"Trickery!" he muttered.

"I beg your pardon, your honor?" Gillian said clearly.

"I—er—said nothing. The objection is sustained."

The courtroom buzzed again. The judge threatened to have it cleared if quiet could not be maintained.

Nellie looked serenely at Gillian. Thus had Gillian thrown an armor about Truth.

BUT ELTON DAWBRIDGE was not to be thrust aside so easily. He could mention incidents which had nothing to do with the defendant. And he did. Although the newspapers had already done so, he savagely laid bare the unfortunate facts of Nellie's origin.

Serenely, truthfully, Nellie answered him. She had nothing to withhold. Her attitude was that she was far from being ashamed of her cloudy origin, and far from being ashamed of having grown up in an orphanage.

His wrath got Mr. Dawbridge nowhere. Thwarted, he turned his witness over to the defense.

Gillian said simply: "Miss Hearthstone, I want you to tell the jury something about your life with the Grundles."

She did so. She told the jury of the persecution of Amos Grundle; of his cruelty to his wife, of his brutality to her, of his meanness to animals.

Dawbridge objected; was sustained. But the facts came out, nonetheless. The courtroom listened and was appalled. There had been rumors of Amos Grundle's dual nature. And there could be no question that Nellie was telling the truth.

Yet, when Gillian dismissed her from the stand, the ugly fact still remained: A chain of circumstantial evidence which could not be broken bound James Truman to the electric chair.

The State rested. Judge Lindley said, almost in a snarl:

"Gentlemen of the jury, we are about to take a recess for lunch. Court will reconvene at two. The Court admonishes you not to speak about this case among yourselves or permit any one to speak to you about it. You will keep your minds open until the case is finally submitted to you. The defendant will retire."

Gillian said: "If your honor please, is it necessary to hold Mrs. Truman any longer?"

Judge Lindley: "Mrs. Truman will be returned to her cell." He beckoned Gillian to the stand and said: "Hazeltine, if this marriage is only a bluff, I will put you away for ten years for contempt."

Gillian smiled. "It is not a bluff, your honor. As you know, perhaps, Mr. Dawbridge has kept the defendant and Miss Hearthstone in adjoining cells, with a Dictaphone concealed somewhere. Yesterday, I brought Dr. Minkin in to perform the ceremony, and he did so—standing in the corridor so that he could look into both cells.

"The dictaphone, I believe, was out of order for about an hour! Shall we say that this marriage was made in heaven and in jail at the same time, your honor?"

CHAPTER XV

THE X-RAY'S STORY

GILLIAN WAS NOW surrounded by reporters, but he would answer no questions. But he invited his old friend Josh Hammersley, of the Greenfield *Times*, to have lunch with him and Seth Peters in the latter's office. Seth had brought down sandwiches, pie and coffee.

Behind the locked door of the office, Josh said: "Gill, you give me a pain in the neck. I could beat the country on this if you'd only give me a hint."

"You can keep on having the neck pain," Gillian laughed.

"But you have a defense?"

"Certainly I have a defense. But I won't talk about it. I'm superstitious. It isn't that I don't trust you, Josh, but I have the foolish belief that spilling a plan before you execute it spoils it."

"You might let me have something exclusive to send out."

"Wait till after the trial. We ought to wash things up this afternoon. See me after the trial, and I'll give you a nice little exclusive story."

"Who's your first witness?"

Gillian hesitated to answer, then said, reluctantly: "Dr. Hoffman."

"The X-ray specialist?"

"Yes."

"What's the big idea?"

"Keep right on guessing."

Josh threw down his half-consumed sandwich, took a final gulp of coffee and ran to the door.

"What's your hurry, Josh?"

"I'm going to file that. You don't mind?"

"Hop to it."

"And you'll have something exclusive for me after the trial?"

"If I win the case—yes."

ELTON DAWBRIDGE was sitting on the edge of his table when Gillian walked in. The county prosecutor said: "Hazeltine, I'm warning you, if you pull any trickery this afternoon, I'll have you disbarred."

"Those are harsh words," Gillian laughed. "And it seems to me I've heard them before."

"I'll smash you flat—I'm warning you!"

"I tremble all over," Gillian answered, "You terrify me, Elton. Really, you do. You know, you're a terrifying man. Something ought to be done about you. If I had any voice in the matter, I'd have you burned at the stake. By the way, you haven't forgotten our little bet?"

"My hundred and fifty thousand is in escrow in the Greenfield First National, isn't it?"

"And you're still going to Washington—Senator?" Gillian gravely asked.

"You know I'm going to win this case. I'm saying again: any of your vaudeville tricks, and I'll mash you flat!"

The judge had come in.

"My first witness," Gillian said presently, "is Dr. Henry Hoffman. Will Dr. Hoffman take the stand?"

This was greeted by a stir of interest which drew glares from several bailiffs. And there was noticeable excitement about the press table. Dr. Henry Hoffman of Greenfield was the foremost X-ray specialist in the state; a man, indeed, of such prominence in his profession that he was frequently called into consultation in all parts of the country. A dangerous man for the defense.

Elton Dawbridge stared at him with fascination. So did Judge Lindley. What did Gillian have up his sleeve? If they had asked him Gillian would promptly and gravely have answered, "The bogey man"—and meant it.

"Dr. Hoffman," Gillian briskly began, "will you kindly tell the jury what you were doing about midnight on September the fourth?"

"I was reading a book in bed," the doctor answered. "At a little after midnight, there was a ring at my front doorbell. I answered and found you standing there."

"What did I want?"

"You wanted me to accompany you here, to check with my instruments an autopsy which had been performed by Dr. Vollmer, the coroner here."

"And did you come here?"

"I did."

"Kindly describe your procedure."

"You took me to Dr. Vollmer's undertaking establishment. I went into the back room, where the corpse of Amos Grundle was packed in ice. I unpacked the ice and made a searching investigation."

"Did you take X-ray photographs?"

"I did. I took ten of them."

"I have the photographic films here," Gillian said, holding up a sheaf of thick, black celluloid sheets. "Will you kindly identify these as the photographs you took that night?"

"Gladly."

GILLIAN HANDED the photographs to him. Dawbridge started forward, but changed his mind and glanced at the judge. Judge Lindley was frowning and his eyes were glittering.

"Will you explain these films and pass them along, first to the judge, then to the jury?"

"I will. The first of them, which has a label on the back of it, numbered one, shows a diagonal view through the chest of the dead man. It shows two interesting things. It shows that the heart of the dead man was not removed, as Dr. Vollmer stated this morning. And it shows that the diamond bullet—or a missile of some kind—lodged, as has been claimed, in the third rib down on the left side, above the heart."

"Would you say, doctor, from your study of that X-ray film, that the impact of the diamond on that rib would have caused instant death to a strong, healthy man?"

"I would not say so," Dr. Hoffman answered. "In fact, I would be strongly inclined to doubt that the impact of the diamond at that point would cause death in a robust man. The rib was fractured at that point. The blow might have driven the breath from the victim's lungs, but I certainly would not agree with any one who stated that such a blow would result in death."

"Might it have resulted in unconsciousness?" Gillian inquired.

"I doubt it very much. I should say emphatically no."

"What do the other photographs show?"

"There are three more, taken at various other angles through the chest, which support my contention. The remaining six are of the bullet wound and the bullet in the back."

The statement came so casually that no one in the courtroom was prepared for it. One reporter dashed out of the room. People were babbling. Judge Lindsey made no attempt to restore order. He was staring at Gillian with indignant amazement.

The county prosecutor had seized Gillian's arm in a savage clutch.

"You damned trickster!" he cried. "This is cooked up!"

Gillian shook him off. When order was restored, Dr. Hoffman continued with his testimony.

"These six films show, from various angles, the course of the thirty-two caliber revolver bullet which entered the dead man's left side above the kidney and broke his backbone—shattered it, in fact—causing instantaneous death."

Judge Lindley was white. His mouth was open, but he could say nothing. Elton Dawbridge shouted:

"That's a lie! Dr. Vollmer performed the autopsy. He found no bullet lodged in Grundle's backbone!"

"Wait a minute," Gillian snapped. "Let me refresh your memory. This morning, under cross-examinations Dr. Vollmer said that he had not examined the lungs or any other part of the body. He lied when he said he examined the heart. His stomach was too tender for him to examine the heart—or lungs. He got that diamond out and—called it a day!"

"He performed a thorough autopsy!" Dawbridge shouted.

Gillian said calmly: "Will the stenographer please read out of the record my question to the coroner which began: 'In other words, your autopsy was complete when you had removed the diamond,' *et cetera?*"

The stenographer thumbed back through the record and read:

"In other words, your autopsy was complete when you had removed the diamond and, later, examined the heart. As an expert, you saw no need of examining lungs or other vital organs or other parts of the body, naturally. In your opinion, the diamond did it. You had the burned hole in the shirt to prove it. Am I right on these various points? Dr. Vollmer: 'Yes; that's right.'"

"THAT WILL do," Gillian said. "It is clearly established, is it not, that Dr. Vollmer's delicacy prevented him from performing a thorough autopsy?"

"I deny it," Dawbridge snapped. "Where is that shirt?"

"Ah, that shirt," Gillian sighed. "Where, indeed, is the shirt? Why didn't Dr. Vollmer examine the shirt, and he would have seen the bullet hole down on the left side, in back?"

"There was no other hole in the shirt!" Dawbridge roared.

"All you have to do," Gillian said quietly, "is to prove it by producing the shirt!"

"Your gang of gunmen stole the shirt!"

The courtroom roared with laughter. When order was restored, Gillian said:

"If his honor please, may we have some ruling? We are entirely out of order. I beg the Court's indulgence for one moment. Can your honor conceive of any man hiring a gang of gunmen, as my esteemed colleague puts it, to steal a shirt?"

But Judge Lindley was speechless.

"Is it any fault of mine, your honor," Gillian went on, "that neither shirt nor corpse can be produced as 'material evidence.' Alas, the shirt is gone—and the corpse has long since been cremated."

The judge found his voice; barked: "Are you through with this witness?"

"If your honor please, I beg leave to introduce these films as Exhibits A, B, C, D, E, F, G, H, I, J for the defense."

His honor looked on the verge of apoplexy, but he was compelled to admit the exhibits as material evidence. But his eyes sought out the white face of Coroner Vollmer across the room and crucified him. That unfortunate man looked as if his stomach were troubling him still.

"Could this bullet have been fired from a silenced gun?" Gillian asked.

"There is no way of proving the contrary," stated Dr. Hoffman.

"I want your expert opinion on these two wounds, Dr. Hoffman," Gillian continued. "The point I wish to establish is this: In your opinion, did the diamond in the rib or the bullet in the backbone cause the death of Amos Grundle?"

"Unquestionably, the bullet caused instant death," the doctor answered. "The spinal cord was torn in twain."

"In your opinion, was Grundle dead when he fell into the water?"

"The X-rays prove he was dead," the witness answered. "If you will examine those which show the lungs, you will see—at least I can see—that those lungs contain no water."

"And your expert opinion is that the diamond would not have caused the death?"

"That is my opinion."

"That will be all. Does the State wish to cross-examine?"

Most decidedly the State did. Elton Dawbridge shouted at Dr. Henry Hoffman until he was hoarse. He took him up and down his direct testimony; tried to shoot holes in it, tried to trap the doctor into making contradictions.

The famous Roentgenologist remained unshaken. Coolly, calmly, with icy politeness he turned the shafts aside.

Dawbridge all but collapsed into his chair.

Judge Lindley said harshly: "Has the defense other witnesses?"

"Yes," Gillian said. "Miss Nettie Jarvis."

Once again the courtroom burst into roars of laughter. Someone in back shouted: "Oh, you bogey man!"

With glowing dark eyes and a complacent smile, the seamstress took the stand for her "courtroom scene."

CHAPTER XVI

THE MYSTERIOUS STRANGER

THE "BICYCLE WOMAN," as Miss Jarvis had been mirthfully referred to by certain of the peach colored newspapers, was fairly glowing with excitement. One did not need be a clairvoyant to know that Nettle Jarvis was realizing her life's ambition. Her words were to thunder across the nation. She was, at last, in her own.

In a voice so thin and excited that it sent titters about the courtroom, Nettie answered Gillian's questions.

Yes, on the morning of Amos Grundle's murder, she had been riding past the Grundle farmhouse on her bicycle a few minutes before ten o'clock.

"Where were you going, Miss Jarvis?"

"I was going to Mrs. Brubaker's, five miles farther along the road, to help make the clothes for her darling new baby, Junior. Mrs. Brubaker will testify to this," the seamstress added with defiance.

"As you were passing the Grundle farmhouse, what did you see from your bicycle?"

"I saw Mr. Grundle walk out of the back door with a rifle under his arm."

"Anything else?"

"Yes!" Miss Jarvis hissed. "I saw a face peering out at him from the bushes—the elderberry bushes. He was a great tall man with a black beard—a thick black beard. As Mr. Grundle started off in the direction of the quarry, this tall man stepped out from the bushes and stealthily followed him."

"Did he creep from tree to tree like an Indian?"

"Exactly!"

"Did you see a bulge in this black bearded man's hip pocket, as if he might be carrying a revolver?"

"I did!"

The face of every man and woman in the courtroom, with the exception of the judge and the county prosecutor, was smiling. They looked grim and uneasy.

"How was this black-bearded man dressed, Miss Jarvis? Like a tramp?"

"No, sir. He was dressed queerly—like a miner—I mean, like the gold miners we see in the movies. He wore a black slouch hat, a black sateen shirt, a vivid red bandanna handkerchief, blue serge pants and a pair of scuffed brown oxfords."

"What else did you see, Miss Jarvis?"

"That was all."

"Did you see this young lady here—Mrs. Truman, *née* Hearthstone?"

"No, sir."

"That will be all. Does the State wish to cross-examine this witness?"

"I want to ask the witness just one question," Dawbridge said sourly. "Do you know, Miss Jarvis, that you have the reputation of being the greatest liar in Clinton County?"

Gillian snapped an objection—and was overruled. Dawbridge and his judge were going to carry the fight to the last ditch.

Miss Nettie Jarvis left the stand to a fluttering and a tittering. She looked very indignant. With nose in air, she disappeared. Her great moment had been crowned with an insult.

DAWBRIDGE DRIFTED over to Gillian. His mouth was a snarl.

"You haven't heard the end of this," he growled. "Those X-ray films were fakes—and you know it! Was there a bullet hole in the back of that shirt?"

"Ask the shirt," Gillian answered.

"I'll cook you yet!"

"I'll make a tough dish—*Senator!*"

"Next witness!" snapped the judge.

"Mary Nolan."

Dawbridge turned in his tracks so sharply that he almost fell, His widening eyes looked at Gillian. He strode back.

"Look here, Hazeltine. What's the big idea?"

"Live and learn," Gillian answered.

"Why are you calling that girl to the stand?"

"You can cross-examine her to your heart's content," Gillian replied, "when I'm through with her. Don't forget the bet!"

The county prosecutor licked his lips, watched the girl on the stand uneasily, and relapsed into silence.

She was a pretty, bright-eyed country girl. She looked wholesome and fresh.

Gillian began firing questions at her:

"Miss Nolan, where did you grow up?"

"Clinton Orphanage," Miss Nolan said briskly.

"Was Mrs. Truman, formerly Nellie Hearthstone, there with you?"

"Yes, sir."

"What was and is your opinion of the orphanage superintendent, based on your personal experience and observation?"

"Mr. Wardell was the finest, kindest man I ever knew."

"Did you ever know him to auction off pretty orphans to the highest bidders?"

"No, sir. That was a vile lie."

"What is your occupation?"

"I am a cook."

"Where are you employed?"

"At present, I am not employed."

"Where was your last position?"

"I worked for Mr. and Mrs. Elton Dawbridge."

A faint hum rose in the courtroom; but fell off into eager silence again.

"Why did you leave his employment?"

"Because I knew too much."

Elton Dawbridge sprang up. His mouth was working savagely. His fists were clenched. His eyes were ablaze.

He shouted: "That girl is lying! She's lying! This is a dirty, cold-blooded frame-up!"

Gillian said patiently: "Your honor, will you please request this gentleman to refrain from interrupting me? He may take this witness for cross-examination in just a moment."

His honor did nothing but stare with hungry fascination at Gillian.

Gillian took advantage of the lull to say: "Miss Nolan, what do you mean—you knew too much? Kindly tell the jury just what you meant."

"I meant simply that I knew how violently Mr. Dawbridge and Mr. Grundle quarreled and fought."

"Fought?" Gillian snapped.

"Yes, sir—fought. They fought terribly. Every time Mr. Grundle came to the house, they fought. And one time, just a few days before the murder, Mr. Dawbridge shouted that he was going to kill Mr. Grundle."

"Your honor—" Dawbridge began, and choked.

"What did they fight about?" Gillian asked.

"The graft."

"What graft?"

"Well, you see, Mr. Dawbridge had put Mr. Grundle on the board of education and the board of charities, and he grafted. And Mr. Dawbridge thought Mr. Grundle was holding out on him."

"OBJECTION!" ROARED Mr. Dawbridge, who was now purple.

"Sustained!" cried the judge somewhat hastily.

"And then," the girl went on sweetly, "I suppose I knew too much about the masquerade party."

"What masquerade party?" Gillian gently prompted her.

"The firemen's ball, held in Hook and Ladder Company Number Seven's firehouse last Washington's Birthday."

"Did Mr. Dawbridge attend that masquerade party?"

"Indeed, he did, sir. He won the second prize."

"How was he dressed?"

Dawbridge sprang up. But the girl answered so rapidly that he could not even force words out of his throat.

"He was dressed as a gold-miner. He wore a thick black beard, a black sateen shirt, a bright, red bandanna handkerchief, a black slouch hat, and scuffed brown oxfords."

"Could you identify the costume if you saw it?"

"Yes, sir."

Gillian opened a paper package on his table; held up, in turn, a thick black false beard, a black sateen shirt, a bright red bandanna handkerchief, a pair of old blue pants, and a pair of scuffed brown oxfords.

"Where," Mr. Dawbridge roared, "did you get those?"

"Out of your bedroom closet," Gillian snapped.

Mr. Dawbridge now found his voice. He shouted objections. He insisted that every line of Mary Nolan's testimony be stricken from the record. He shouted at the girl that every word of her testimony was a flagrant lie, manufactured testimony.

"Didn't you wear this costume at the Firemen's Washington's Birthday masquerade party?" Gillian demanded.

"Yes! What of it? What does it prove? You dirty trickster! Your honor—"

But his voice was lost in bedlam. He was still fighting, not knowing that the battle was over. Judge Lindley, however, was fully aware that Elton Dawbridge's powerful machine was smashed. The judge was, in fact, the first rat to leave the ship.

He demanded order. He gave instructions to the jury so brief that his address consumed no more than five minutes. What he told them, in so many words, was to bring in an acquittal verdict for James Truman, and to bring it in on the jump.

Dawbridge had the look of a man distracted beyond all normal mental bounds. His face white, his hair and eyes wild, he attempted, in the hubbub, to denounce Gillian. He used the word trickster, with profane and picturesque variations, forty times in two minutes.

"Am I accusing you of the murder?" Gillian finally countered. "My dear Elton, I am not a detective or policeman—I am not even suggesting that the State prosecute anyone for Grundle's death. I am merely a hard-working lawyer, struggling to bring the light of justice into the dark places of the land."

The frantic county attorney left him and pleaded with the newspapermen. Nettie Jarvis had seen him at the party; she had been coached; he had been framed, he declared. The reporters laughed at him.

Mr. and Mrs. James Truman seemed in a daze. They sat at the table, holding hands and gazing into each other's eyes.

No one heard what Nellie said to her husband: "Isn't it marvelous, darling? You won't have the slightest shadow on your conscience, because there's not the slightest doubt about it. Mr. Hazeltine's proved that it was the bullet—not the diamond."

Her husband looked ten years younger already.

YET THERE was just a shade of doubt, just a suspicion of suspicion, in more cynical quarters.

Josh Hammersley had Gillian in a corner.

"Come clean, you old vulture," he was saying. "You know damned well that whole bogey man story, including Hoffman's films, is phony. Your secret will be safe with me, Gill. Come clean."

"Josh," Gillian protested, "you astonish me. You hurt me."

"Yeah? Are you going to follow this up and get out an indictment for Dawbridge?"

"Why should I?"

"You mean, you've smashed him for life. Sure, you have. But are you going to follow it up?"

"No, Josh. I am going abroad with my wife, and spend part of the hundred and fifty thousand dollar profit I made recently in a business deal. We are going to London—Paris—Florence—Rome."

"Listen! What was that exclusive story you were going to hand out?"

"Ah, yes," Gillian murmured. "It's a nice little story. It's about Jim Truman and his bride. It's about their honeymoon. They are going to the same little village in southern France where my wife and I spent our honeymoon. Villeneuve. It's in the rose orchards, Josh. It's near the champagne orchards, too, Josh. What a wonderful, romantic spot for a honeymoon—with the azure Mediterranean before you, the glorious snow-capped Alps behind you! And what charm. And after the honeymoon, we are all going to meet in Paris—for a little whoopee."

"Listen, Gillian, just satisfy my personal curiosity, won't you? Was that Nolan girl telling the truth?"

"Didn't she take an oath?"

Josh scratched his head. "You know damned well that Jarvis woman is the worst liar in the world. She could have seen that costume when Dawbridge wore it, and remembered."

"Don't forget," Gillian said sternly, "that, at least once in their lives, the worst liars in the world may break all laws and tell the truth."

Gillian fought his way out of the courtroom, posed resignedly to pose for several hundred feet of motion picture film, and then walked over to the telegraph office.

To Governor Judson Withrow he sent the following cryptic telegram:

THE RAT WEARS A BELL

ABOUT THE AUTHOR

THE DECISION TO become a writer of fiction was made for me by fate. In 1914, in Panama, where I spent a week when I was a wireless operator on a little steamer that creaked up and down the Central American coast, I met an author who painted the joys of free-lancing so vividly that I could not resist the call. We were drunk. I was twenty. Since then, I have been trying to catch up with all of those joys he mentioned.

Starting to write stories in 1914 and, four years later selling my first one, marks up, I suppose, a very poor batting average. But in those years I was getting experience, seeing the world, and acquiring knowledge. I "punched brass" as a wireless operator all over the Pacific. I entered Columbia University in 1915, and one year later left because I didn't believe in higher learning. I still don't believe in it. I became a newspaper reporter, later a magazine editor.

Then came the war, which I won practically single-handed by writing high-pressure publicity to induce patriotic Americans to send books to Washington for camp libraries for soldiers and gobs. Books came by the carload, by the ton: McGuffy's readers, old almanacs, spellers, arithmetics, out-dated novels and just trash. The soldiers and sailors who read those books soon hated the war so bitterly, that they promptly got busy and ended it. That's how I won the war.

After the war, I wanted another look at China, and was sent

to the Far East by *Collier's* to write articles on China, the Philippines, India
and Malaya.

George F. Worts

The first story I sold was written
while I was editing a motion picture
trade paper. It was bought by the
Argosy, and it was about a wolf named
Murg. Don't ask me why. In the inter-
vening years I have written millions of
words. Perhaps it is Murg who sits so
patiently at my door!

I started writing fiction under the
pen name of Loring Brent, because it would have annoyed the
owner of the motion picture magazine to learn that I was writing
fiction out of hours. He thought I fell asleep at my desk because
I was working so hard for him! When my income from fiction
exceeded my salary, I quit the job. Since then I have been free-
lancing exclusively, except for a two-year period when I lived
in a Florida swamp town and added to my writing the duties
of postmaster, game warden and deputy sheriff. Out of that
experience came a long series of stories about a Florida town I
called Vingo.

I have enjoyed most writing stories about certain established
characters. Apparently the most popular of these have been the
Peter the Brazen, the Vingo and the Gillian Hazeltine stories. I
stopped writing about Peter the Brazen (a swashbuckling wireless operator on ships in the China run) about ten years ago.
He was, incidentally, the subject of the only novel I have had
published in America. I am now starting a new series about him.

When I am not traveling I live in Westport, Connecticut. My
interests are horses, sailing and flying. I took up flying about a
year ago to write some articles on how it feels to learn to fly, and
was badly bitten by the bug. I can make a three-point landing
about five times out of ten.

I like New York, but would prefer to live in Honolulu. I smoke sixty cigarettes a day. I like murder trials. I have never mastered the noble game of poker, although I once wrote a book about it. In my spare time I study law and medicine. I have two young sons and a still younger daughter; an able crew for my sailboat—except that there is usually mutiny aboard the lugger!

THE ARGOSY LIBRARY ™

SERIES 5 INCLUDES:

* WORTS * SHEEHAN * SERVISS *

* BRAND * PERRY * ROSCOE *

* BEECHAM *

* WIRT * FORSYTH *

* ROUSSEAU *

THE BEST FICTION
FROM THE FRANK
A. MUNSEY LINE

Made in the USA
Las Vegas, NV
08 April 2022